# NOBODY RIDES FOR FREE

## AN ANGUS GREEN NOVEL

# NEIL S. PLAKCY

**DIVERSIONBOOKS**

Also by Neil S. Plakcy

*The Next One Will Kill You*

Diversion Books
A Division of Diversion Publishing Corp.
443 Park Avenue South, Suite 1008
New York, New York 10016
www.DiversionBooks.com

For more information, email info@diversionbooks.com

First Diversion Books edition October 2017.
Print ISBN: 978-1-63576-052-1
eBook ISBN: 978-1-63576-051-4

LSIDB/1708

# 1.
# DISTURBING EVENTS

The bullets didn't pierce my Kevlar vest, but they hit me with enough force to fracture a rib. Even now, two months later, I can still feel the occasional ache in my shoulder and chest.

Everyone said I was lucky. The bullet that hit my stomach could have gone into my arm or leg, damaging nerves or muscles. A difference of a few inches in the trajectory of the second bullet, the one that caught the bottom edge of my vest, and I could have bled out through my femoral artery.

I had to rest in bed for a few days and be careful when I began to exercise again. When I returned to work as a Special Agent at the Miami office of the Federal Bureau of Investigation, I was assigned to a team that visited local colleges to discuss the ways vulnerable young people could be approached by foreign governments. I showed a video about a case we had investigated where a student studying in China had been hired to write position papers about how Americans felt about various issues. He had eventually been pressured to engage in espionage and was sent to jail.

When I spoke in community college classrooms, I could see the students' eyes glaze over. The idea that they would have the opportunity to study and travel in China was as remote to them as being selected for a mission to Mars.

I stuck out the college program for over a month, meeting every week with a Bureau-approved psychologist to review my mental state. I didn't tell her, or anyone else, that every time I heard a loud noise I flinched, regardless of if it was a baby crying or the clatter of a dish hitting the floor in a restaurant. When I twisted too quickly, pain zinged under my left armpit—where the vest had pressed against a nerve.

The nightmares stopped but I still had trouble sleeping. I backed away from my roommate, Jonas, avoided my other friends, and broke up with the guy I'd been dating. My instinct was to hibernate until I felt better, but at the same time, I hated my assignment and longed to get back to real duty.

That wish came true on a Monday morning in mid-January. Roly Gutierrez, a senior agent I'd worked with in the past, buzzed me and told me to meet him ASAP in the main lobby of our office building. "I need you, Angus," he said. "Another face-eating zombie. And this one's on federal property."

There had been a couple of cases in the news where otherwise ordinary guys overdosed on synthetic drugs, which did crazy things to their bodies and minds. It caused their core temperature to rise, forcing them to shuck all their clothes, and something short-circuited in their brains, leading them to attack innocent citizens and begin gnawing at their faces.

Even for Florida, where the crimes are wacky and the criminals wackier, this was extreme.

Roly hung up before I could ask for any details. He had been my mentor on the case when I'd been shot, and he was my best hope to get off the college engagement team and back into the field. I was glad to jump when he said to. On my way out of the office, I grabbed a couple of evidence bags, in case there was something we needed to collect.

When I got to the lobby, he was on his cell phone. He was a Cuban-American guy who'd been in the Miami office for a dozen years, turning down promotions to stay near his family. Like most days, he wore an immaculately tailored suit—black with a charcoal gray pinstripe—and a red tie patterned with American eagles.

He ended his call and I followed him outside. "911 got a call about twenty minutes ago about a naked man on the premises of the Department of Labor," he said. "He attacked a woman in the parking lot and tried to bite her face. The Broward Sheriff's Office is on site and has him cornered."

As we walked to the garage where his SUV was parked, he said, "We need to respond because it's a federal building, and in case there's some terrorist component. Doesn't sound like one, but you never know. And this gives us a chance to have a chat. How's your current assignment working out?"

"Confidentially?" I asked, and he nodded. "I hate it. The promotional copy for the college event is misleading, so the students and faculty who attend get confused because they don't learn what they expect. I know it's important to reach out to the community about what we do, but this particular project feels like a waste of time."

"I'm not surprised. Most of the agents who end up on that detail are ones who've been shunted off the main track, either because they screwed up or because nobody wants them on a team."

"Did I screw up?" I asked. "By getting shot?"

"Not at all. You been seeing the department shrink?"

"I have," I said, making sure that my voice didn't waver. I wasn't going to give Roly, or anyone else at the Bureau, the idea that I wasn't fully recovered. "She says I'm ready to jump into a case as soon as someone needs me."

"Good to know. Depending on what we find at this site, I may need your help."

There were enough police and fire vehicles in the parking lot of the Department of Labor building to handle the arrest of a dozen suspects and the medical treatment of a dozen victims. However, most of the officers stood on the shore of a man-made lake behind the building, along with about thirty or forty people who probably worked in the building. They all watched as two officers in scuba gear stood in the middle of the shallow lake and tried to wrestle a naked man back to shore.

I could see why it was taking them so long to get the guy out of the water. He was skinny, but looked awfully strong, and the way he growled and clawed at the officers reminded me of one of those Animal Planet programs where park rangers tried to subdue an angry predator. As the scuba officers dragged the man closer to shore, another pair in uniform waded in to help out.

Roly went off to confer with a guy he knew from the DEA, and I walked over to a Broward Sheriff's Office deputy I knew, a broad-shouldered Haitian-American guy named Hercules Dumond. "Hey. You know what happened here?" I asked.

"Way I heard it, this white guy comes charging out the building, buck naked," he said. "Grabs this woman coming in for a job interview, knocks her to the ground, and starts chewing on her face."

"That is the creepiest part of these cases—the face-chewing part."

"I got you, brother. Couple of guys from this financial services company across the way spotted him, pulled him off her. One of them got scratched up pretty badly. Ambulance took the woman and the guy who got scratched away a few minutes ago. Then, the crazy man jumped into the lake and started splashing around."

The officers were finally able to wrestle the man out of the water. The guy's erection made the scene look like it was something from a porn movie, and I wondered if the drug enhanced sexual desire, too.

Because I wanted to prove to Roly that I was more than ready to come back to work for him, I started showing my badge to onlookers and asking if they knew who the man was. When I reached a stylishly coiffed African-American woman in her mid-thirties, she said that his name was Brian Garcia, and that he worked in her office.

I called Roly and told him I'd found someone who could ID the zombie, and he joined us a moment later. The woman's name was Shirley Thomas, and she was a supervisor in the Department of Labor. Garcia was a wage and hour technician, a staffer in her office who responded to complaints about wage inequities.

"Do you know what set him off?" I asked.

She shook her head. "I can show you his cubicle if you want. Maybe there's something there. We're on the second floor."

I turned to Roly and asked quietly, "Do we have grounds for a search?"

"An employee in a federal office has no expectation of privacy with regard to his workspace. So this is just like a house. If she's responsible for the area, and she agrees to let us look, then we can. This is a federal facility, so we can assert jurisdiction if we choose. When I spoke to my buddy from the DEA, he said he's got five different investigations into local distribution of drugs that could have caused this situation, and he's happy for any help we can provide."

I nodded. "What do you want me to do?"

"Secure his workspace and then talk to his colleagues as they come back inside. Figure out what happened here and see if you can identify what he took and where he got it from. I'm going to make some calls to follow up with the victim and see how the zombie's doing at the hospital."

I was back on Roly's team. It was the opportunity I'd been waiting for and I was psyched.

I followed Ms. Thomas up to the room on the second floor where Garcia worked. All six of the cubicles were empty, as everyone seemed to have gone outside to watch the circus. Ms. Thomas provided me with Brian's home address. "He lives with his father," she said. "I think his mother died a few years ago, and his father's sick with something, I'm not sure what."

I thanked her and went to Brian Garcia's cubicle, trying to put myself into his shoes. I didn't need to see rainbow flags to know he was gay—the sexy postcards from Provincetown and Key West that were pinned to the fabric walls told me that. I sat behind his desk and looked around. He had a huge plastic tumbler with a couple of ice cubes in it beside his computer monitor. Condensation dripped down the sides, pooling on a stack of government forms.

Overheating was one of the symptoms of an overdose of the synthetic drugs that had been implicated in the previous attacks. It made sense that Garcia would have tried to drink ice water to cool down.

I made a note to find out how fast those drugs took effect. Had he taken something the night before—or this morning—and still been suffering from the effects? In that case, might there be traces in the cup? I put it in an evidence bag to take back to the office.

I heard voices as Brian's coworkers returned. I started with the woman across from him, who had the clearest view of his cube. I showed her my badge and asked her to describe what she'd seen this morning.

"Brian looked exhausted when he came in, and I asked him if he'd been out late at a club last night. He said yes, and that this morning he was feeling empty. I thought it was a strange word to use, empty."

"Do you know which club?"

She shook her head. "I told him to get some coffee, but he said he had something better. I said that he shouldn't be messing with drugs but he insisted he knew what he was doing. Then I saw him about a half-hour later and he looked like crap. He was pale and sweaty. I asked why he didn't take a sick day and go home but he said he didn't have any banked."

"He give you any indication of what kind of drug he was going to take?"

She shook her head. "I sat down at my computer, and the next thing I knew Brian was standing up, fanning himself. He said something about going outside to cool off and then he took off."

The other staffers had little more to add. Brian was a quiet guy, a good worker. He'd never shown signs of drug abuse, though most of them agreed that he was pretty raw on Monday mornings. "Never this bad," an older Asian man said. "He'd usually just swig a couple of those power drinks and be OK."

Garcia had a personal laptop in a case beside his desk. The rules for law enforcement searches are pretty clear—I was allowed to search his laptop without a warrant only if there was evidence on it, and if that evidence was in danger of being erased.

I made a decision. Roly had directed me to find out what Garcia had taken, and where he'd gotten it from. The evidence might be in a message from one of the services that regularly deleted posts, like Snapchat, or in an e-mail in his trash folder. Depending on the way he'd set up his account, his trash could be emptied regularly by his server. That meant the evidence was in danger of disappearing, right? And finding out what he took, and when he took it, could potentially help the doctors in the emergency room save his life.

It was a stretch, and I ran the risk that if the case ever came to court, a judge could rule my search inadmissible. But I decided to take that risk, and I opened the laptop, hoping that he hadn't protected it with a password. I was in luck, because it came right on and I was able to access his social media accounts, to figure out where he'd been and who he'd been with.

At ten o' clock the night before, Garcia had "checked in" on Facebook at Cosmopolitan, a gay dance club near the Fort Lauderdale airport. He had also uploaded a couple of photos of him and a group of friends. I didn't recognize any of them, and I'd never been to that club myself. I saved and forwarded the photos to my Bureau e-mail account in case I needed to find those guys in the future.

I logged into his Gmail account—fortunately, he'd saved the password. I scanned through quickly, looking for any messages that might indicate what he was on, or where he got it. It was slow and tedious work. Brian wasn't big on spelling or punctuation, and I felt like a teacher of remedial English as I read his complaints about work, his plans for hook-ups, and so on.

Then I came to a thread of messages between Brian and someone whose address was ohpee@hotmail.com. The subject line was "high as a kite."

According to the message, Ohpee lived in a house where there were lots of drugs, and at the time he was writing, he was high—on weed, though. Someone in the house was selling flakka, one of those opiates that had caused previous zombie attacks, and had given him some to try, but he didn't want to take it.

"I've taken flakka before and it's great. Gives you this high that lasts and lasts," Brian had written in response. "You don't want it, send it 2 me."

Ohpee had about an ounce of the stuff in a zipper-lock bag, and he had offered to mail it to Brian, who'd supplied his address, in Hialeah. "In the mail today," Ohpee then wrote. "P.O. lady says only a day from Lauderdale to you."

The most recent message was from two days before. Brian had written to thank Ohpee for the flakka. "I owe you big time, dude," he wrote. "Any time you need something, just ask."

Was that what Garcia had taken? I did a quick Internet search and discovered that flakka was part of a group of drugs called bath salts, because that's what they looked like. The main ingredient in the compound was alpha-PVP, a chemical that blocked the brain from absorbing the overflow of dopamine, the feel-good substance that is generated when you enjoy anything, from a piece of music to a lover's kiss.

That meant that your brain was awash in good feelings—but it also might mess with your fight-or-flight instincts, leading you to excessively violent behavior.

All that made sense in light of what Brian Garcia had done. He was feeling down, and according to his coworker, took a drug to perk him up. Flakka was often mixed with other drugs like tran-quilizers and anti-psychotics, so you never knew exactly what you were taking. Even though Garcia had taken flakka without adverse effects before, this batch could have caused the overheating and the violent behavior he'd displayed.

I went back to the chain of messages. After Garcia had written to thank him, Ohpee had responded that he was unhappy where he was living, and he might need Garcia's help to get out.

"At first it was cool to live here in the house and get paid to have sex," Ohpee wrote. That surprised me. So Ohpee was one of those exhibitionists on webcam sites? No wonder he had to get high a lot.

"I'm creeped out about all the guys out there watching me, getting off on the fact that I'm not even sixteen yet," Ohpee continued. "But where could I go? I haven't seen my dad since I was five years old, and with my mom dead, I got no other family. Guess I have to stick it out here."

I stopped cold. Not only had Ohpee supplied the flakka to Brian, he was fifteen, and being forced to have sex online. From his post office message, it appeared he was living in Fort Lauderdale—maybe even near where I stood, or where I lived.

# 2.
# HIALEAH

I closed Brian's laptop and placed it back in its bag. I verified with Ms. Thomas that I could take it with me, along with the tumbler from Garcia's desk. Then I called Roly and arranged to meet him at his SUV. "I've got a couple of pieces of evidence that need more evaluation," I added.

When I linked up with Roly a few minutes later, he was with a guy he introduced as Colin Hendricks from the DEA. Hendricks was about my age, late twenties, skinny, in jeans and a T-shirt that read: "Brains are awesome! I wish everyone had one." His forearms were covered with tattoos and his dark hair had been shaved close around the sides, leaving a big mop at the top.

"Don't mind the undercover look," he said, as he shook my hand. "I was in the middle of something else when I got called out here." He nodded toward the evidence bag I was carrying, and Garcia's laptop. "What have you got there?"

I explained, and reluctantly offered to turn over what I had to his custody. He shook his head. "You hold onto it, see what you can get from it."

"Garcia's at the hospital," Roly said. "It's going to take a while to test his blood, hair, and urine to confirm what he took, but all the indications point to flakka. They've put him in a medically induced coma to minimize the danger of a stroke or heart attack and preserve his kidneys, so no one can talk to him for a while."

I was pleased that I'd been able to figure out that Garcia had taken flakka myself. "There's a message on the laptop from the guy who supplied the drugs to him."

"Forward that to me," Hendricks said. "This isn't the first case where someone either took too much of the stuff and moved into overdose territory, or took something purer than expected, or ingested a bad mix of flakka and something else. I'm working an investigation into local manufacturing and distribution and I'm seeing more and more cases like this."

"You find out where he got the stuff that quickly?" Roly asked me.

"I searched through his e-mails." I explained my rationale, that his server might be deleting messages regularly and that therefore there was an expedient need for me to look into them. Roly looked doubtful but he let me continue.

"Looks like he got the flakka from someone who says he's a fifteen-year-old who does online porn for a gay sex site."

"That's a new twist to me," Colin said. "But it's so damn easy to get flakka if you have access to the dark web. You click a couple of buttons, find a supplier in China, and then wait by the mailbox."

I'd heard the terms "dark web" and "deep web" used interchangeably. An analogy I read compared the Internet to an iceberg. Only about 10 percent of all networked material was accessible through search engines and web crawlers. Techies called that the surface web. The rest included password-protected sites for illicit activity, as well as things like your bank account information—anything that wouldn't easily show up in a search engine.

"It's pretty easy to get into the dark web, isn't it?" I asked. "Just get the Tor Browser, right?"

Using the Tor Hidden Service Protocol, your surfing requests stay within the Tor network so you maintain anonymity. You don't know where the server you're accessing is, and it doesn't know where you are. It's perfect for political activists in repressive regimes, and for people who want to share and/or sell illegal materials—like drugs or kiddie porn.

"Too easy. You know how to find this kid?"

"Not yet. But he mentions that he mailed the flakka to Brian Garcia from a post office in Fort Lauderdale. There are a lot of personal details in the e-mail chain, and I believe that if I follow them I can find him, and then whoever is dealing drugs from the house where he's living."

"Any dealer we can put out of business is progress. If you guys take point on the gay porn angle, I'll go through my usual sources, and we can connect in a day or two."

Roly agreed, and Colin walked away. "Be careful what you assume, Angus," Roly said, as we drove. "You know as well as I do that strippers and porn performers and sex workers lie as easily as they breathe. This 'kid,' as you called him, could be in his twenties, stringing Brian Garcia along for money."

"I don't think so. They really bonded. They're both Cuban-American, they went to the same middle school in Hialeah, though Brian is ten years older, and both of them were molested by family friends when they were young." I took a deep breath. "This kid sounds like he's in real trouble—and if I can find him, maybe I can help him out, and we can track down a flakka supplier."

"This is the most fired-up I've seen you since you got back from being shot," Roly said. "I'll request you back on my team and I'll give you some leeway to do your research. But you've got to come up with real, verifiable data quickly. I know you want to save this kid, but don't get sidetracked. Focus on the drug distribution. That's where we have jurisdiction."

"I'll work my ass off," I said.

On our way back to the office we discussed approaches I could take. "I'm glad to see you back in the saddle," Roly said, as we walked into the building. "I'm sure it was tough getting shot the way you did. But remember that it's a rare occurrence for an agent to be wounded in the line of duty."

"Uh, Roly?" I pointed to the electronic display in the lobby as we passed it—a computer program that showed all the agents who had died while working for the Bureau.

"I'm not denying the job can be dangerous. But you're an

accountant by training—run the numbers. Consider how many agents have been with the Bureau since it was founded in 1908. Then see what percentage of them are on that screen."

"I know. And I worked through all that stuff with the shrink."

He stopped as we reached my office. "You've got to tread lightly with this investigation, Angus," he said. "Be aware that you might get a reputation as only being able to work cases in the gay community."

I was the only openly gay Special Agent in the office. Though there were other LGBT employees in supporting roles, I'd been able to leverage my knowledge during the last investigation I'd worked with Roly, where I was able to get information and make intuitive leaps that a straight agent might not have been able to.

I was glad to crack that case, even though it had left me with those bullet wounds. "Would that be so bad?" I asked. "I want to be the best agent I can be, attack every case I'm given with all the skills I have. But there's something to be said for protecting my community. If no one else is going to step up and do it, then I will, and I won't give a damn what anybody thinks."

He laughed. "You remind me of myself. You know my background, right? I'm a first generation Cuban-American. When I graduated from Quantico I was assigned to New York and my first assignment was to go undercover and investigate a protection operation being run by Cuban émigrés. One of the guys in charge reminded me of my own *abuelo*. It freaked me out."

He leaned against the doorjamb. "I wondered how come they'd put me in this position. I was reporting on my own people. It was like they were exploiting my background. But I recognized that they put me there not just because I could speak the language, but because I fit in. That my job was to uphold the law and protect the people—some of them Cuban-American, some not—who were being victimized."

That was how I felt, too.

"You may be forced to investigate, or arrest, other gay men.

You have to be able to make that separation between your personal life and your career."

"I can do that," I said, though even then I recognized my arrogance. How would I know until I was faced with a situation?

"Good. Then you'll succeed no matter what kind of case you're assigned to."

I appreciated Roly's faith in me—but it was time to demonstrate his faith was warranted. This case was my ticket off the academic team and back to being a real FBI agent. But more importantly, it was the chance for me to be the big brother to a boy who might not have someone to look out for him.

One of my high school classmates, Tommy Carlton, was an overweight effeminate boy, and other kids made fun of his mannerisms and called him every kind of nasty name. They beat him up after school, gave him chocolates that were actually laxatives, and generally made his life miserable.

I was afraid to stand up for him because I didn't want anyone to know I was gay, and I didn't want to make waves that could upset my new stepfather. So I did nothing, and during our senior year Tommy committed suicide by shooting himself with his father's rifle.

Our high school staged a memorial service, and I could see that the kids who'd bullied Tommy felt bad. But I was gutted because I worried that if I'd done something to help him, I might have prevented his suicide.

Now maybe I had the chance to make up for it.

I dropped the cup I'd brought from Garcia's office at the lab and asked to have it checked for flakka. Then I took Garcia's laptop to the evidence locker and checked it in. The guy in charge raised an eyebrow at my explanation of how it came into my possession, but I filled out the paperwork, then carried it back to my office.

Before I went back to the laptop, I wrote up an FD302, the field report used to summarize interviews with subjects. I began with the people I'd spoken with at the Department of Labor office and followed the standard conventions, putting the first and last name of each person I spoke with in all capital letters. When I came to the bottom of the page, I inserted the date and the location of the investigation, the file number and the date created. It always gave me a thrill to type SA Angus Green on the last line.

When I'd finished that, I set up Brian Garcia's laptop and went back to the e-mail chain from Ohpee. The easiest and quickest thing to do was to send an e-mail to Ohpee from Brian's account. "Took the flakka this morning," I wrote. "Really messed me up. Don't take any of that shit yourself."

I hit "send," and almost immediately I got a response back from the Gmail mailer-daemon that the account had been closed.

I could put together a subpoena to Gmail to get whatever details they had for the account, but it was pretty easy to set up one of those accounts, and if Ohpee was into porn and drugs he had probably used false information. So I went back to the e-mail chain. There had to be a clue that would lead me to the site where Brian had first encountered him. And from there, I could get Ohpee's face, maybe his name.

As I read, I realized that Ohpee also performed in videos— Brian mentioned one that he'd seen with Ohpee and another guy. "Were u really in locker room @ Hialeah racetrack?" Brian had asked. "That was so hawt."

Ohpee had responded that the producer had shot the exteriors at the racetrack, but the locker room where they'd filmed the scene was at a gym near the house after hours.

I opened up a browser and searched for "gay porn Hialeah racetrack," and got 21,600 results—most of them missing one or more of my search terms. I slogged through two pages of links before I hit pay dirt, a free preview of a porn movie that began with a sweeping shot of flamingos taking flight from a pond in front of a grandstand at a racetrack.

Quickly the scene shifted to a jockey in purple and white racing silks walking into a locker room. He was a short, skinny guy, with a rounded face and no facial hair. He tossed his cap onto a bench in front of a locker, then pulled off his jersey, revealing a hairless chest. I leaned forward, trying to get a view of his face, but he sat down on the bench and the camera focused on him removing his knee-high boots.

He stood again, this time dropping his white breeches, revealing a purple jockstrap the same color as his jersey. He began to peel off the strap—and then the preview ended with a pop-up window that offered me the chance to see the whole movie if I signed up for a membership with the website.

It had to be Ohpee, right? What were the chances that there were two gay sex flicks with the same setup? I'd seen my fair share of porn, with all the common tropes—student/teacher, coach/athlete, job applicant/interviewer, and so on. But I'd never seen one with a jockey before, and certainly the addition of the Hialeah track made it unique.

But I couldn't see the guy's face or establish his name. And the website that wanted me to sign up was a well-known one that didn't produce videos, but instead collected them from many sites.

The movie had been produced locally—I was sure of that from Ohpee's e-mail. I didn't know anyone who acted in or produced porn locally, but I knew who to ask, starting at Lazy Dick's, the gay bar where I'd hung out a lot with my roommate Jonas before I got shot.

He had tried to drag me out to Lazy Dick's nearly every weekend once I was off the pain meds and could drink again, but I resisted. It seemed frivolous to go out partying when I'd had a near-death experience. But now, it was different. I had a mission.

# 3.
# GREEN HORNET

The FBI office in Miami is in Miramar, in the southwest corner of Broward County. It was a long hike from there to Wilton Manors, the neighborhood of Fort Lauderdale where I live. I often wondered, as I sat in bumper-to-bumper traffic, if I'd be better off moving closer to work. But that would mean giving up the gay-centric community where I had begun to feel at home.

The long drive usually gave me a chance to shift gears from Special Agent Angus Green to off duty mode, but that afternoon I kept thinking about my case and wondering what I could find out at Lazy Dick's. I doubted anyone would admit to watching underage porn, but a lot of good-looking guys hung out there, and I could see one of them might have been approached to act in something, especially if the production facility was local. Or it was possible someone might know about the existence of this house through a friend or a casual trick.

I was finally able to exit the highway at Sunrise Boulevard, driving past a wasteland of used car lots and fast-food operations. The sun was glaring off the rear of the car ahead of me, and rap music blasted from a low-rider with heavy-duty speakers.

It was a relief to turn onto Wilton Drive, where the trees made a canopy over the street. I knew I was home when I started to see bars advertising drag nights, rainbow flags on nearly every business, and a cluster of brand new buildings, full of businesses ready to exploit the pink dollar.

Lazy Dick's was a landmark, a gay bar by night and the go-to restaurant for Saturday and Sunday brunch. The sprawling low-rise building was surrounded by shaded patios. Jonas and I had spent a lot of time hanging out there, drinking and chatting and looking in an idle way for Mr. Right—or perhaps Mr. Right Now.

I pulled into the parking lot, took off my suit jacket and laid it carefully on the front seat, then removed my Penn State tie and folded it. I undid the first two buttons of my white oxford-cloth shirt, pulled tail out of my white shirt to cover the thumb holster at my waist, checked my hair in the mirror, and I was ready to go.

The patio bar was hopping that evening, with lots of guys in the same kind of work drag I was wearing, along with a mix of older, retired men in Hawaiian shirts and jeans. Kelly Clarkson's "Heartbeat Song" was playing on the speakers and I felt the rhythm moving in me.

After working my way through Penn State at an Italian restaurant with an active bar, I knew that the best place to start when looking for information was with the bartender. A good one knows his clientele—not only what they like to drink, but whether they want to talk, and if they do, what they're interested in. And despite the noise and activity, the bartender often overhears more than the patrons assume.

But there was a line at the bar, guys eager to get cheap drinks before happy hour expired, so instead I started a circuit of the room. I recognized a lot of the regulars and I jumped into conversations with a bit of banter.

A few months before, I had investigated the death of one of the busboys at Lazy Dick's. I'd come out as a Federal Agent to the denizens of the bar and though there had been an initial buzz and some predictable jokes, eventually my job had ceased to matter to anyone. I was no different from the Lauderdale cop with the ripped physique and lots of body art—or the travel agent or the marketing exec.

I asked everyone I knew about companies that might be filming porn in the area, but got nothing more than vague memories. "I saw a call for guys a few months ago," one of the men said.

He was a beefy man in his forties with a pelt of dark hair that peeked above his shirt. "But I'm not exactly porn material so I didn't pay attention."

"Hey, there are lots of sites that would take you," his friend said. "Just hunt for fat guys fucking."

"If I wanted to see guys like you, I could search for tiny dicks fucking," the bear said.

I left them to their squabbling and moved on. Finally, the crowd around the bar cleared and I could get in. The bartender on duty that evening was a rail-thin Trinidadian with cocoa-colored skin, a smooth island accent, and the habitual runny nose of a coke addict. He was in his early twenties, and wore a skin-tight tank top with the Lazy Dick logo. "Hey, Raj, what's going on," I said as I slid onto a bar stool.

"Green Hornet," he said. "Good to see you, mon."

Raj had a nickname for everyone, usually a riff on the person's real name. When he learned my last name was Green, he'd come up with that reference to the super hero. At least he didn't call me Angus Cattle.

"I'll take a Rum Runner." Because it came out of a machine it was watered down enough that one wouldn't even begin to get me drunk.

"Coming up. Long time you been away. You better now?"

From what Raj said, I realized that the gay grapevine had been working during the time I was gone, spreading the news of my shooting. It was probably Jonas' fault—talking about me gave him something to say, a reason for better-looking guys to talk to him.

"Yeah, back to work. Say, you know any companies making porn locally, Raj?"

"Why you ask, mon? Uncle Sam not paying you enough?"

I could have told Raj about the flakka, but questions about drugs often cause guys to shut down. I thought I'd get more information by focusing on Ohpee. "I got a tip that there might be an underage guy performing for one of those sites, based here in Lauderdale. Trying to track him down and make sure he's not being victimized."

"I haven't heard of nobody filming locally. If they do it, they on the down low. And for sure nobody using kids." Raj sniffed and wiped his nose. "Still tough being a gay kid these days," he said. "You see all this stuff in the paper, kids coming out early, joining queer clubs and all. But still a lot of trouble for so many of them." He shook his head, then went on to the next customer.

I did another circuit with no result, and I was draining the last of my Rum Runner when I spotted Jonas. "I'm surprised to see you here," he said. "I thought you'd given up on the bar scene."

I explained about the case, but he didn't know anything about flakka, or about anyone making porn in the area. "That's creepy, taking advantage of a kid like that," Jonas said. "I ever tell you about the guy who approached me at the beach?"

"No. Somebody wanted you to act in porn?"

"You don't have to look so surprised," Jonas said. "I was skinnier then and I wasn't so hairy. Plus, I looked really young. One day—I was fifteen—I was online and I read something about the gay, nude beach at Haulover."

I'd been to Haulover Park only once, briefly, because of my fair skin and tendency to burn quickly. I'd walked out to the long sandy beach and past the sign at the northern end that warned novices that they might encounter nudity beyond that point. Most of the men were ones you didn't want to see naked, but it was still a forbidden thrill to be in the middle of so much casual nudity.

"You went to a nude beach when you were fifteen?" I asked.

He nodded. "I hadn't done anything more than fool around with a friend, and I had this idea that I'd go to the beach and meet some kid like me, and we could be boyfriends."

He looked down.

"I wish I'd had a place like that when I was a teenager back in Scranton," I said, thinking of myself and Tommy Carlton. "You were lucky."

He shrugged. "I took three buses to get there from my house

and then I had to walk a long way from the bus stop." He got a wistful gaze. "It was amazing, Angus. All these naked men. I got hard right away and that made me too scared to pull my clothes off.

I finally managed to pull my shorts down and lay down on my belly. But almost as soon as I did, this guy came over to me."

"Another kid?"

"An old guy. Now that I think of it, he was probably only in his forties, but he was like my dad's age and I kind of freaked. He sat down on the sand next to me and started talking. Casual stuff, you know, like what a beautiful day it was, how great it was to go into the water and cool off after lying in the sand."

"What did you say?"

"I didn't say anything at first. He asked me what my name was, how old I was, where I went to school. Then he asked me if I'd ever wanted to be in movies. He said I had a sweet ass and it was almost a crime not to share it with other guys. I thought he was kidding at first, because I didn't have muscles or anything, but he was serious. He told me I could make a lot of money to be naked in front of a camera, and he asked me to turn over so he could see me from the front."

"Did you?"

"I told him I didn't want to because I was hard, and he said that was OK, that I could turn on my side and he'd be the only one to see." He smiled. "He said all kinds of nice stuff, and he gave me his card and told me that whenever I wanted to make some money, I should give him a call."

"Did you?"

He nodded. "A couple of weeks later. He gave me his address and I said I'd go over there on a Saturday afternoon. I found the right bus route and rode almost all the way there, but at the last minute I chickened out. I wonder what would have happened if I'd had the balls to get off that bus."

"I think it took bigger balls to stay on it," I said. "You realized that you had too much respect for yourself."

"That's nice of you to say, but I was just scared. Though he hadn't said anything I knew there was going to be more than taking my clothes off for pictures and I wasn't ready for that."

"However it happened, I'm glad you didn't let someone take advantage of you. This kid wasn't as strong."

I should have hung around the bar for a while longer, asking more guys about local porn producers, but I had triggered something in Jonas and I had a responsibility to look after him. I shifted the conversation to his day at work, and after a while, we walked across the street to a take-out Mexican place. We got a couple of wraps and then drove home and ate at the kitchen table.

The house we shared was a run-down ranch in a rapidly gentrifying part of Wilton Manors. The huge oak tree in the front yard kept the grass from growing, and the exterior walls were painted puke green, but it was home. Our rent would probably go up a lot when our lease was up, if the landlord didn't sell the place as a tear-down.

Inside, the furniture looked like it had either come from a thrift shop, or belonged in one. In the living room there were mismatched metal chairs around a linoleum kitchen table, an overstuffed couch and a couple of easy chairs in the living room, beds and dressers in the bedrooms. At least Jonas had brought an oversized plasma screen TV with him.

As we ate, we settled down together to watch TV. About halfway through, a commercial came on for a local car dealership called Exotic Imports. The owner was a strange old man with white hair. He had a pet cheetah on a leash. In the ad, he strolled around the lot, pointing out the Jaguars, Ferraris, and Lamborghinis. Sales people stood beside the cars, as if they were ready to sell you one right away.

Jonas peered forward at the TV and pointed to a tall, dark-haired guy beside a midnight-blue Porsche Spyder. His muscles bulged out of his logo polo shirt. "Look at that guy," he said. "I'm sure I've seen him at the gym. You think he's gay?"

"Well, the gym we go to probably has the highest percentage

of gay guys of any in town. Why don't you ask him the next time you see him?"

"If I do, I'm definitely mentioning this commercial. That's a good way to start a conversation, right?"

"Absolutely."

I could tell from the glow in my roommate's eyes that he was already planning his wedding to the hunk—or at least a hot date.

When I left my bedroom the next morning dressed for the gym, I wasn't surprised to see that the guy in the commercial had motivated Jonas to accompany me.

Jonas had never been much of an athlete, and he'd only joined the gym as a way to meet cute, fit guys. Since he rarely exercised, that wasn't working out for him. But a couple of weeks before, he had started eating a healthy diet—no more late night fast food binges or buckets of fried chicken. The cafeteria at his office building had a good salad bar, and he'd been grazing there at lunch.

If it took seeing a guy on TV to get him to work out, it was all good, right?

As Jonas drove us to the gym, he asked, "You want to go to Lazy Dick's on Saturday night? They're doing dollar margaritas all night."

"I'll see." When we walked into the gym, I pointed at the line of machines. "Where do you want to start?"

He looked around, and then turned back to me. "It's him!" he said in a loud whisper. "The guy from the commercial. I was right! He's here!"

"Put your tongue back in your mouth." It sure looked like the same guy we'd seen the night before in the Exotic Imports commercial. "Well, you were going to tell him you saw him on TV. Give it a try."

Jonas shook his head. "He'd shoot me down."

"You never get anything you want if you don't try. Offer to spot him while he lifts."

Reluctantly, Jonas walked over. The guy wore a T-shirt that read RUN MORE THAN YOUR MOUTH in block letters, and his pecs and biceps strained against the fabric. I watched as Jonas approached him and spoke. The guy shrugged, then got down onto the bench and began lifting. Jonas stood beside him as the guy began his reps.

He had a lot of weight on the bar, and I hoped he wouldn't need Jonas's help because I was sure my roommate couldn't manage it.

I got onto a treadmill and set the timer. I wasn't working my upper body much because I still felt the occasional twinge from the muscles damaged when I got shot, and I didn't want to overdo it.

As I worked my calves and thighs, I thought about the way Jonas and I had both grown up, and how lucky we'd been.

My dad had died when I was ten and my brother Danny six, and my memories of him were growing hazier with time. I remembered sitting on his lap with the atlas open, him pointing to all the exotic destinations he wanted to visit. He had a thing for island chains—the Azores, the Seychelles, the Abacos. I hadn't been to any of those places yet, but I'd gotten out of Scranton, which was more than he'd ever been able to do.

Once my mom married my stepdad, we moved into a bigger house where Danny and I each had our own room. We always had food and clothes, and I mowed lawns and washed cars for spending money. I was able to get an academic scholarship to Penn State, where the LGBTA Student Coalition enabled me to come out in a supportive atmosphere, and though my mom and stepdad weren't thrilled to learn I was gay, they didn't abandon me or try to force me into therapy. I'd been able to stay in school, thrive, and build friendships and personal relationships that helped me succeed.

Jonas's story was similar to mine. His parents were divorced, and he'd come out to his mom when he was in high school. She had immediately joined PFLAG, the group for parents and allies of gay people. He was embarrassed about how enthusiastic she had been, but her support had been crucial to his adjustment.

What might have happened to me if I hadn't had the opportunities I had? Suppose my stepdad had discovered I was gay while I was still living under his roof, and he'd kicked me out? Where would I have gone? There weren't a lot of social services for LGBT teens in Scranton, so I'd probably have gone to either New York or Philadelphia.

The thought of being an outcast on my own in one of those big cities was frightening. I could have turned to prostitution, been raped, infected with HIV or other venereal diseases, or gotten addicted to drugs.

That reminded me of the boy who had supplied Brian Garcia with the flakka that caused him to go crazy. Was the kid an addict too? Or part of a supply chain?

I was getting too depressed, so I put my ear buds in and zoned out to Survivor's "Eye of the Tiger." I was a tiger, strong and smart and tenacious. I was going to find that kid and from him whoever was distributing flakka on my turf.

# 4.
# GAY GUYS ONLINE

The next morning a stiff wind tossed around the palm trees alongside the highway as I drove the forty minutes south and west to the office. As I drove, I thought about the conversation that I had with Raj the night before. I knew that as kids identified as queer earlier and earlier, they became exposed to other gay kids and adults. That could be negative, because they could be more vulnerable to predators. The adolescent brain isn't fully formed, particularly when it comes to impulsive behavior and understanding the consequences of actions.

But it could also be positive, as they could meet role models and have safe spaces to express their feelings. There had to be groups in South Florida that would protect kids the way the ponds and stands of sawgrass, as well as the iron fence and security gates around our office, protected us from terrorist attacks. As soon as I got into my office I began to research services for LGBT teens. Someone at one of those groups might be able to give me a lead on Ohpee—and I knew that if I found the kid, I could find the drugs.

I called a shelter in Fort Lauderdale that I'd heard of. It was a branch of a national organization, and the guy I spoke with was emphatic that he knew nothing about local porn production. When I asked if I could come speak to the kids staying there, he said, "Privacy is very important to our kids, many of whom are not out to friends or family members. Though I recognize your need, we do not bring in guest speakers."

Thanks a lot, I thought.

I called a couple of other places I found through a resource website for gay teens and got similar responses. The last on my list was a shelter for runaway LGBT teens in Fort Lauderdale called Lazarus Place. From its website, I saw they had a facility off Sistrunk Boulevard near downtown, in the heart of a historically black neighborhood that had suffered a great deal of blight.

I called the phone number on the website, but got a voice mail system. I left a message, introducing myself as an FBI agent and included my request. I didn't expect to hear back, but if I didn't, I'd try again.

Time for a different approach. The newspapers and TV stations had been all over Brian Garcia's episode. From the reports, I learned that flakka was a man-made drug that had originated in China a few years ago. It was ten times more powerful than cocaine, and simulated the effects of both cocaine and methamphetamine, without the price tag. That's why it had become so popular with young adults and impoverished addicts.

One article noted that Broward County was turning into a center for flakka abuse, but there was little more information than that.

I called Colin Hendricks at the Drug Enforcement Agency and asked if I could come to his office in Weston and talk to him. He agreed, and I drove up I-75 to the building, a generic low-rise sheltered by tall oak trees.

Hendricks looked much more like an agent that day, in pressed chinos and a long-sleeve dress shirt that covered his tats. "You make any progress?" he asked, as we sat down at his cubicle.

"I haven't been able to track down the kid Brian got the flakka from," I said. "But I've got feelers out."

"I'll leave that angle to you, then. You've obviously got the inside track. Let me know if you come up with anything."

"Can we speak to Garcia yet?"

Colin shook his head. "Still in the coma while they monitor his body temperature. I've spoken to his father who he lived with in Hialeah. The father knew nothing about drug abuse and he admitted that even though they live in the same house, they don't communicate much. I get the sense the father isn't happy that Brian is gay, but can't do anything about it."

"Parents never can," I said. "All they can do is accept and love."

"I hear you, brother. Got the father to authorize a search of Brian's room and the rest of the house, but we couldn't come up with any drugs. Just a bunch of porn I'm sure he wouldn't want his father to know about."

I nodded. It was one thing to know that your kid was gay, and another entirely to see physical evidence of what kind of practices turned him on.

"I've also been compiling some statistics, looking for patterns," Colin said.

"Now you're talking my language. What did you find?"

"I noticed an upsurge in incidents involving flakka that began about two months ago," he said as he turned his computer screen toward me. "I started with arrest reports that included possession of anything that looked like gravel or bath salts."

Flakka was often called gravel because it looked like small pebbles or big grains of sand.

"Then, I started looking for flakka in ER visits at local hospitals. Routine drug testing doesn't detect it, but doctors are starting to recognize the symptoms of overdoses and use an advanced testing kit to detect it. Then I put each incident onto this map."

He pointed at the screen. There was a cluster of dots on the screen—many of them around Holy Cross Hospital—the closest emergency room to Wilton Manors—and others in a rough circle spreading out from that area.

"Do you have someone undercover in gay bars in the area?" I asked.

"Not specifically gay bars, but we have agents who work the bars. You think there's a gay connection here, beyond the kid who gave Garcia the flakka?"

I pointed at the screen. "An awful lot of these incidents take place in Wilton Manors," I said. "There's a big gay population there."

"You ever do undercover work?" Colin asked me.

I shook my head. "And I can't do it here. My last case outed me as an FBI agent and the red hair makes me pretty visible."

He nodded. "I have a guy I can put on it. Thanks for the connection."

• • •

As I drove back to the office I thought about what Hendricks had said. Did I have the inside track because I was gay? Or was it because I'd been following up the chain of e-mails? Was there something in the Hialeah racetrack video I'd be able to spot because I was gay, and because I had my own history of watching porn?

When I got back to the office I opened the teaser video, but after staring at it for a while, I still had nothing.

I watched the clip three times, the flamingos taking off over the racetrack, then the quick jump to the locker room as the jockey walked in and began to strip. My eyes were glazing over when I finally paid attention to the picture hanging on the front of one of the lockers.

It was a bright orange triangle, like a yield sign, only brighter and had big black letters on it that read "Ice and Snow." The font had mounds of snow on top of each letter, reminding me of the big white drifts that piled up back in Scranton every winter. The words "take it slow" were printed in smaller block letters at the bottom of the sign.

What an odd picture to hang in a locker room in South Florida. It was very visible—had it been put up specifically for the video shoot? Was it a shout out to people in the Snow Belt? A warning to masturbators to take it slow? Don't rub your dick too fast or you'll get friction burns?

I sat up with a start. What if it was an instruction to viewers to watch the video slowly?

At Quantico I'd studied a bit of steganography—the science of concealing information in non-secret text, pictures, and videos.

There were all kinds of sophisticated mechanisms, but the simplest were to insert coded text in a message header, or intersperse it between the frames of a video.

I had Microsoft's Movie Maker software on my computer, and I opened the movie clip in that program so that I could view the individual frames. I flipped through them quickly until one jumped out—a single frame with an orange background and the same font as the one in the image on the wall—black letters with white snow caps.

At regular speed, the image would have flashed on the screen for a fraction of a second because most digital video was shown at around twenty-four frames per second. So unless you followed the instructions to watch the video slowly, you'd miss it.

The text read: "FOR MORE BOY LOVE ACTION GO TO" followed by a URL. It was one of those anonymous links with a bunch of letters and numbers. I tried the address, but a password window popped up before I could get any further.

I tried various combinations of "ice" and "snow" as the password but got nowhere. I kept getting a message that the password was incorrect—but at least I was encouraged to "try again."

The password had to be hidden in the video. There was no reason to give viewers an address, only to lock them out. I went back to my frame-by-frame analysis, and after another couple of dozen frames of the jockey slowly stripping, I found another orange screen, a single frame with the words M4N B0Y L0V3 in that same snowcapped font.

I went back to the password window and typed that in. Immediately, it was replaced by a very professional-looking series of screen captures. It was a webcam site, a supermarket of gay guys looking for action. Some were clothed in everything from T-shirts to business suits, while others were naked. Some had teaser videos you could watch, while others displayed lengthy chunks of text beneath their faces, promising they were "sweet company, with an awesome smile," or "playful and funny with a little bit of dirty mind." They were lonely, horny, and eager to meet new people.

Many of the guys looked young, but I couldn't tell if that was because they were underage, or made to look that way.

About halfway through the list I found the boy I was looking for, but he wasn't online at the time. I took a screenshot of his picture and saved it to a folder I'd created for the case, and then printed a copy, too.

I checked with a domain name website, where I discovered that the URL for the site was registered to a company called gayguysonline.net. The e-mail contact—admin@gayguysonline.net—wasn't helpful. But right below it on the registration site was the company name, street address, and phone number.

My pulse raced. The address was in Wilton Manors. "Gotcha!" I said out loud.

I quickly popped the address into Google Maps, only to find that it belonged to a company that rented mailboxes. Disappointing, but not surprising. I punched the phone number into a database program and discovered that it was one of many assigned to a company that sold no-contract cell phones through electronics stores.

I used my own phone to dial the number, pressing *67 before I dialed so that if I was calling a cell phone or a caller ID unit, the recipient wouldn't see my incoming number, only "private" or "unknown."

After a couple of rings, the call went to an automated voice-mail message. I hung up, then turned to the Florida Department of State's website, where I found the records for the administering organization behind the website, a company called Gay Guys Online LLC.

Most of the information there made no sense to me—entries like "document number" and "last event." I clicked through each of the hyperlinks for corporate annual reports, but unlike the ones I was accustomed to dealing with in my days as an accountant, these contained nothing more than what was in the state's records. Even the articles of organization were useless.

The only real information was under the heading "Registered

Agent Name and Address." The agent was an attorney named Alexei Verenich, with an address on Collins Avenue in Sunny Isles Beach.

His company's website was very simple: the name of the practice and the address, along with a headshot of Verenich himself. There was no indication of the kind of law he practiced, no glowing recommendations from clients, or marketing copy encouraging you to hire him and his firm.

Before I called his number, I did some more research. There wasn't much online about Verenich, though he was a member of the Russian-American Chamber of Commerce and several other professional organizations. I went back several years through the monthly summary of discipline actions provided at the Florida Bar's website, but I couldn't find any complaints registered against him.

Verenich's name appeared in the records of numerous real estate transactions, all of them in either Sunny Isles Beach, a city on the barrier island at the tip of Miami-Dade County, and Aventura, another independent city right across the causeway from it.

As a last resort, I looked him up in the FBI database, where I was surprised to find that he was the subject of an ongoing investigation. The agent on the case was listed as Ekaterina Gordieva, from the Miami office.

Even though I'd only been there about eight months, I thought I knew all the agents in my office by name, but I'd never heard that one. I went down the hall to speak to Roly about her, but first I wanted to see if he'd heard anything about Brian Garcia.

"Still in the medically induced coma. You find anything about that boy he was e-mailing?"

I told him about the progress I'd made. "I found a video like the one Ohpee mentions in his e-mail to Brian, and that led me to a company domiciled in Wilton Manors. The site is owned by an LLC and the registered agent is a guy called Alexei Verenich. According to the database, he's the subject of an ongoing investigation led by an agent named Ekaterina Gordieva. You know her?"

"Katya. She's a transfer from New York working undercover on a money laundering case. This guy must be involved in that. I'll send her an e-mail and ask her to reach out to you. It may be a day or two though, depending on what she's got going on."

He leaned forward. "Remember, what you have is still circumstantial. I'm not seeing any evidence that there's an actual teenage boy in trouble. Talk to Katya, but remember to keep your eye on the flakka distribution. That's your case and you need to focus on it."

I nodded, but I remembered Tommy Carlton, and the way I had stood by while he was tormented. I wasn't going to make the same mistake with this boy.

# 5.
# FRONT MAN

I returned to my office, and opened another FD302 to report on the guys I'd interviewed about local porn companies at Lazy Dick's the night before, and then added information about the movie, the website, and Alexei Verenich.

It was grim to see how little I'd accomplished, and I realized that the form made it look like I'd only been focused on finding Ohpee, not on the drugs. That reminded me to add the results of my conversation with Colin Hendricks at the DEA.

By the time I'd finished, the agent that Roly had mentioned called me, and we arranged to meet at a coffee shop near where she was working. I hoped she'd have some insight into Verenich and his possible connection to drug dealing and pornography.

As I drove south on I-75, past vast tracts of undeveloped land at the edge of the Everglades, I wondered how Ohpee had ended up at the porn house. I was pretty sure by time I was a teen that I liked boys more than girls, but I hadn't acted on any impulses and I wouldn't do so for another couple of years. I'd grown up in a safe, healthy atmosphere, and it was sad to think that other kids didn't have that opportunity. I had strong memories of my dad and I'd always felt that my mom loved me and Danny. We didn't have a lot of money, but we always had food on the table, heat in the winter, and clean clothes to wear to school.

How would we have survived if our mother had died while she was still single? My dad was an only child and had no close relatives. Would we have been shipped off to my mom's sister, who had four kids of her own? Sent to foster care? Would we have ended up on the street, lost and abandoned?

When I-75 crossed the border into Miami-Dade County and then died into the 826, the landscape around me changed to industrial and commercial buildings. Most of the signs and billboards were in Spanish, advertising everything from *lo mejor musica* to ambulance chasers asking if I was *lesionado*. I could buy *teléfonos móviles, comida latina,* or *seguro de salud*, health insurance under Obamacare.

After a long drive east, I landed in Wynwood, a neighborhood north of downtown Miami. The area was once a decaying warehouse district home to a large Puerto Rican population, but now boasted hipster coffee shops, craft beer outlets, and tons of artistically rendered graffiti. It was all mixed with run-down apartment buildings and small stucco houses with elaborate grillwork over the windows and doors.

The coffee shop where I was supposed to meet Agent Gordieva was in a repurposed gas station. I parked by an old pump, ordered a café mocha, and sat down with my laptop. I initiated the VPN software and began catching up on department e-mail. I was reading a long treatise on armored car robberies when I heard a woman say, "You must be Angus."

She was very pretty, with honey blonde hair and a luscious figure poured into a business suit with a short skirt. "What gave me away?" I asked. "The red hair?"

She shook her head. "I didn't know what color your hair was. But you have FBI written all over you."

I must have pouted, because she said, "Don't worry, it's a good thing. You look honest and trustworthy. I've had to work hard not to let my Bureau training show through when I'm undercover."

The barista called "Katie!" and the blonde walked over to retrieve her drink.

"I thought your name was Katya?" I asked when she returned.

"I prefer Katya. But try getting a barista to spell that on your cup. I Americanize when I have to."

She took a sip of her coffee. "Thanks for coming over here to meet me. I'm working undercover as a sales agent for one of the Russian brokers in Sunny Isles Beach, and right now I'm dealing with some nutty clients who won't stop calling and texting me. It's hard for me to get enough free time to go all the way out to Miramar."

I gave her the rough outline of my case. "The reason why I reached out to you is because a name came up, and when I looked him up in the Bureau database it said you're investigating him, too. Alexei Verenich."

She nodded. "Yeah, he's the front man for a bunch of LLCs that invest in real estate, primarily in Sunny Isles Beach. How did he come up in your case?"

"As the registered agent for a company running a porn site."

"Sleazy is sleazy," Katya said. "You'd be surprised at how many different things a group like the Russian mafia is into."

"Whoa. That's what you're investigating? The Russian mafia?"

"My investigation is targeting money laundering through real estate purchases, and a lot of the money passing through comes from people here in South Florida we suspect have connections to the Organizatsya."

"Can I talk to Verenich?" I asked. "To ask him about his connection to the LLC that operates the porn site? He's the best lead I have to this boy who's being exploited."

"Can you hold off on that, please? I understand your concern, and believe me, I hate the idea of kids being sexually exploited, too. But I don't want to spook Verenich with a visit from the FBI, even if it's something different from my case. Give me some time to dig into his business and talk to people."

"Does he have other porn clients?"

"I don't know. I've only been investigating the real estate companies, not him specifically."

"Do you know anything about him personally?"

"Divorced with two adult sons. He was dating a much younger girl named Lyuba Sirko, but I think they've broken up."

Verenich was my best lead, and it was frustrating to be told I had to hold off, though I understood that was the nature of the game at the Bureau—triage to give priority to the more important case. My interest in Verenich was only peripheral at best—I had no direct knowledge he was involved in drug distribution, only the tenuous connection to the porn production company.

"So there's nothing I can do?"

She looked at me. "You busy Friday night?"

I shrugged. "Not particularly."

"Want to go clubbing with me? Lyuba often hangs out at Russian bars in Sunny Isles Beach. If we cruise around and find her, I can introduce you, and you can see if she'll tell you anything about Verenich's business."

"I don't know," I said. "I'm not that good on sweet-talking girls."

"Trust me, you don't have to say anything. Just smile and look handsome and you'll reel Lyuba right in."

I wasn't going to out myself to this stranger, so I agreed.

"Good. You can be my wingman, too. I've been snooping around a guy named Yevgeny Berdichev, who owns a convenience store in Sunny Isles Beach that might be a front. He makes large cash deposits regularly and then makes transfers into offshore accounts. He also owns a couple of car wash businesses, a Laundromat, and a liquor store—all cash-intensive businesses."

She picked up her coffee and took a sip. "I heard a rumor from one of my contacts up north that a bigwig from the Organizatsya in New York is going to be in Miami this weekend. We've never been able to pin so much as a traffic ticket on him. I'm hoping that he'll show up at one of the bars where the Russian mafia hangs out. If I can catch Berdichev entertaining him, that will help me make connections between the New York operation and the one here in Florida."

I liked her, and I thought it would be fun to hang out with her for a while. And good for me to get out somewhere new, away from the small world of Wilton Manors, where everybody knew my name and knew that I worked for the FBI. If I wanted to avoid the

NEIL S. PLAKCY

ghettoization Roly and I had talked about, it was important that I be able to operate effectively outside my comfort zone. Could I schmooze and flirt at a straight bar as easily as I did at a gay one? I'd see on Friday night.

# 6.
# BACK FROM THE DEAD

As I was leaving the coffee shop, my cell phone rang with a call from an unfamiliar number, from an area code in West Virginia. I assumed it was a robo-call but I answered anyway.

"My name is Shane McCoy and I'm calling from Lazarus Place," the man on the other end said. "Can I speak to Angus?"

I introduced myself, and he said, "I'm so glad you called. I've been talking to the police but I can't get anywhere with them."

"Talking to them about what?"

"It's complicated. Can you come over here and talk?"

I looked at my watch. It was late afternoon, and I didn't need to head back to Miramar. "I can be there in about forty-five minutes," I said.

We hung up, and I remembered the nickname Raj, the bartender at Lazy Dick's, had given me. The Green Hornet. I'd need all my powers to be the superhero these kids needed.

• • •

My car was like an oven, and I took off my jacket for the ride north and blasted the air conditioning. It was late afternoon by the time I reached Fort Lauderdale. The sun was a giant orange globe that glowed from behind one of the high-rise towers. Long shadows spread in front of Lazarus Place, a three-story building with a white-washed stucco exterior, grills on the first and second floor windows, and a rainbow flag over the front door. The high-rises of downtown Fort Lauderdale loomed in the background, but the distance between those million-dollar condos and this run-down neighborhood was greater than the few blocks that separated them.

I put my suit jacket back on to cover my shoulder holster, locked my car, and walked up the cracked concrete sidewalk.

The guy who answered the door was in his late twenties, broad in the chest, with a sexy five o'clock shadow, and dark brown hair that hung down to his shoulders. He wore faded Bermuda shorts, a T-shirt that read: "Prayer, the original wireless network," and a pair of bright green Crocs.

He was sexy in a friendly, effortless way. I showed him my badge and said, "Thanks for agreeing to meet me."

"No, thank you, for looking into this," he said, as he ushered me into the building's foyer. "I'm glad someone cares enough."

Shane locked the deadbolt behind me. "This isn't exactly the safest neighborhood," he said.

"I should tell you I'm armed," I said.

"I'm glad. But don't tell the kids—it's going to freak them out enough knowing that there's an FBI agent in the house." He pointed to the room to our right, where a mix of African American and Hispanic teenage boys were sprawled on thrift-shop sofas and bean bag chairs, reading or playing a video game. "That's our lounge, and to the left is our classroom."

The building had a warm but shabby feel, with Spanish tiles on the floor and inspirational posters on the wall. The one in front of me read, "Aim for the moon, and even if you miss, you'll be among the stars."

"The kitchen is straight ahead. Can I get you something to drink? Sorry I don't have anything alcoholic to offer you. We keep things substance-free around here for the kids."

"I'd love some water." We walked through to a kitchen that reminded me of my grandmother's, with an avocado-colored refrigerator, a pop-up toaster, and a couple of lights hanging from the ceiling in plastic globes.

He pulled a couple of bottles from the fridge. I felt guilty for taking supplies from a non-profit. I made a mental note to make a donation to Lazarus Place when I could.

"So why have you been talking to the police?" I asked.

"A boy who stayed with us for a while disappeared a few weeks ago. He left behind some of the stuff he'd been given, which made me think that he didn't move on. But the police detective insisted that if he ran away from somewhere else, he probably ran away from here. I tried to explain what we do but she wouldn't listen."

The cold water felt good going down. "Why don't you start by telling me what you do here," I said, as we sat at the Formica-topped kitchen table. "I know Lazarus was the guy Jesus raised from the dead but that's about it."

"Do you know why Jesus did that? Why he made Lazarus the subject of his most awesome miracle?"

"You got me there."

"Lazarus was a bachelor living with his two spinster sisters," Shane said. "In the book of John, chapter eleven, when Lazarus was dying, his sisters sent word to Jesus saying 'Lord, the man you love is ill.'"

"Hold on. Are you saying Jesus was gay?"

"Not at all. Other translations say either 'the one you love' or 'your friend,' and there's a whole raft of commentary that insists this was just brotherly love. But he cared so much for Lazarus that he raised him from the dead. That's a metaphor for what we're trying to do here. We're a shelter for runaway LGBT teens, mostly gay boys who end up on the streets of Fort Lauderdale. Though we're a Christian ministry, our focus is on helping these kids feel better about themselves, get back in school, or get jobs."

He drank some water. "The first Lazarus Place was founded about twenty years ago in Seattle by a Catholic priest who wanted to reach out to homeless kids. Pretty quickly he figured out that many of them were on the streets because they were gay and had been rejected by their families. That caused him to shift his focus. We usually have about twenty kids in residence at any given time.

There are two dormitory rooms on the second floor, one for the boys and one for the girls."

We heard some cheering from the living room as one of the boys apparently won the game they'd been playing. Shane smiled.

"Franny and I are both full-time resident counselors. We have rooms on the third floor, and we're always available if the kids need help. I spend a lot of time talking to homeless kids and convincing them to come here. Franny runs the house and teaches life skills like money management and how to be safe on the Internet. We work with a counseling group that gets the kids under eighteen back into school, and government aid if they qualify. We have a network of doctors and dentists who see them pro bono, and we have arrangements with a couple of local thrift stores to get them proper clothing."

I pulled out the screen capture I'd taken of the boy's face. "Do you recognize this kid?"

Shane gulped. "Yup, that's Ozzy Perez. The boy who went missing."

Ozzy Perez. Ohpee. Finally, a lead on who he was.

"Where is Ozzy now?" Shane asked. "I need to talk to him."

"I don't know yet. As far as you know, was he sexually active?"

Shane crossed his arms over his chest. "Why do you ask?"

"I think he might have been forced into doing porn." I left out the flakka for the moment.

"We talk a lot to the kids about having safe, responsible sex, but unless they volunteer the information we don't quiz them on whether they're sexually active or not." He took a deep breath. "But I know that Ozzy was molested by a neighbor when he was younger. That kind of assault can lead kids into continued sexual activity."

Ozzy had mentioned that molestation to Brian Garcia—further evidence that he was the Ohpee I was looking for.

Shane stood up. "I have Ozzy's intake form up in my room. There might be some information on it you could use."

Shane and I climbed a switchback stair to the second floor,

where he pointed out the two dormitory rooms—boys to the left in the larger room, girls to the right. We kept climbing to the third floor, where Shane's bedroom nestled under the eaves with a slanted ceiling. His bed was a futon, his desk a wooden door spanning two short file cabinets.

There was only one chair, and Shane motioned me to it while he looked through his files. "I have to fill out a form for each kid who checks in," he said. "We never know if what they tell us is a hundred percent accurate, but at least it gives us a place to start."

He handed me Ozzy's intake form, which had a photo stapled to it. Ozzy looked tired, and his hair was shaggy and plastered down to his head. He looked underfed and scared. In the video he appeared to have filled out a bit, but it was clearly the same kid.

I was fascinated by how complicated the form was, not only in the information it requested, but in the way that the reliability of each piece of data had to be certified. For example, there were boxes to check if the client didn't know each piece of information, chose not to provide it, or if the interviewer hadn't asked for it.

Ozzy's full name was Oswaldo Yuniesky Perez, his ethnicity was Hispanic/Latino, and his race was white. The list of genders was one of the most comprehensive I'd seen on a government form, including male, female, transgender MTF, transgender FTM, other, client refused to answer, or client doesn't know.

That stopped me for a moment and I turned to Shane, who was sitting on his bed. "How can you not know your gender? Don't you just look down?"

"It's not that easy. Gender is a lot more than the equipment between your legs, especially to teens going through puberty. I'm talking about kids who might be confused, or might eventually be trans. And then there are people who are gender fluid."

"Which means?"

"It's when your gender identity is a dynamic mix of boy and girl. Some days you might feel more masculine, and some days more feminine. But you always have parts of both. It has nothing to do with what kind of genitals you have, and it's not about sexual orientation, either."

"Wow." I shook my head, marveling at how complicated the world could be, and then went back to Ozzy's form. His sexual orientation was "questioning/unsure," he was homeless, and had been living in a "place not meant for habitation, such as a vehicle, an abandoned building, bus/train/subway station, airport, or anywhere outside." I was fascinated that there were almost thirty choices, from nursing home to jail to foster care to couch-surfing.

Ozzy had been born in Cienfuegos, Cuba, fifteen years ago. The last school he attended was Hialeah Middle, where he had dropped out during seventh grade. His overall health was good, though his dental health status was poor.

Interestingly he had refused to answer the questions about whether he had been persuaded to have sex in exchange for anything.

Poor Ozzy. He'd been lucky to end up at Lazarus Place, and I wondered what had caused him to leave. I looked up at Shane. "Ozzy was here for what, three months? What else can you tell me about him that's not on the form?"

"His mom and dad were never married, and apparently his dad died in Cuba when Ozzy was about five. His mom brought him here after that. She was some kind of engineer but she couldn't speak much English, so the only work she could get was cleaning houses. Ozzy grew up around a lot of anger."

"You think his mom beat him?"

"He had a couple of burn scars on his back, and there was something about the way he held his right arm that made me think it had been broken and maybe not set properly. But he wasn't here long enough for us to get him a comprehensive medical exam."

Shane leaned forward. "Ozzy was almost painfully shy, and he never liked to look you in the eye when he spoke to you. It was hard to get him to open up, even about simple stuff, like what kind of food he liked. He told me that once he got into middle school, kids started to give him a hard time for being gay. He stopped going to class around the time that his mother got sick, maybe a year and a half ago, and when she died he had no place to go, so he started living on the street."

"No social services?" I asked.

"Once he dropped out of school he didn't have a teacher or a counselor to talk to, so he had no idea what was available. He went over to Miami Beach but he said it was too crowded and there were too many cops. Another kid told him he could live easier in Lauderdale so he came up here."

I went back to Ozzy's form to check something. Under "refer-ral source" he had checked "outreach project."

"What does this mean?" I asked Shane. "Did someone refer him here?"

"He tried to hustle me one day. You know Fort Lauderdale beach at all?"

"Some. My skin burns pretty easily so I don't go out to sun-bathe or anything."

"The beach area here is a barrier island between the Atlantic and the Intracoastal Waterway," he said. "A1A runs right along the ocean, and that's where all the big hotels are. But if you go a block or two west, you'll find a bunch of small motels and older apartment buildings. Some of those motels have been renovated into gay guest houses."

I nodded. I'd seen ads for a couple of those in bar magazines.

"Ozzy was hanging around one of the motels scrounging from guests when I met him. I convinced him to come over here and try us out. I was upset when he disappeared because I thought we could make a difference for him."

He leaned back against the pillows. "I think his early history of abuse, and the way he was raised—being afraid to question anything or ask for anything—might make him particularly vul-nerable to being victimized."

I stood up and gave him my card. "I appreciate the help." He stood too, and there was an awkward moment when neither of us knew whether to shake hands or hug. "Can I talk to the kids? Maybe one of them has been in touch with Ozzy since he left."

"I doubt it, but sure, you can ask. Go easy on them, all right? Remember, they're only kids."

"I'll hold off on the waterboarding then."

Shane looked alarmed.

"I know what it's like to be a gay teen," I said. "Don't worry."

He led me back downstairs and into the lounge. A half dozen kids, a mix of boys and girls, black, white, and Latin, looked up and I felt their eyes on me. "This is Angus, and he works for the FBI," Shane said. "You guys hang here while I round up everybody else."

From the way they looked at me, I assumed that most of their experiences with law enforcement hadn't been positive. "You for real?" one of the boys asked.

I nodded. "I'm a for real FBI Special Agent." To cover my own nerves, I told them a couple of stories about my experiences at the Bureau, and the kind of training I'd gone through at Quantico.

Other kids began filtering in, both boys and girls, followed by Shane and the other social worker, Franny. She was a thirty-something-year-old woman with dime-sized holes in her earlobes and other piercings in her nose and right eyebrow.

I explained that I was looking for Ozzy. "Did he say anything to any of you before he left the house? Like maybe he met someone who was going to take care of him?"

"Shit. Ain't nobody gonna take care of us besides ourselves," a boy named DeAndre said. "And Shane and Franny."

"Anybody?" Shane asked. "Any of you have any idea where Ozzy went?"

A slim kid in a baggy plaid shirt looked down at the floor and said, in a low voice, "He was happy."

My gut reaction was that they were female, but I had no idea what pronoun they preferred.

"Happy about what, River?" Shane asked.

"He met some guy by the beach," River said. "The guy seemed nice and told Ozzy he could give him a place to stay, all the food he wanted to eat, new clothes, and stuff. Ozzy wanted an iPhone and the guy promised him one."

No one else had anything to offer, though I thought maybe the kids might open up more if I wasn't around. "Can you follow up with them?" I asked Shane as he walked me out. "Ask any kids who weren't there tonight?"

He nodded. "I cover Friday nights here at the house and Franny covers Saturday," he said. "You free this weekend?"

I nodded, though I was confused. Was he asking me on a date? Or setting a time to check in? Either way, if he had information about Ozzy Perez I'd make it my business to see him. "I'll call you, all right?" I said.

He nodded. "Be careful out there."

As I opened the door and walked out into the humid night, I wasn't afraid. I felt a bit like Lazarus myself. This investigation had brought me back to life after I was shot, and after I'd closed in on myself.

I had a full name for this boy and now I was sure he was underage. From the e-mails he'd sent Brian Garcia, I knew he wanted to get out of where he was.

Hold on, I thought. I'm coming for you. And once I get you somewhere safe, you're going to tell me all about the flakka distribution and whatever other drugs there are in the house where you're living.

# 7.
# JOCKEY AND GROOM

The next morning, just after dawn, I went out for a quick run before leaving for work. The houses around ours were shabby bungalows or ranches like the one we lived in, and I couldn't help wondering what went on behind their curtained windows. We knew a few of our neighbors, including a middle-aged gay couple and an elderly black woman with a Rottweiler. But we'd never been inside anyone else's home. Could Ozzy be living in a house in my own neighborhood?

As I ate breakfast, I checked the latest media reports on Brian Garcia. Coverage had moved from the front page to the local section. Reporters had spoken with his father, who, like Colin had told me, had no knowledge of his son's drug use. Co-workers cited his promptness, his good rapport with clients, and so on. They were all surprised at what had happened. An unnamed police source said that the cops were waiting for Brian to come out of his medically induced coma to interview him.

When I got to work I wrote up another FD302 on what I'd learned at Lazarus House last night. I began with a visit to the shelter's website and copied out some information about it and inserted it into my report. In as much detail as I could, I wrote paragraph after paragraph about speaking with Shane and the kids, and his identification of the boy in the screen capture as Ozzy Perez.

I included everything from the intake form as well as what River, a resident of the house, had said about Ozzy meeting a man who would take care of him. I was careful to avoid the need for any gendered pronouns in River's case.

Then I accessed an immigration record with the date that Ozzy had come to the United States with his mother, sponsored by her sister under the Cuban Family Reunification Parole Program. I found a record of his mother's death the year before, and verified that Ozzy had attended Hialeah Middle School and dropped out during the seventh grade. But after that, nothing. I searched all the databases I had access to in case Ozzy had been arrested or was in custody. No one of his name showed up anywhere.

After the form was complete, I went back to the only piece of concrete evidence I had—the video of the jockey in the locker room at Hialeah Race Track. Time to use my credit card to access the full video.

It was weird to watch porn in the office. I skimmed through the movie until I came to the place where the free preview had stopped. Ozzy finally looked at the camera and it solidified his identification as the boy whose screenshot was on the webcam site and whose photo was stapled to Shane McCoy's file.

He stood there naked for a moment, his purple and white silks pooled around his feet, then began to play with himself. He was getting into it when the door behind him opened with a bang, and a dark-skinned young man came in.

He wore a western-style plaid shirt, jeans, and a black cowboy hat. They talked for a moment—it appeared that the black guy was the groom who took care of the jockey's horse. "You're a good rider," the groom said. "You want to ride me?"

He dropped his jeans, revealing a long, slim dark purple dick that was already hard. He sat down on the bench and Ozzy lowered his ass over him. They engaged in some basic sex—nothing I hadn't seen before. I was intrigued, though, by how smoothly the black boy occupied the space around him. He had great posture, and when he stood, he kept his spine erect and moved his long legs with a sense of grace. Though I didn't know much about classical dance, there was something about him that made me think he'd had ballet training.

I wondered if his height, close to six feet, indicated that he'd gone through puberty already. But his body was hairless and his face was rounded, not demonstrating the angularity that came with those body changes.

The boys romped together for a while, and then an older man walked into the locker room and started yelling at them for fooling around. He whipped out his dick and Ozzy sucked him while the man played with the black boy's nipples. The video ended with the man pulling out of Ozzy's mouth and spraying his face with semen.

I hit the buttons to grab a capture of the black boy and the man's faces, and then a screen popped up offering me more videos. None of the teasers featured either of the boys, though, so I closed the window.

Who was the other boy with Ozzy? Was he local, too? And if he was, could he lead me to Ozzy, or to whoever was distributing the flakka?

I did the same thing I'd done with Ozzy—I put his face into Google's image search function. After a lot of hunting, I found him at the edge of a group shot of young male dancers, ranging in age from little boys to teenagers. I recognized the teacher with them—a guy named Nathan who I'd met a couple of times at meetings for an LGBT political action group Jonas and I had joined.

It was another example of the small world of Wilton Manors. If you moved around from circle to circle—from a bar to a civic group to meeting friends of friends—you could get to know a wide range of people.

Of course I didn't have Nathan's phone number; that would be too easy. But the political group had an online site, with a spreadsheet listing names and phone numbers of members so that we could coordinate rides to rallies and so on. I found Nathan's cell number there.

I called him and reminded him of how I knew him. "I'd like

to ask you a couple of questions about a boy who's in a photograph with you," I said.

"This isn't a good time," he said. "I have a dozen budding ballerinas waiting for their afternoon class, and as soon as I finish I have to head over to the bar where I work nights."

"If I came up to your studio, could we talk for a couple of minutes before you have to go to work?"

He hesitated. "What's this about?"

I explained that I was trying to track down a couple of boys I suspected were being abused. "One of them is in a picture with you. I'd like to find out his name and how you know him."

He agreed that if I met him at the studio in Pompano Beach, he could talk to me for a few minutes before he had to leave for his restaurant gig.

When I left the office a few minutes later, the skies were gray and threatened rain. A flock of white egrets rose gracefully from one of the retaining ponds, and I was reminded of the way the boy moved in the video. You didn't come by those moves naturally. They were the result of years of dedicated training. What had happened to turn him from that path and into the grip of a porn producer? Had he been seduced by the promise of money and security, the way Ozzy had? Had he, too, lost his home and family?

Traffic on I-95 crept north through Fort Lauderdale onward to Pompano Beach—a grimy area of car repair shops, chain retailers, and fast food restaurants. In my Mini Cooper, I felt small and insignificant in a sea of semi-trailers, oversized SUVs, and RVs with Canadian license plates.

Between the gray skies and my gloomy thoughts, I was in a dark mood by the time I reached the address Nathan had given me. The School of Modern Ballet was located at one end of a 1950s-era shopping center. The grocery at the other end had ceded its property to a Haitian Apostolic Church. The street's remaining tenants included a cell phone retailer, a tax outfit, and a dollar store.

I parked in front of the studio and recognized Nathan at the front of the class facing the full-length windows onto the parking lot. He was in his mid-twenties, and had a slender, graceful body and a mop of brown hair that flopped in his face as he danced. I didn't want to interrupt, so I sat in my car and watched the class.

About a dozen girls and one boy, stood around the room beside a waist-high bar attached to the mirrored walls. They watched as Nathan grasped the bar on the back wall and lifted his right leg up, his foot extended. Then he stopped and the kids imitated his movement.

He walked around the room, adjusting the set of a spine or the height of a leg. The session seemed to be finished when all the kids applauded him, and a barrage of moms approached the studio to pick up their kids. I walked inside against the tide of giggling ten-year-olds in tights and toe shoes. Nathan had a towel around his shoulders as he bent over to replace the CDs in their cases on a shelf. The wood floor was scuffed, the room smelled of sweat and mold, and the mirrored walls made the room seem larger than it was.

"I was watching from outside for a couple of minutes," I said. "You're incredibly talented."

"If I was that great I'd be dancing Balanchine with the Miami City Ballet instead of teaching ten-year-olds and waiting tables on the side. But that's a whole other conversation. What did you want to ask?"

I pulled out the screen capture I'd taken of the ballet class with Nathan on one side and the boy from the video beside him. "Oh, yeah, I remember that," he said. "A friend of mine got a stress fracture in his foot and had to stay off it for a few weeks, so I took over his classes at the New World School of the Arts in Miami while he was laid up."

"Do you recognize this boy?"

He peered closely at the photo. "Like I said, I only taught there for a short time. I think his name began with D. Derick? David? Something like that. Manny could probably tell you more. Manuel Arristaga. It was his class I took over."

He folded up his towel and stuffed it into a gym bag. "You can call the school tomorrow and find out when he's teaching," he said. "The kid may still be studying there. That picture was taken last year and I don't think he was a senior."

"The New World School," I said. "Another dance academy like this one?"

He shook his head. "A performing arts high school, like the one in the movie *Fame*. You have to audition to get in, and you have to have talent." He tapped the photo. "This kid was good but raw, like he hadn't had much training when he was little. But he could imitate any move you showed him."

He looked at his watch. "I wish I could stick around, but I have to be on shift in fifteen minutes and that's barely enough time to drive there." I thanked him and walked back out to my car.

Here was a kid with talent, who'd been in the right place to develop what God had given him. Manuel Arristaga might hold the key that would unlock the mystery of this boy, and perhaps Ozzy Perez as well. Too bad I'd have to wait until the next day to get hold of him.

So far I'd found two boys involved with the same website. Were there more? What if there was a whole stable of these kids performing? And how did the flakka distribution figure in?

# 8.

# DANCING WITH THE DEVIL

After a shower and a quick breakfast the next morning, I joined the flow of rush hour traffic heading south, instead of my normal south-west route to the office. After a long slog, the towers of downtown Miami appeared on the eastern horizon like a kind of Shangri-La by the Sea. For a boy like me who'd grown up land-locked in the industrial Northeast, Miami seemed like a paradise of sunshine and palm trees, even though in my eight months there I'd already begun to explore its darker corners.

I turned off the highway and into the maze of one-way streets that characterized downtown. The New World School of the Arts was housed in a nine-story building surrounded by parking lots and low commercial buildings. I'd read that the dance studios were housed in the main building, along with the academic classrooms and administrative offices, so after I parked in a city garage that's where I headed.

I walked in under the theater-like marquee and marveled at how clean and bright the building was. The walls were splashed with color and student art work—from woven tapestries to graffi-ti-like murals. It sure didn't look like the high school I'd attended back in Scranton.

I showed my badge to the young woman on duty at the sleek wooden reception desk and had her establish that Mr. Arristaga was in the dance studio. I filled out a form and got a visitor's pass.

It must have been between classes, because the halls were filled with a diverse group of teens that could rival the United Nations.

Boys, girls, and those whom Shane had called gender fluid, were dressed in everything from T-shirts and low-riding jeans to tight outfits I'd expect to see in a club, not a high school. Every color of hair was represented, from scarlet to purple to green.

They all seemed so happy, as if at every moment they realized how lucky they were to be in such a great environment. I took the elevator up to the dance studio level with two boys and a girl, and the girl began singing the chorus of Adele's "When We Were Young" a cappella. Then the boys joined in with her, all three of them completely unself-conscious.

Their enthusiasm was infectious, and I was humming the song myself as I made my way to the main studio, where I spotted a slim man in black slacks and a white shirt exercising at the bar along one mirrored wall.

The contrast to the studio where Nathan taught was striking. This room was high-ceilinged and bright, with a baby grand piano in the corner instead of a CD player. The wood floor was the same, but here it had been polished to a high gleam, and the room smelled of makeup, canvas, and rosin.

I waited until the dancer turned and noticed me. "Can I help you?" he asked.

He was older than I'd expected, probably fifty or so, with graying black hair. As I approached him I said, "Nathan Clemens suggested I speak with you. My name is Angus Green and I'm a Special Agent with the Miami office of the FBI."

"The FBI? Is Nathan in trouble?"

"Not at all." I explained that I was trying to track down a boy who might have been one of his students, and I showed him the photo of Nathan and the group of students. "I'm interested in this young man here," I said, pointing.

"That's Dimetrie," he said. "Why are you looking for him?"

Once again, I chose not to mention the flakka—at least not right away. I thought I'd get more from Arristaga by focusing on the boy. Now that I knew he was young, like Ozzy, there was a compelling case to be made that he needed rescuing.

"I think he's being exploited."

I explained about the video featuring Dimetrie. I showed him a head shot from the video, and he confirmed that it was the boy he knew.

"That's awful. If you find him, let him know that he can call me. The school has a counselor who could try and get him into foster care, at least so that he can finish high school. I'll do whatever I can to help him."

"I will. Do you know his last name?"

"Beauvoir." He spelled the first and last name for me. Then he stopped. "Technically, I shouldn't release any information to you without Dimetrie's written permission. We have to follow the Family Educational Rights and Privacy Act guidelines."

"If I knew where Dimetrie was, I wouldn't need your information," I said. "But can you at least give me his family contact? That's not protected."

He agreed and led me through a doorway to a small office behind the studio. The walls were plastered with posters from dance competitions, and there was a brand-new box of toe shoes on the visitor's chair. "Sorry for the mess," he said as he walked behind the desk and began tapping on the computer keyboard.

A moment later, the printer beside the desk began to hum, and he handed me a single sheet of paper. "You're in luck. Dimetrie updated his information at the beginning of the term."

His guardian was Racine Beauvoir, with an address on Northeast 60th Street, in the heart of Little Haiti. Dimetrie had been born in Miami on April 11, 1999, which made him a few months shy of his seventeenth birthday.

"I'm going to this address," I said. "But it would help me a lot if you could give me some background." I hesitated, wondering how far I could push. Then I decided. "If you insist, I'll go back to my office and get a warrant prepared. But that can take time, and if I'm correct, then Dimetrie is being sexually abused, and every day that we delay adds to the danger that he's in. There is documented evidence of the connection between sexual abuse and anorexia, self-harm, and suicide. Do you want that on your conscience?"

Arristaga blew out a deep breath. "Dimetrie started here in ninth grade. His raw talent blew us away in his audition. He said he'd studied on and off with a woman who was a friend of his mother's. Over the years I had a few heart-to-heart talks with him and he told me that his father was a white man who disappeared as soon as his mother got pregnant. She turned to prostitution and eventually was infected with HIV."

He crossed his arms over his chest. "That turned into full-blown AIDS when Dimetrie was about ten. They say AIDS is no longer a death sentence, that it's a manageable illness now, but that's true for rich white men," he said. "Not for poor black women like Dimetrie's mom. Eventually, she got so sick that she couldn't work anymore, so he had to stop taking those dance classes, but his mother encouraged him to apply here. She was so proud of him. And we loved having him here, because not only was he talented, but he was tall."

I cocked my head in curiosity.

"When our female students go up en pointe, on their toes, some of them reach nearly six feet," Arristaga said. "We need tall boys to partner with them."

I nodded. "Is he still enrolled?"

Arristaga shook his head. "He showed up for the first couple of weeks of his senior year this past fall, but he told me that his mother died over the summer and he and his sister had to move in with their grandmother. She's very religious, and she didn't approve of him dancing. She said something like, he looked possessed by a devil when he did. It was a shame to lose him. I assumed he transferred to one of the mainstream high schools."

"Are there any students around I could talk to? Anyone who might have kept in touch with him?"

"I don't know offhand," he said. "There are about forty kids in the program who might know him, and they're all in their academic classrooms right now. If you leave me your card I'll speak to them this afternoon and see if I can get any information from them."

"That would be great." I handed him my card, and scrawled my personal cell number on the back. "Call me anytime." Before I left, though, I had to ask about the flakka. "Was Dimetrie into drugs at all?"

"Not as far as I know. These kids, their bodies, are everything to them, so they tend to eat carefully, exercise, take care of themselves. Why? Do you think Dimetrie is involved in drugs now?"

"I think he knows someone who's dealing flakka," I said.

"So this isn't about saving Dimetrie, is it?" Arristaga demanded. "You assume that a young black man has to be a criminal?"

"That's not what I said. I've been very clear to you about what I know. I have seen a video of Dimetrie performing sexual acts with another boy whose name is Ozzy. Both of them are under the age of legal consent. That's wrong, and against the law, and part of my investigation is to find both these boys, and any others who are underage, and get them away from these porn producers."

I took a breath. "As part of this investigation, I have discovered that this other boy supplied flakka to a young man who went crazy on Tuesday morning."

"The face-eating zombie? I read about him."

"So you see why it's important that I find Dimetrie, and through him, this other boy, and then through him, whoever is distributing the flakka. I don't care if they are black, white, or green. I'm going to stop them."

My tirade seemed to have placated Arristaga. "I meant what I said. If you get hold of Dimetrie, please let him know that I want to help. Today is a half-day for most of the school system, so if you wait until about one o'clock, if he's enrolled in another high school, he might be at his grandmother's place by the time you get there."

"That's good to know." I thanked him once again, and returned to my car, full of righteous indignation I was prepared to unleash on Dimetrie Beauvoir's grandmother if she wasn't willing to tell me what I needed.

# 9.
# LIKE A MARIONETTE

I went back to the same coffee shop where I'd met Katya, opened my laptop, and used the secure VPN software to get on my Bureau e-mail. I'd gotten a few more messages from groups that helped LGBT kids, but none of them were able to shed any light on local pornographers.

There had to be something else I could do. But what?

Colin Hendricks at the DEA had implied I had special insight into the gay porn connection. Was there any other way to leverage that?

I sat back in my chair. What if I wasn't an FBI agent, just a gay guy in Fort Lauderdale looking for some fun. Would I be willing to experiment with flakka?

That required too much of a shift in my outlook. I'd never been much into drugs in college, and even if I was still working as an accountant, I doubted I'd dabble into anything so dangerous.

But Jonas was another story. He got high occasionally, though he'd promised never to bring drugs into the house, or even have them in a car we were driving in together. Getting caught with drugs in my vicinity, even if Jonas vouched for them, could be the end of my law enforcement career.

Would Jonas try flakka? Based on what I knew of him, I had to say yes, especially if a guy he was interested in offered it to him.

And what if he did, and he liked it? Where would he go to look for it?

Jonas had a profile on Grindr, the gay hook-up app, and one

night a few weeks before I got shot, he'd convinced me to sign up as well. I'd never logged in since then, but I pulled out my cell phone and opened the app.

I was surprised at how many men were nearby and online. It was the middle of the morning, and I wasn't in what I thought of as a very gay neighborhood, yet the first profile that popped up was for a man less than a thousand feet away.

I looked furtively around the coffee shop, as if I'd been caught sneaking a peek at some guy in the locker room. No one around me matched his description, so perhaps he was in one of the other stores nearby.

I started scrolling through profiles, looking for anyone who liked to get high. I found a couple of guys, but I hesitated to contact any of them. As a Federal Agent, if I initiated a conversation about drugs with someone, and that later resulted in legal proceedings, my role could easily be construed as entrapment.

It also didn't seem fair or moral to contact a guy through a hookup app when I had no intention of hooking up with him. It was enough to learn that a gay guy like Brian Garcia or Ozzy Perez could find a drug source that way.

I checked the URL for the webcam site, hoping I could catch Ozzy online, but he wasn't one of the performers available at the moment.

By then it was one o'clock, and I logged out of the app and headed west into the heart of Little Haiti. Like many of the inner city neighborhoods around Miami, it was undergoing gentrification, with newly renovated houses right next to vacant lots and derelict properties.

I passed a restaurant painted in bright yellow and green, with a stylized palm tree painted over the door. The large-scale menu outside showed pictures of a pork dish called *griot* and a bowl of bright-orange liquid called *soup joumou*.

The address in Dimetrie Beauvoir's file was on a side street, and I cruised along, searching for house numbers on a row of small bungalows, all in various stages of disrepair. The stucco on his grandmother's mustard-yellow house was stained with leaks from a rusty water pipe. It was surrounded by a chain-link fence, with a sparse patch of grass inside. Iron grillwork covered the two small windows.

I parallel parked a few houses down and sat in my car for a moment with the air conditioning blasting. My gun felt heavy against my chest, in the shoulder holster hidden by my suit jacket. Despite the steps toward gentrification, Little Haiti was still the kind of neighborhood where drive-by shootings occurred on a regular basis, often taking out innocent children. One girl had been killed while she sat on a front porch while her aunt braided her hair.

A pair of boys who were about seven or eight passed my car, looking in curiously. Ahead of me, a heavy-set older woman in a brightly flowered dress pushed a grocery cart loaded with pineapples and mangoes.

I stepped out of the car, straightened my tie, and locked the door. I felt very conspicuous as a white man in a suit in an all-black neighborhood, and I sensed people watching me—including a skinny guy leaning against the wall of a grocery on the corner. A low-riding car passed me, the speakers blasting fast tropical music.

Despite the sunshine and the bright colors, I felt an ominous gloom in the neighborhood that contrasted sharply with the joy I'd experienced at the New World School. What had it been like for Dimetrie to commute between these two worlds?

With a smile plastered on my face, I walked down the cracked sidewalk to Mrs. Beauvoir's house, let myself in through the gate, and rang the bell on the front door. To my right was a large crucifix with Jesus grimacing in pain, his body twisted and drops of blood were painted on his hands and feet.

"Who are you?"

The voice that came from behind the door was high-pitched, with a heavy French accent. I held up my badge to the eye hole. "Special Agent Angus Green from the FBI," I said. "I'd like to talk to you about your grandson, Dimetrie."

The latch slid and the door opened a fraction. A short, wizened woman in a faded housecoat peered up at me. "He izz not here no more."

"I'm looking for Dimetrie," I said. "Do you have any idea where I could find him?"

"He have bah-won in him," she said. "Pulling him strings like marionette." She mimed a jerky dance move that seemed far from Dimetrie's grace and I wondered if that bah-won was the Haitian demon that Manny Arristaga had mentioned.

Out of the corner of my eye, I spotted a skinny, flat-chested girl who was about thirteen, lurking by the street. But I ignored her for the moment to concentrate on Dimetrie's grandmother.

"Dimetrie may be in danger now. I'd like to help him."

"No help for heem," she said. "He izz like heem mother, full of demons."

She tried to close the door, but I stuck my foot in it. "Do you know any friends he might be with? Any other relatives he'd go to?"

"No one." She pushed the door against my foot, and when I stepped back she slammed it and I heard the deadbolt click.

Had she given up on her grandson because she feared that the demon had lured him into debauchery? Did she know that he had become involved in porn?

I slid one of my business cards into the door handle, though I was sure Dimetrie's grandmother would throw it away as soon as she saw it. It was sad that she had abandoned her own flesh and blood, a boy with so much talent.

After waiting a moment in case Racine Beauvoir changed her mind, I turned and walked back out to the sidewalk. The skinny girl I'd noticed was gone, and the only sounds I heard were trucks on I-95 a few blocks away.

I looked up and down the street. Did no one care enough about this boy to try and help him? Or were they sure I was trying to arrest him rather than rescue him?

I looked down at the pavement, where a tiny yellow flower pushed up through the cracked concrete. It reminded me of the ones I'd picked with my friends—buttercups, I think they were. We'd rubbed them on our chins to prove our sweetness.

Such innocent days. I'd lost that innocence at Quantico, when I learned how awful the world could be. It was sad to think that Dimetrie Beauvoir and Ozzy Perez had lost theirs even earlier.

# 10.
# BARON SAMEDI

I'd only gone a few feet back toward my car when I heard a voice behind me. "You a cop?"

I turned around. The skinny girl was there, her hands on her hips.

"I'm an FBI agent." I smiled at her, trying to establish that I was a good guy. "My name is Angus."

"Why you looking for my brother?"

"Because I want to help him. I think he's in trouble."

"He's fine. My grand-mére, she hates him because he likes to dance. She say both of us remind her too much of our mother."

She did look a lot like Dimetrie, with the same deep set eyes and flat black hair.

The small grocery store, where the guy in the wife-beater had been lurking, was half a block away. "It's really hot out," I said. "Can I buy you a soda and ask you some questions about your brother?"

She looked around furtively. I was sure that people were watching us from behind barred windows, but Dimetrie's sister seemed to decide to trust me. "All right," she said, and she started walking down the street.

I hurried to keep up with her. I didn't have a lot of experience talking to kids her age, and it was important to get her to open up to me if I had a hope of finding Dimetrie.

One of the skills we'd studied in Quantico was elicitation, using apparently casual conversation to collect information that a target might not willingly provide. There were more than two dozen specific techniques, from simply being a good listener to making provocative statements in order to fool the target into rebutting.

The first thing I wanted to do was establish a rapport with the girl. "What's your name?"

"Lucie."

"You look a lot like Dimetrie," I said. "But I've only seen pictures. I have a couple that I printed out. Maybe you'd like to see them."

"Old pictures?" she said dismissively.

"I don't know. You can help me figure out how recent they are. But then again, they're poor quality screenshots. You might not even recognize him."

We reached the store and I opened the front door for Lucie and ushered her in ahead of me. The air conditioning was set to frigid and it felt great after being in the heat of the sun.

"Screen shots?" she asked. "You mean from the Internet? Is he dancing?"

I didn't answer. I was afraid that if I told her the truth, she'd deny it, shut down, and I'd never get anything else from her.

She pulled a can of Coke from the cooler and put it down on the cashier's counter. I did the same thing, then paid for the two sodas.

She grabbed her can and walked a few feet to the back of the store, where she sat down at a small table. "Dimetrie's going to dance with a real ballet company."

I sat across from her. "I spoke to his teacher at the New World School of the Arts and he agrees with you. He said Dimetrie's very talented." The soda can was ice-cold in my hand. "Do you know where he's living?"

She shook her head. "He won't tell me. But it's somewhere in Fort Lauderdale."

"How do you know?"

She looked down at the table. "He sends me money orders sometimes."

My heart sank. Lucie almost certainly did not know what Dimetrie was doing to earn that money. "He does? That's great."

"He won't tell me where he is or what he's doing. But he says he's still taking free dance classes." She looked down at her soda can. "I like to sing, and he says I should use the money to pay for my lessons. That one day we're gonna sing and dance together."

"That sounds awesome," I said. "But here's the thing. I'm afraid that someone is taking advantage of Dimetrie. I want to find him and make sure he's OK."

"You don't want to arrest him?"

I shook my head. "He hasn't done anything wrong." I paused. "You said he's sending you money orders from Fort Lauderdale?"

She nodded.

"Your grandmother doesn't know?"

"He sends them to my friend's house," she said. "I take them to this check cashing place where her brother works and he cashes them for me."

I knew that a money order had to indicate the specific location where it was sold. If I could see one, I might be able to track Dimetrie down through it.

"The next time you get one, could you call me?" I asked. "I'd like to see where the money order was issued."

She looked down at the table and didn't say anything for a moment, but then she reached into her pocket and pulled out a folded envelope. "My friend gave me this one this morning."

She held the envelope, but didn't move to give it to me.

"There's nothing wrong with your brother sending you money," I said. "You won't get in trouble, and neither will he. But it would help me to know where the money order came from."

She handed me the envelope and I unfolded it. The postmark read "South Florida," which wasn't helpful. She had already opened the envelope so I was able to pull out the money order, wrapped in a piece of lined white paper, obviously a note from her brother.

I put the note aside and looked at the money order for fifty dollars. It had been issued at a Publix grocery store on NW Fifteenth Avenue in Fort Lauderdale, at the border of Wilton Manors.

I wrote down all the information on the money order and then handed it back to Lucie. "Does he send these regularly?" I asked. I thought perhaps I could stake out the Publix if he had a pattern.

"Every few weeks," she said. "The last one was maybe two weeks ago."

There went the idea of watching the Publix. "Is that a note from Dimetrie?" I asked, nodding toward the white paper.

"You can read it if you want."

It was a quick scrawl, sending his love to her, and at the bottom he had written what looked like "*rete bonjan*." I pointed to it and asked, "What does that mean?"

"It's Haitian creole," she said. "It means stay strong."

I tried to pronounce it, and Lucie laughed. She said it out loud for me, and I mimicked her. "Thank you, Lucie." I gave her my card. "If you ever have the chance to get word to Dimetrie, tell him that I want to help him, all right?"

She took the card and nodded shyly. "You said you have pictures of my brother?"

I pulled out my phone and showed her the head shot I had taken from the racetrack video. I'd cropped the shot from the scene where Ozzy was blowing him. Dimetrie's head was tilted back showing his face. He was still wearing the cowboy hat, and his eyes were glazed over with lust.

"Why is he wearing that stupid hat?" she asked. "Is that for a dance?"

"He's playing a role in a video."

"Is he dancing? Do you have a link to the video?"

"I don't have the link," I said. There was no way I was showing a ten-year-old girl her adored older brother having sex on camera.

I had a feeling she knew my reasoning without telling her. She grabbed her soda and said, "I have to go. My grand-mére will be looking for me." Then she hurried out of the store.

I sipped my soda and considered what I had learned from Lucie and her grandmother. Mrs. Beauvoir had kicked Dimetrie out because she thought he was under the influence of a Haitian demon called the "bah-won." He was obviously being paid for his movie work, because he had enough to send regular money orders to his sister. And he said he was still taking dance classes, too.

Was it possible he was performing in porn without being forced? Either way, at sixteen, what he was doing was still illegal—whether he was being forced or not. I still had to find him. The address of the Publix in Fort Lauderdale was a good clue that he might be living somewhere in the Wilton Manors area—maybe right in my own neighborhood.

When I got to my car, I turned on the engine and kicked the air conditioning into high gear, then drove back to the office. When I got there I opened a new FD302 and entered all the details of what I'd learned from Manuel Arristaga, Mrs. Beauvoir, and Lucie. It seemed like a lot of information, yet little of it was going to help me find Dimetrie and Ozzy. And none of it had anything to do with flakka distribution.

I was falling into the trap that Roly had warned me about, worrying too much about these boys when my case, and our jurisdiction, was the drug angle. But I couldn't help myself. I needed to find Dimetrie and Ozzy, and my gut told me that once I did, I'd find the drug distributors.

Dimetrie had told his sister that he was still taking dance classes, so I did some searching and found a bunch of different offerings in the Wilton Manors area. I ruled out the ones that were clearly for amateurs—Dimetrie was too much of a professional already to bother with a group that learned different dances each week to explore self-expression. I didn't see him at a bar learning to line dance, or taking swing lessons at a senior center.

The Broward School's adult education department offered a range of classes for kids and adults, including a free ballet class at Lauderdale High, on the edge of Wilton Manors. It met on Tuesday evenings and was led by a rotating series of volunteers. I put that in my calendar. It seemed like my best bet to find him based on what I knew.

What about the demon that Racine Beauvoir had mentioned? The bah-won? I'd worked with a Haitian agent on my last case,

Ferdy Etienne, so I walked through the narrow corridors of our office building until I found his office.

He was a round-faced guy with a bald head, a mustache and a goatee, who favored neatly tailored suits with nipped waists. "You ever hear of a Haitian demon called the bah-won?" I asked.

"Sure, Bahwon Samedi," he said, giving the words the full French pronunciation. "In English he's called Baron Samedi. He's the spirit who accepts you into the realm of the dead. What's your interest in him?"

I explained the way that Racine Beauvoir had described her grandson as a puppet of the demon.

"Makes sense." He typed on his computer and then swiveled the screen around to show me. "This is a picture of him. See the top hat, black tail coat, dark glasses, and cotton plugs in the nostrils? That's the way we dress a corpse for burial in the Haitian style."

Just looking at the character's skull-like white face creeped me out.

"I can see why this grandmother would be upset if the Baron has possessed her grandson," Ferdy said. "He's known for outrageous behavior, swearing, and making filthy jokes to the other spirits. And he lures people into debauchery."

"Sounds like what has happened to this boy."

"Baron Samedi is a *loa*, one of the gods of Haitian voodoo. They say that Papa Doc Duvalier, the Haitian dictator, modeled his personality on that of the Baron, speaking in a nasal voice and wearing sunglasses."

I thanked Ferdy for the help and walked back to my office. It must have been tough for Dimetrie to be torn between the crucified Jesus on his grandmother's front door and the voodoo spirits inside. Would I end up in a tug of war between the two for Dimetrie's soul? Where was he, and how did he and Ozzy tie into the distribution of flakka?

# 11.
# SEXY GIRL

It was already Friday evening by the time I called it quits, and I went home to change clothes for my evening with Special Agent Katya Gordieva, trolling a Russian bar in search of bad guys and ex-girlfriends.

I took I-95 south from Fort Lauderdale and got off at 163rd Street in North Miami Beach, then headed east. As I crossed the bridge over the Intracoastal Waterway, the familiar detritus of check cashing places and dollar stores gave way to a vista of skyscrapers in so many odd shapes—cylinders with wrap-around balconies abutted ziggurat towers which were next to sleek glass rectangles. You'd think the view was a geometry quiz.

Evening had fallen as I turned left on Collins Avenue, the north–south road that paralleled the beach. The tourists lining the sidewalks had swapped their bathing suits for Hawaiian shirts and tasseled shawls over sleeveless dresses. I found the bar where I was supposed to meet Katya and snagged a tiny spot near the street. As I walked toward the entrance, I passed an elderly couple in matching track suits, and an Orthodox Jewish woman wheeling a double stroller, accompanied by two young boys wearing yarmulkes. It was a different world from Wilton Manors.

I peered in at the bar and didn't see Katya, so I ambled around the center for a couple of minutes, passing a cell phone store, a Russian deli, and a women's clothing store with sparkly dresses on skinny mannequins in the window.

I saw Katya coming through the parking lot and waved to her.

She looked smoking hot in a tight black mini-dress, with a couple of gold chains around her neck. "Have to fit in with the crowd," she said, when I mentioned how good she looked. She tucked her arm in mine. "Come on, I'll show you some fun."

The bar, Tovarich, was little more than a double-wide store-front—much smaller than Lazy Dick's—with a u-shaped bar lined with high stools and a glittering glass bar-back filled with one of the most extensive displays of liquor I'd ever seen.

Katya led me up to the bar and peered forward, scanning the bottles behind it. She nodded, then turned to me. "You like oranges?"

"Sure."

She spoke to the bartender in Russian and he nodded. We watched as he mixed a premium Russian vodka, Lillet, orange liqueur, and bitters, then topped both drinks with extravagant orange peel curls. She handed him a platinum credit card and said to me, "This is on me. I'll say you're a client considering buying a condo here."

She lifted her glass to mine. "This is a Snow Queen Martini. I got hooked on them in New York."

The martini was miles better than the cheap beer and watered down margaritas I was accustomed to drinking. "Wow," I said.

"See? You've got to know what to order in a place like this. Otherwise, they'll give you the cheapest vodka and charge you the highest price."

She leaned toward me. "Let me give you some background on this neighborhood. Ten or fifteen years ago, this part of Collins Avenue was a long strip of fifties motels. Then, somebody recognized it was undervalued beachfront property, and the building boom kicked off. The Russians moved in during that first wave, so the neighborhood got the nickname Little Moscow."

"Everybody here is Russian?"

She shook her head. "Lots of other groups, too—South Americans, Cubans, Romanians. But because the Russians are concentrated here, rather than spread around, their presence is more visible. Last statistic I saw was that seven percent of residents here speak Russian as their first language."

She lowered her voice. "Look around. Tell me what you think of the clientele."

Most of those at the bar were men in their thirties and forties, in groups of two or three. They looked like they'd come from work, a mix of corporate-logo polo shirts and business suits. When I listened closely, I realized that the only language I could hear was the guttural tones of Russian.

I told her that, and she nodded. "Most of these guys are from the southern part of Russia—I can tell from their accents."

"Is there that much of a difference?"

She shook her head. "Only in the way they pronounce certain consonants, or their occasional word choice. When I was in college, I spent one semester in Moscow and another in Volgograd, so I learned the difference."

"Is the guy you're looking for here?"

"Nope. But those two guys up at the bar, with the close-cropped blond hair? They're Berdichev's drinking buddies, so he might be on his way. Let's order some food and give him time to show up."

Katya called over a waitress and ordered for us in Russian. After the waitress left, I asked, "So what's your story?"

"Born in Boston to Russian immigrant parents. Bachelor's in Russian studies from NYU, recruited to the Bureau right out of law school at Georgetown. I've never worked in a field office; I've always been undercover."

"Wow. What's that like?"

"Long periods of boredom interspersed with brief moments of pure terror." She smiled. "What's yours?"

"Bachelor's and master's in accounting from Penn State. Crunched numbers for a company in Philadelphia for six months and hated it. Joined the Bureau as an analyst, did that for two years. Then I went to Quantico. Landed here eight months ago."

"After you e-mailed me, I spoke to Roly Gutierrez about you. He says you're very smart. And fearless."

"I don't know about that." I told her how I'd been shot during a takedown at the Miami Beach Convention Center, as a case I'd been investigating came together. "I felt like the Terminator, you know? These guys in a big SUV were trying to kidnap a jewelry dealer, and they had assault rifles out. I walked toward them, firing at anything that moved. It was an out-of-body experience."

"Good agents work on instinct," she said. "That's what you did."

"Yeah, that's what they say."

"What brought you to Miami?"

I shrugged. "It's where the Bureau assigned me. How about you?"

"I needed to get away from the cold and snow."

There was something about her posture that made me ask, "And away from a man?"

She cocked her head. "Have you heard something about me?"

"Nope. Just a guess."

"Yeah. I got in too deep with a guy I was cultivating as a source. I go for the bad boys, you know?"

"Must make it tricky for you."

"You don't know the half of it. What about you—you like the bad boys too?"

So she knew I was gay. Well, that wasn't a shocker. I hadn't been hiding at the Bureau, so either Roly told her or she'd figured it out on her own.

"My dad died when I was ten, and I had to step up and be the man until my mom remarried. I was the good boy, never got a note sent home from the teacher, never failed a class, or got drunk or high. Bad boys scare me."

She smiled, and I could see how seductive she could be. "Sometimes being scared is the best part."

We talked more as we ate. Katya had ordered a bunch of different food for us to share—a spicy borscht topped with a dollop of sour cream, red peppers stuffed with ground beef and rice, and lamb meatballs. It was a real change from the grilled chicken, salad, and pizza I usually ate.

As we talked, Katya observed the people around us, listening to conversations and making mental notes. She was livelier and more open than most agents I'd worked with, and we bonded as she introduced me to a side of South Florida I'd never seen before.

By the time we finished eating, her mark still hadn't shown up, nor had Verenich's ex-girlfriend Lyuba. I was about to call the evening a wash when Katya said, "Wait here."

She stood up and walked to the bar. I watched as she leaned in beside one of the buzz cut guys she'd said was Berdichev's friend. She spoke to the bartender, then the two guys joined the conversation. Katya laughed and put her hand on one guy's shoulder.

When she returned to me she said, "There's a special party at a Russian bar called Krasotka," she said. "Those two guys are going there in a few minutes. That's probably where Berdichev is taking the New York bigwig."

Krasotka was tucked away on a side street a couple of blocks away, Katya said. She paid the bill with her platinum card and we walked out into the warm night. There was a steady stream of traffic, with tiny Fiats and Smart cars squeezing between monster trucks and huge RVs beside us as we made our way over to the bar. The night buzzed with honking horns, laughter, Latin music, and revving motorcycles.

We turned a corner and Katya pointed to a glittering building with two huge wooden front doors. "Krasotka is Russian slang for sexy girl," Katya said. "Think I fit the bill?"

"Absolutely."

We stood at the edge of the parking lot and Katya analyzed the crowd. "That girl there," she said, pointing at a blonde with shoulder-length straight hair and large-framed glasses. "Fresh off the boat. See how loose her dress is? And she has no boobs. Give her a year here, and she'll have contacts, breast surgery, and a full wardrobe of bandage dresses."

She took my arm, said something in Russian to the bouncer

at the door, and we walked inside. Swoops of tiny glittering blue-white lights hung from the ceiling. The bar and all the banquettes along the sidewalls were black and bright blue, and the music was loud.

We walked around the perimeter of the room. Then Katya pulled me off to the side. "I don't see Berdichev yet, but do you see that black-haired girl over there—the one in the tight red dress? That's Lyuba."

Lyuba had short dark hair cut in a pageboy. She held an empty martini glass in her hand as she tapped one of her red high heels against the floor and swayed to a Rihanna song. "I guess I'm on, then," I said.

I walked up to Lyuba and motioned toward her tapping foot. "You want to dance?"

She smiled and put her arm in mine. "You bet!"

I led her to the dance floor and we danced to a mix of contemporary American music and what seemed like Russian pop. I went to a bunch of LGBT dances when I was at Penn State, so I'd mastered a few moves, though I'd always danced with men before. Lyuba was shorter than most of the guys I'd danced with, and of course bustier. It was odd having her ya-yas pressed against my chest, and she was curvy in places guys weren't.

I'd always assumed I was pretty far down on the Kinsey scale, a five or more probably a six, because I'd never fantasized about girls, and I'd never been to bed with one. But with Lyuba, my dick didn't seem to get the memo. It was stiff and I liked the way it felt as she moved against me. If only I could fantasize she was a guy—but from her frizzy hair, sweet perfume, and insistent hips, she was all woman.

One of the speakers who'd come to Penn State when I was in school was a salesman from the suit department at a big department store, and he'd given us pointers on the clothes we'd need for our first jobs. He'd asked the guys in the audience who knew which way they dressed, and one guy raised his hand. "To the right," he said, and I realized the salesman was talking about the way your dick fell to one side or the other.

Luckily for me, I dressed to the left—which meant my gun was on the opposite side of my body, and it wasn't difficult to keep Lyuba from realizing I was armed.

After our fourth or fifth dance, Lyuba fanned herself. "I could use drink," she said. It was the first time I got a hint of her accent.

"Sure, me too," I said. "What do you want?"

She asked for a Heineken, and I managed to snag the bartender's eye and order one for her and one for me. She stayed right behind me, as if I'd sneak away if she let me out of her sight.

When we got the beers I motioned her over to a quieter place by the wall, where we were able to slip into a side-by-side banquette. She knocked her beer against mine and said, "I am Lyuba. What your name, handsome?"

I began to say Angus, but stopped on the first syllable. "Andy," I said. To cover for the blip, I added, "They call me Andrew at work. But it's not work hanging out with you."

"You are slick one, Andy," she said. "What kind of work you do?"

"I'm an accountant." I named a big company whose offices I often passed on the highway. "Internal audit. Very boring. How about you?"

"Doctor's office. I do Medicare billing. Even more boring." She looked at me. "I have not seen you here," she said. Her Russian accent flattened out the hard *e* so that *seen* sounded like *sin*. Or maybe I was getting that sin thing from the way she leaned in close to me, her breast pressing against my upper arm. "You just move here?"

I shook my head. "I don't live around here. Just checking out the scene." I took a breath. "A lawyer I met through work told me about this place, said there were lots of sexy ladies here." I smiled at her. "He was right."

"Ah, these other girls are *tyolki*," she said, making a face. "Me,

I am good girl. Except when not." She pressed against me to make the meaning of her statement clear.

"Hey, you're Russian, aren't you?" I asked, as if it had just occurred to me. "Maybe you know my lawyer friend. I was hoping he might be here. His name's Alexei."

"Are a million Alexeis here," she said. "Is common name in Russian. You know his last name?"

"Verenich," I said, though I deliberately mangled the pronunciation like a clueless American would.

Lyuba pulled back, her mouth open. "You know Alexei?"

"Why? Is that a problem? You're not his girlfriend or anything, are you?"

"For while, yes. But no more," she said. "He have bad temper."

"He seems like such a nice guy. Always talking about his rich friends and clients."

She leaned in close to me. "Alexei take stupid risks, cheating clients then bragging about it. I am scared what will happen so I say goodbye."

She picked up her beer and took a long drink. "But no more bad talk. You want to take me out sometime, Andy? We go to dinner, have good time."

Suddenly, an uproar erupted near the bar. Two men were arguing, and the crowd had cleared around them. One was a younger guy with black, curly hair that reminded me of 70s afros, though this guy was white. The other was a man in his forties, wearing a bright patterned nylon shirt.

Shirt guy shoved curly hair in the chest, and curly hair tried to punch him. People around them began yelling and the bouncer appeared and tried to separate them.

My cell phone buzzed with an incoming text.

GTG, ASAP, Katya texted.

"Crap," I said to Lyuba. I held up the phone so she could see the message but not who it was from. "My buddy needs to clear out and I'm driving. Maybe I'll see you here next time."

I leaned forward and kissed her quickly on the lips. Then I put my bottle on the table and hurried for the door, darting through the middle of the dance floor. *Staying Alive* by The Bee Gees was blasting through the speakers and a glittering ball had been lowered from the ceiling. People were making hokey disco moves and singing along with the lyrics and I felt disoriented by the periodic flashing lights from above.

It was a relief to reach the front door and step outside into the warm, humid night. "Sorry I had to pull you out so quickly," Katya said. "But I saw someone I didn't want to recognize me and I needed to get out. Did you get anything from Lyuba?"

"More than I expected. I guess I don't look gay. Lyuba responded right away."

"You don't look gay at all." Katya fingered my cotton shirt as we hurried from the bar. "These are straight guy clothes. Too bland and boring to be gay. And even if they know, maybe they think they can change you, or at least have some fun with you."

"Lyuba said that Alexei has a bad temper, and that he takes stupid risks—cheating clients and then talking about it."

"Wow. You got all that so quickly?"

"What can I say? I'm an interrogation whiz."

"I guess so."

"How about you? Did you see Berdichev?"

"Yup. He was with Doroshenko, the Russian bigwig. But also someone else. My ex. The one I left New York to get away from."

"What would he be doing in Miami?"

"I think he might be Doroshenko's bodyguard. But honestly, he's the last person I expected to see down here. He always told me how much he hated the heat."

We reached the parking lot where we'd left our cars. In the light of a street lamp Katya looked scared, the way Lyuba had when she mentioned Verenich. "You going to be OK?" I asked.

"Yeah, I'm just shaken. I'll be fine."

We said goodbye, and as I drove home, I wondered why Katya had been so spooked by seeing her ex. If she'd met him through her previous case, she had to know he was involved with the

Organizatsya, and she could have anticipated he might be accompanying this honcho from New York. Was there something more?

Not my business. I had learned that Verenich had a bad temper and cheated his clients, but how did that connect to the LLC behind the porn videos? And to the distribution of flakka?

# 12.

# MEMBERS OF THE TRIBE

Saturday morning I went to the gym for a long workout. By the time I was finished, my arms were like jelly and my legs wobbled, but I was on the road back to full strength. It was a great feeling. Throughout the day, I checked the URL for the webcam site, but it seemed like Ozzy wasn't performing. Had he heard about what had happened to Brian Garcia and gotten freaked out? Maybe he'd admitted to giving the drugs to Brian and had been pulled from the roster—or something more.

Later in the afternoon I got ready for my meeting with Shane McCoy. Was it a date? Technically, I was following up with him on my case. But there had been a vibe between us on Wednesday night, one that both of us seemed interested in exploring.

I dressed carefully, from my sexiest boxer briefs to a pair of button-fly stonewashed Levis and an oxford-cloth short-sleeve shirt that I could wear tails-out to cover my holster.

Shane had said that he'd be at a gay teen group meeting at the Pride Center in Fort Lauderdale. He thought I might be able to get some information from the kids. Again, I realized I was focusing on the two boys rather than the flakka, but at least I was on my own time that night.

• • •

It was a two-story building that could have passed for doctor's offices, across from some single-family homes and empty lots. I parked and walked inside, where Shane and a bunch of teens sat on hard plastic chairs in a meeting room.

I recognized DeAndre and River from Lazarus Place, but the others were strangers. As Shane introduced me, a couple of the kids shifted uncomfortably when they heard I was from the FBI.

"I want to show you some pictures," I said. "These are boys your age who are being exploited, and the man I think might be doing it. I don't want to arrest the boys, just help them get out of these situations and put whoever's taking advantage of them behind bars. Can you guys help me out?"

No one said anything.

"Guys," Shane said. "This is important."

A heavyset black girl with red and blue strands in her thick braids said, "What you care what we think? We ain't nothin' to you."

I turned to her. "I came out when I was about your age," I said. "Ten, eleven years ago? So I remember what it was like to be a gay kid. Hell, I'm still struggling with the same things I was dealing with in high school and college. Worrying about coming out to people, figuring out if a guy likes me, getting pissed off or maybe even scared when I hear somebody make a faggot joke. So you're not nothing to me, girlfriend. You are my tribe and I stand for you whether you like it or not."

"I look at your pitchers." The boy who volunteered had a heavy Spanish accent, shoulder-length dark brown hair, and an almost feminine bearing.

I handed him the screenshots I'd taken of Ozzy and Dimetrie's faces. "What's your name?"

"Yunior," he said. I smiled at him, and as he smiled back his face lit up.

The other kids agreed to look, and I passed around copies of the pictures. A moment later, Yunior said, "I recognize dis guy." He held up the picture of the older man. "He come up to me once by the bitch."

It auto-corrected in my head to "beach." "What did he say?"

"He ask me if I want to make money, be sexy. But he scare me so I run away."

"Good move," Shane said. "That's great advice for all of you. If you get a bad vibe from someone, get out of there as soon as you can. Head toward other people."

There was a general murmur of assent from the group.

With his smooth skin and lack of facial hair, Yunior could easily be presented to viewers as younger than he probably was. "That's the only time you saw him?" I asked.

"I di-int see him, but I was talking to Dorje and I tole him this man come up to me, and he say dat guy was bad news," Yunior continued. "He say dat guy always out looking for boys."

Because of Yunior's heavy accent I wasn't sure of the name he'd mentioned. "George?" I asked. "He another kid on the street?"

"Dorje," Shane repeated. He pronounced the name door-juh, and I had no idea what that implied about the kid's background or ethnicity. In South Florida it could be almost anything. Shane spelled the name for me as I pulled up the Notes app on my phone.

"Dorje knows everything that goes down on the beach," another boy said. A couple of them seconded that. Shane looked at me and nodded his head a bit to the side, and I took that to mean he'd tell me more about Dorje later.

None of the other kids had anything to add, and the meeting broke up a few minutes later. "Thanks for inviting me here," I said as Shane and I walked out into the tree-shaded parking lot. The sun glittered through the leaves and a nice breeze blew through. Hard to remember what dangers lurked in the shadows. "You know this other kid they were talking about?"

"Dorje's a beautiful guy," Shane said. "I think he's probably in his early twenties, and is half-Tibetan, half-Caucasian, but he's very cagey about his background. He hangs out in the area around the beach. I've tried to point him toward social services, college scholarships, that kind of thing, but he's not interested."

"He lives out there?"

"So I gather. From what I've heard, he makes deals with contractors renovating buildings to bunk down there. When he can't do that, he has a tent and a bunch of solar-powered stuff hidden away somewhere. He hustles tourists now and then for cash but mostly he meditates and breathes in the beach vibe."

"Sounds silly."

"He's anything but. He's very sharp underneath the whole new-age thing. I get the feeling he's waiting for some rich guy to come along and swoop him up."

"You know how I can find him?" I asked.

"He could be anywhere on a Saturday night," he said. "If you want to head over to Las Olas we could look for him there."

Las Olas Boulevard ran through the heart of downtown Fort Lauderdale. A couple of blocks were lined with restaurants and shops so it was a go-to destination for locals as well as tourists. If Dorje was as good-looking as Shane said, he might be there panhandling or looking for a sugar daddy to take him back to a hotel room.

Shane agreed to let me drive, and slotted himself easily into the passenger seat of my Mini Cooper. On the way, he told me about a neighborhood community meeting he'd gone to, and how he had met with one of the benefactors of Lazarus Place. He also spent his time cruising the back streets of Fort Lauderdale looking for homeless kids to bring into the shelter.

"It must be emotionally draining," I said, as I turned onto Las Olas and began looking for a place to park. "Dealing with all that sadness."

"It's tough sometimes," Shane said. "But the rewards are awesome. One of the kids I brought in from the street graduated from Broward College in December with a certificate in office systems. He's got a job in a doctor's office now and is sharing an apartment with a friend. He came by a few days ago on his way home from work to say thanks."

I agreed with Shane that it was great the kid had been able to turn his life around as I simultaneously swung into a city garage at the far end of the street. I found a space on the fifth floor, and while I put money in the automated machine, Shane walked over to a window.

I joined him there. Below us, fairy lights twinkled in the trees and cars and SUVs trickled slowly down the street. In the distance, the hotels and condo towers along the beach radiated a welcoming glow. "Sometimes I forget what a beautiful place this is," Shane said.

We stood close to each other and I resisted the urge to put my arm around him because I was afraid we'd both want to go too far too fast. Instead I said, "Yeah. I'm still in awe that I get to live here, when most people have to work all year somewhere cold and grim to afford a week's vacation in the sun."

"But where there's sun, there's shadow." Shane leaned out over the concrete windowsill. "See that alley down there?"

He pointed to a narrow space between a French restaurant and a store selling ladies' clothes. "A dealer hangs around there so junkies can steal wallets on Las Olas and turn the cash into instant fixes."

"The police know about that?"

"You never see him unless he wants to be seen," Shane said. "A lot of homeless kids are like that, too. They blend into the background and you don't realize they're there unless you're looking the right way."

"I'll count on you to be my guide," I said.

We strolled down the sidewalk for a while, weaving around the straight couples and people walking small dogs. I spotted the occasional gay couple, and a group of young friends around my age, but no kids who looked homeless or vulnerable.

Shane and I walked through a gallery of handmade art—from letter-press cards to fancy glass and metal sculptures—and we window shopped at a male underwear boutique. "Boxers or briefs?" Shane asked me.

"Boxers. My mom used to buy all my clothes, and one day, when I was about fourteen or fifteen, she came home with some boxers for me. 'You're a man now, Angus,' she said. 'You should wear men's underwear.'"

Shane laughed.

"I was mortified," I said. "I worried that maybe she'd seen come stains in my briefs when she washed them. She had just started dating the guy she was going to end up marrying and I obsessed that she was talking to him about me going through puberty." I turned to him. "How about you?"

"I'm kind of obsessed with skimpy briefs, weeny bikinis, jock-straps too." He looked right at me. "I like the way the strap feels against my ass."

Yowza. My dick stiffened in my pants and I turned away from him to re-position myself. When I looked back I said, "I'm getting hungry. Want to stop somewhere?"

"I could eat." He licked his lips.

We chose a French restaurant and settled into an outdoor table only inches from the passing promenade. I made it clear that the dinner was my treat, and encouraged Shane to order what-ever he wanted. He smiled and caught my eye—once more my dick stiffened.

We ordered onion soup and then crepes as our main course. When the waiter left, I asked, "Do you think Dorje might be out by the beach tomorrow?"

"When I get back to Lazarus Place I'll ask the kids if anyone knows where he's squatting and I'll give you a call or a text. We could go out there tomorrow afternoon."

I agreed with that, as our crocks of onion soup arrived, crusted with melted cheese. I leaned down and inhaled. "I hate to keep using all your time," I said.

"It's what I do. I find kids and talk to them and sometimes, I can even help them. It's not work if you love what you're doing."

We continued to chat, sharing bits and pieces of our back-grounds as we ate. "What brought you to South Florida?" I asked.

"I went to community college back in West Virginia," he said. "I was struggling with some issues and I gravitated toward my sociology professor, a kind, motherly woman. She encouraged me to consider a career in social work or counseling, and she helped me look at bachelor's programs and fill out my applications. I got a scholarship to Barry, in Miami Shores, and that was that. I majored in social work there, and when I graduated, I got the job at Lazarus Place."

"So you've been there a while," I said, calculating the difference between Shane's apparent age and how old he would have been when he graduated college.

"Not so long," he said. "It took me longer than normal to get my AA, between family stuff and money stuff and failing a bunch of courses because I wasn't mature enough, I finished at Barry about a year and a half ago."

"I imagine that's not an uncommon story for the kids you counsel," I said. "I was lucky that my mom pushed me to go to college, and I was able to get scholarships and part-time work. My brother's in the same situation right now and I try to send him some money when I can to make it easier for him."

"You're a disciplined kind of guy," Shane said. "I can see that. I'll bet you never failed a course or dropped out of one, did you?"

I shook my head. "Part of ignoring my sexuality when I was in high school was that I knuckled down and focused on homework and grades. By the time I got to college, that attitude was stuck in me."

We finished dinner and Shane looked at his watch. "I ought to get back to Lazarus Place," he said. "Sometimes we hear about kids, our own or ones the cops pick up, who let loose and have too much fun. Jessie and I are both on duty from eleven on Saturday night until noon on Sunday in case of emergencies."

I paid the bill, and we walked back to the garage in silence. I'd thought there was something building between Shane and me, but then he'd shut it down. What was up with that? Had I not responded strongly enough? Had I said something to put him off?

Traffic was difficult and it took a while to get out of the garage and then away from the crowded downtown area, so neither of us spoke until I drove into the parking lot of the Pride Center, where Shane had left his car.

It was dark and his car was the only one left in the lot. I pulled up beside it, then turned in my seat, expecting him to face me so that we'd share a good night kiss. But instead, he opened the door and stepped out.

"Thanks for dinner," he said. "I'll text you tomorrow morning if I get any leads on where Dorje is."

"You're welcome. Like you, this is what I do. Go out and talk to people and look for information. Let me know if you hear any more about that guy Yunior mentioned running into out at the beach, too."

Had I made any progress? I thought so. Yunior recognized the man from the video and established that he preyed on kids. It was all anecdotal data so far, but I could feel it accumulating and knew that eventually it would lead me forward, to find the boys and then the flakka distributors.

Tomorrow I hoped I'd go out with Shane again, find this kid Dorje, maybe even run into the older man on the prowl. And then—gotcha!

# 13.
# INVISIBILITY

Sunday morning Shane texted me that he had a lead on where Dorje might be living, and asked if I could pick him up at one. I replied that I would, then I went out to the kitchen, where I found Jonas drinking a tall glass of orange juice.

"You go to Lazy Dick's last night?" I asked.

"It was great! I talked to that guy from the gym. His name is Eric. I asked him if he worked at the car dealership and he said he does odd jobs for the owner and for some of the customers." He smiled. "He even asked me if I go to the gym a lot and said that he appreciated me spotting him."

"That's great," I said. "Are you going to meet up with him there sometime?"

"His schedule's funky, depending on what people need him to do. But he said he'll keep an eye out for me when he's there." I was glad that Eric had been friendly toward Jonas; I'd seen how down my roommate got when guys dissed him.

Neither of us felt like going to the gym, so Jonas and I went for a run around our neighborhood.

A couple of older men were working on their yards, cutting grass or planting flowers, and I got a warm feeling, especially as we passed the houses with rainbow flags. I liked Wilton Manors a lot, and I appreciated the role models the older couples were. Was a relationship like that in my future?

Would I end up with a guy like Shane McCoy, who was as committed to his work as I was? Honestly, I couldn't see myself dating Shane. He was a good guy, but the vibe between us had petered out. And though he was sexy in a laidback way, he wasn't the kind of guy who really floated my boat.

The first gay club I went to was in an old movie theatre on South Street in Philadelphia. It was called Clouds at the time, though it changed names and themes and owners every few years. When I walked in the first time I felt high—so excited by the pounding music, the gyrating half-naked bodies, and the overwhelming smell of male musk.

I stood awkwardly in the corner for a couple of minutes, clutching a beer, and tapping my foot to the beat, before a broad-shouldered guy a few years older than me—and a few inches taller—came over and smiled.

Something zinged in my brain, and I said, *this*. This is what I want.

The guy in front of me looked like he might have played football in college and still took care of himself. His upper body was nearly square, his pecs pressing out against his shirt. He didn't have much of a waist but his legs were like tree trunks.

We talked for a few minutes but the music was loud, and when I finished my beer he motioned to the dance floor and I followed him out there. We danced for a while, moving closer to each other until I was swaying in his arms.

Sadly, he was a sales rep in town for a convention, and after we went to his hotel room, I never saw him again.

But that encounter set the pattern for the guys I was truly attracted to. My most recent boyfriend, Lester, had fit that bill—he was big and strong, a bouncer at a bar, and I felt safe and protected in his arms. Too bad I'd broken up with him when I crawled into my cocoon after getting shot.

By the time I returned from my walk, I was ready to leave the past behind and move forward. After a shower and a brunch of French toast with maple syrup, I went back online. Ozzy still wasn't performing at the webcam site, and all the other men with pictures there looked well over legal age. I spent the rest of the morning looking for information on homeless kids in Fort Lauderdale and where they might hang out, in preparation for my trip to the beach with Shane.

When I got to Lazarus Place, Shane was waiting at the curb for me. "Where do we go?" I asked, as he got in beside me.

"Head for Las Olas again," he said. "Only this time, keep going all the way to the ocean. I'll show you some of the nooks and crannies where homeless kids hang out, and we'll see if Dorje is still staying at the place I heard about."

It was a gorgeous day to be outside—temps in the mid-seventies, low humidity, and bright sunshine. Once we passed through the restaurant zone on Las Olas Boulevard, we entered a neighborhood lined with stately palms, high-rises to our right, and a series of finger islands to our left.

"Wow, it's pretty here," I said. "Must cost a bundle to live on one of those little islands."

"You'd be surprised who lives there," Shane said. "Yeah, those new houses cost a couple million dollars, but there are still longtime Fort Lauderdale families in the smaller houses, and a lot of those condos are vacation spots for snowbirds. It's a weird mix."

The traffic was slow going because of the ongoing construction work on the road and the cars full of folks heading to the beach. When we stopped at a light, Shane leaned forward and pointed. "You see how nearly every place has a dock behind it with a boat?"

I looked where he pointed and saw all kinds of watercrafts, from small canoes and kayaks to muscular cigarettes, tall-masted sailboats, and luxury yachts.

"Most of those boats don't belong to the people in the houses," he said. "They rent the slips out to other rich people. I used to know a kid who stumbled into one of those yachts, which was owned by some people from New England. Nobody used it most of the year, and the house it was behind was the same deal, snowflakes who only came down for the occasional weekend. He was able to sneak on board and live there while it was unoccupied."

As traffic began to move again, I asked, "Can you do that?"

"These kids have learned how to be invisible. They sleep during the day and only go out under the cover of darkness. They use public restrooms and showers by the beach. They have bedrolls or sleeping bags or plastic sheets. If it gets real cold they'll go to a shelter for a night or two. They scrounge food from dumpsters and they'll panhandle if they spot somebody likely to give them spare change. Especially, around the gay guest houses."

"That's so sad." Looking at the beautiful homes, I realized that if I stayed with the Bureau I'd never make enough money to live anywhere fancy. If I was lucky, I'd end up with a guy who made decent money, too, and we'd be able to afford our own house or a condo. But a mansion like these? Never. Nor could I envision a time when I'd go on those big bucket list trips I longed for— an African safari, to see those clay soldiers in China, the beaches of Tahiti.

A woman I'd been in accounting classes with back at Penn State had moved to Silicon Valley and joined one of those Internet startup companies after graduation. At the time, it looked like a dicey move, and I felt smug that I'd landed a good job with solid benefits.

Since then though, the company she worked for had blossomed, and she'd moved up the food chain to controller. The last time I saw her mentioned in the alumni magazine, the company had gone public and made her a paper millionaire.

Shane had clearly chosen his career in social work so that he could help those who might otherwise be invisible. Katya had said she'd gone to work for the Bureau as a way to make a difference. My college friend had gone for the money. Me? The role of big brother had become ingrained in me. After my father died, my relatives had told me I had to look after my mother and Danny, even though I was only ten. I'd done that for so long it had become an integral part of my psyche. Was that why I'd joined the FBI? To look after victims?

When I decided to take the analyst job in Philadelphia, I told everyone that I wanted to do something more exciting than sit at a desk and crunch numbers, to see the world like my father wanted to. But since then, the job had morphed into something more.

Those big questions popped up again—what did I want from my life? What kind of job, money, relationship? At least I had the opportunity to make choices, which so many of the kids Shane worked with didn't have.

After another stall for a red light, we made it past the construction zone, and Shane directed me to cross the bridge and turn north on A1A. On our right, the beach was packed with sunbathers and big umbrellas, men, women, and kids out splashing and swimming in the Atlantic. To our left, the bars and restaurants were jammed.

Shane pointed out three kids—two boys dressed Goth and a heavyset girl with frizzy hair—hanging at a corner in front of a beach bar. "If we weren't on our way somewhere, I'd stop and talk to them," he said.

"You think they're homeless?"

"Can't tell until I talk to them. But they have a vibe, at least the one in the baggy shorts does. He might be living on the street but hooking up with his friends for the day."

"So that's what you do? Go up and talk to kids you think might be in trouble?"

"Part of it. You have to develop a sense of what people are like, what they're doing." He pointed ahead. "Turn left at the next light."

The atmosphere was different as soon as we turned away from the beach and left the oceanfront high-rises and foot traffic behind for a neighborhood of two-story apartment buildings and small hotels. We turned north again, and as we drove, I caught glimpses of the Intracoastal through the side streets.

The cars parked on the side of the street often had surfboards on their roofs, bike racks, or decals advertising stand-up paddleboard companies. "It's an interesting area," Shane said. "Right in the middle of gentrification. Soon all these low-rise buildings will be leveled and replaced with million-dollar condos for foreign vacationers. All the regular people who live here will get shoved out." A couple of high-rises looked new, and one of the few single-family houses was up for sale, with a sign proclaiming it the perfect site for a boutique hotel or condo development.

As we passed the occasional rainbow flag, Shane pointed out that those buildings were gay guest houses that catered to a mix of Canadians, Europeans, and men from cold climates in the states. "They're part of the reason why gay kids hang out here," he said. "The owners can be kind, and the tourists take pity on the kids."

I drove slowly, looking at the occasional empty lots for places where kids might hang out. Every so often, I saw a cluster of palm trees that looked like a good place to crash, especially after dark when there wouldn't be much street light.

"Pull up over here," Shane said, pointing to a spot across from a building under renovation. It was Art Deco-style, with eyebrow windows and a vertical sign, that looked like it belonged on one of the side streets of South Beach. "This is where Dorje might be crashing."

There were surprisingly few people on the street around us, considering we were only a couple of blocks inland from the beach. "One of the kids told me Dorje made a deal with the contractor here," Shane said. "He can crash at night and on weekends as long as nobody in the neighborhood sees him coming and going."

The building was surrounded by a chain link fence with a padlock, and I wondered if the contractor had given Dorje a key.

Shane looked around. "Down there at the end," he said. "See the way that Dumpster is placed beside the fence? And how there's a big plastic trash can on the other side?"

"Yeah?"

"That's probably Dorje's front door. Follow me." We walked up to the Dumpster and Shane looked around to make sure no one was watching us. Then he hopped up onto the top of the can, caught his balance for a moment, then vaulted over the chain link fence and onto the other can.

I followed him up and over the fence. "Interesting," I said as I landed beside him on the sparse grass. "You're sure he lives here?"

"Nope. But if he's not here, he's somewhere like this."

We walked along the fence, in the shade of the palm trees, as we approached the building. "If he's here, he may be asleep," Shane said. "We don't want to be rude."

A flicker of movement from a second-floor window caught my attention. "He's awake," I said, though I wasn't sure who I had seen at that window. "And watching us."

"Good. Then we can hang out here and wait for him to join us."

A couple of plastic chairs rested in the corner where the building met the fence, and Shane and I sat down there. A moment or two later, a slender dark-haired guy stepped out of the building's side door, wearing a pair of faded Bermuda shorts and a loose tank top. "Make yourselves at home," he said.

I was struck by the guy's beauty, if that's what you want to call it. His skin was a few shades lighter than Yunior's, like a solid tan, but with a tinge of brown. He had an oval face—broader at the cheekbones and narrower at the chin and forehead—and deep-set dark eyes. He could have stepped out of the pages of a fashion magazine.

"Hey Dorje," Shane said. "This is my friend Angus."

Dorje inclined his head slightly, put his palms together, and said, "Namaste."

I repeated his motions, and felt as if I was about to begin a yoga class. "Namaste."

"Angus works for the FBI," Shane said. "He's looking for an older man who may be victimizing teenage boys. Yunior said you might know something about him."

I stood up and showed Dorje the picture.

"He calls himself Frank. He hangs around the beach sometimes, looking for boys." He smiled. "They have to be very good-looking, though."

Dorje was very aware of how handsome he was. He was the

kind of guy you sometimes see at Wilton Manors' gay bars, who broadcasts a "look, don't touch" vibe, expecting everyone to admire him. I hated the way guys like that made Jonas, and others like him who weren't picture-perfect, feel.

I disliked Dorje, from his vibe to the phoniness of his yoga greeting, but I had to rein in my feelings to get information about Ozzy and Dimetrie. "You know any way to reach Frank?"

Dorje shook his head. "I don't want that kind of darkness in my life. Haven't seen him around for few weeks. He must have enough boys for now."

"You think they're all boys?" I asked. "Underage?"

"If they're over eighteen, then they sure don't look it," he said.

I showed him the pictures of Ozzy and Dimetrie. "You know either of these two?"

"I know Ozzy. I'm the one who told him to look up Shane. You're saying he went with Frank instead?"

"I think so." I told him about the video I'd seen, and went overboard in describing how Frank had violated Ozzy, trying to see if I could get a reaction from Dorje.

"That's hella sucky," he said. "Dudes like that should get their nuts cut off."

It was interesting to see Dorje drop the whole "cooler than you" attitude. Maybe he wasn't bad after all.

I handed him my card. "If you see Frank again, or hear where he could be, will you get word to me?"

"If I'm still here. I might not be around much longer. My destiny is on a fashion runway."

"You model?"

"I've been trying to break in, but I don't have the cash for the headshots and all that crap, and I'm not going to let somebody take advantage of me." He struck a haughty pose and I could see him strutting his stuff in some of those weird-looking clothes you see in magazines.

"Good luck with that," I said. "And call me if you hear anything."

Shane and I walked back down along the wall. "You think he knows how to get in touch with that guy Frank?" I asked Shane.

"I wouldn't be surprised. Dorje's got a lot more going on than he wants to admit."

• • •

As I drove Shane back downtown, neither of us said much. It was interesting that the sexual tension between us was gone. Was that my fault? In being too focused on the case, had I missed some signs from Shane?

Or maybe, as I kept insisting to Jonas, I wasn't *so* cute that every guy I met wanted to get into my pants.

I pulled up in front of Lazarus Place. "Thanks for your help this afternoon," I said.

"I want to find Ozzy," he said. "I care about those kids, you know? It hurts me when one of them gets into trouble."

He opened the car door. "If you find him, you'll let me know, won't you?"

"Of course. And it's not 'if' it's 'when.' I'm sure of that."

"Oh, I'm sure you'll find him someday. I just worry what shape he'll be in."

He got out of the car and I watched him walk up the concrete path. Was he afraid I'd find Ozzy dead? Or that Ozzy would be so messed up from being abused that he couldn't recover?

The front door opened and one of the kids I'd met reached out for Shane and dragged him inside. He had his job, and it was up to me to find Ozzy and Dimetrie and any other boys who might be being abused at the same place. I only hoped I'd be able to find the source of the flakka, too, to justify all my involvement in the search for the boys.

# 14.
# GRUESOME FIND

Monday morning I was determined to spend some time looking for the source of the flakka. Not just to keep Roly happy—but in case there were other guys out there like Brian Garcia who might be taking a mix of drugs that would drive them crazy.

I kept a computer window open with the webcam URL, and checked it periodically, but got no results, so I spent most of the morning on an FD302 about my meetings that weekend, and going back over everything I had found. I even drew a diagram with Gay Guys LLC at the center and spokes running off it for each piece of information that connected to it.

Alexei Verenich's name stuck out. Could he be Frank, the guy Dorje said was out cruising for boys to perform in the videos? I went looking for his photo online, even though the picture on his website didn't match the photo of the man in the videos. But if he was the registered agent for the business where Frank worked, he had to know Frank, didn't he?

I'd promised Katya that I wouldn't interview Verenich until she'd had a chance to put her case together, but I could still research him on my own. I went back over his law firm's website but I didn't see any mention that his company had LLCs or other types of shell corporations.

What could I discover if I called the phone number listed on the website? I'd need a decent cover story in order to learn anything. I remembered the first bar Katya and I had visited on

Friday night. It had been full of Russians. What if I pretended one of them had referred me to Verenich's office?

"Good morning," I said, when a woman answered the phone. "I need to set up an LLC in order to purchase a condominium in Sunny Isles Beach. A guy I was talking to at Tovarich the other night referred me to Mr. Verenich."

"We are not taking new clients," the woman said in a heavy Russian accent. "Sorry." She hung up.

I sat back in my chair. Not a very friendly attitude. Did that mean that Verenich worked only for clients he already knew? Or was his office merely a front for illegal activities? What else could I discover without affecting Katya's investigation?

There was nothing on his website about his personal life. If I discovered that Verenich was gay, for example, or lived in Wilton Manors, I could make a stronger connection to the porn operation, beyond his acting as the registered agent for the LLC.

I copied his head shot and pasted it into Google's image search. A bunch of results appeared, and it took a couple of minutes to scan through them until I found one that looked like it matched. The photo was of a man standing beside a sport fishing boat, holding a huge fish in his hands.

The site that hosted the picture was titled *Alexei's Fishing Blog*. Though it never indicated his last name, the Alexei who ran the blog was an avid sport-fisherman, and owned a fifty-three foot Hatteras yacht, with long fishing poles attached to the sides. He bragged about his abilities to handle big fish, and the one he was holding was labeled as three feet long, with a weight of fifty-two pounds.

I zoomed in on the picture of him holding the fish. He was bare-chested, and on his right breast, I saw a tattoo in the Cyrillic alphabet. I'd heard somewhere that members of the Russian mafia sported a lot of tattoos.

My brain kept buzzing with connections. Katya had indicated there were members of the Organizatsya involved in her money laundering case. If this man's tattoo was indeed one that Russian mafia members sported, it could be a very strong connection for her.

I copied the picture of the man holding the fish, then cropped it to focus on the tattoo. I uploaded the cropped image and once again had to sift through a lot of results. Many images of bare-chested men with similar tattoos over their hearts or on their arms. One man even sported the tattoo on his back above his waist, like a tramp stamp.

What a strange and wondrous place the world was, I thought, as I kept skimming through the photo results. I stopped at an article from the previous Friday's *Palm Beach Post*. The headline read, "Beach Walker Stumbles over Gruesome Find."

> *Longtime Palm Beach resident, Stanley Gummer, has found many interesting and unusual items walking along the beach from his home on Seabreeze Avenue for the last twenty years, but Thursday morning was the first time he discovered a dead body.*
>
> *"At first, I thought it was just a big pile of junk and seaweed," Gummer said. He collects unusual pieces of drift-wood for his son-in-law, who was a sculptor. "But when I got closer, I saw a human foot sticking out. I called 911 right away."*
>
> *Police responded and uncovered the naked body of a Caucasian male, approximately fifty years of age. His hands had been chopped off at the wrist, and his face had been damaged during his time in the water. The only identifying characteristic was a Cyrillic tattoo on his chest, which police translated as "communism only produces victims."*
>
> *Forensic examiners noted that the man's dental work is consistent with work performed in the former Soviet Union. Anyone with information about this man is urged to contact the TIPS line for the Palm Beach Police Department.*

I went back to the picture of Alexei Verenich and the fish he'd caught. He looked to be the right age, and the tattoo matched.

Then I looked up the registration for his boat, and found that he kept it at the Sunny Isles Marina. Was the boat still there? Or was it lost somewhere at sea?

Had he gone out fishing, and fallen off the boat and drowned? That wouldn't account for his hands being cut off. I went back online and found that if you took a boat out about five or six miles offshore, which was very reasonable for sport fishing, you could hit the Gulf Stream.

Suppose Verenich had gone out that far to fish, and someone on board with him killed him, cut off his hands, and tossed him in the water. Once the gases in his body began to expand after death, he'd float to the surface.

From a meteorological site, I discovered that the Gulf Stream moved at about five miles an hour. Then I checked with the Coast Guard. There was no record of Verenich or his boat being reported as missing.

I called Katya and told her what I'd found. "*Bozhe moi!*" she said.

"Why don't you call Verenich's office?" I asked. "See if his secretary will talk to you?"

"I'll give it a try."

A few minutes later, she called back. "It took some coaxing, but I was able to get her to talk," she said. "He hasn't come to work for more than a week, and she can't reach him. She's very worried."

"Well, we might know where he is," I said. "How would you feel about a road trip?"

# 15.
# ROAD TRIP

I picked up Katya outside the office where she was working. "I want to make a quick detour before we head north," I said. "Do you know how to get to the Sunny Isles Marina?"

She directed me down Collins, past a row of high-rise towers that completely blocked the view of the ocean. "Turn right at the Epicure Market. There's a shortcut back there that will take us out close to the marina."

I turned where she suggested, and we cruised along North Bay Road, past yet another line of fancy condos, this set fronting Biscayne Bay. The narrow lane was lined with towering palms and flowering plants, without the hustle and bustle of A1A.

"What made you start looking into Verenich?" Katya asked.

I told her that I'd been trying to make more connections between Verenich and the porn case, and how I'd done some image fiddling.

"And this detour to the marina?"

"If the local cops already know who he is, they'll have impounded the boat," I said. "That is, if it's there. And if they haven't..."

"Then we can look around," Katya finished. "Good idea."

We came out on the 163rd Street Causeway, and the vast expanse of the bay spread out to the north and the south. "Don't cross the bridge," Katya said. "Stay to the right and go under it."

We drove beneath the arching bridge, the Intracoastal to our right, and I pulled up at the entrance to the Sunny Isles Marina.

The parking lot was empty and a fence with a locked gate surrounded the property.

Four long, skinny concrete docks stuck out into the bay, with a mixture of boats docked in pairs between even narrower wooden finger piers. The air was much more humid by the water, and I took a couple of deep breaths. A steady, warm breeze blew salty air from the ocean, and the sun glinted off the decks, the condo towers, and the mix of powerboats and sailboats tied up along the finger piers. Halyards clanked on the sailboat masts and the bridge reverberated with idling cars and trucks.

You didn't get days like this in Scranton.

I pulled up a photo of Verenich's boat on my phone and we walked along the outside of the fence. "There it is," I said. It was all white, with a line of dirt or mold above the waterline. The name on the transom was *Bolshaya Ryba*, with "Sunny Isles Beach, Florida" beneath it.

"It means Big Fish," Katya said, when I asked her to translate.

Beyond the transom was a well with chairs and fishing rods, and the tall poles I'd seen in the photos online. An interior cabin and a metal ladder led up to a covered platform. Katya pulled out a small pair of binoculars from her purse and peered forward.

After a moment, she handed them to me. "Look at the transom," she said. "What do you see there?"

I focused the binoculars on a pattern of tiny brown specks. They could have been dirt—it didn't look like Verenich was very particular about how he kept his boat. Or, they could have gunk from the last fish Verenich caught. Or something else.

When I put the binoculars down and looked at Katya, it was clear she had the same idea I did. "Blood," I said. "Verenich's?"

We walked back to the car. "If that's Verenich's blood, then someone had to take him out on the boat and kill him," I said. "Then bring the boat back."

"The article you read didn't mention a cause of death, did it?" Katya asked.

I shook my head as we got into the Mini Cooper. "I figured

we could get that information from the police more easily if we went up there."

"I agree. Though we should call and find out who the detective is and make sure he or she is available to talk to us."

I waved my arm in her direction. "Make it so."

"Very Jean-Luc Picard," she said, as she pulled out her phone. "Are you a *Star Trek* geek?"

"Not particularly. I just like pop culture."

While she made the call, I concentrated on getting us headed in the right direction for I-95. Traffic along 163rd Street West was heavy and again I found myself wondering why there were always so many people out on the roads in Miami in the middle of the day.

Growing up in Scranton, every adult I knew worked a day job, either in the mining industry, stores, or offices. When we went on the occasional school field trip it felt like a real holiday and traffic was always light. Our only rush hour was a short time in the morning and the evening, with the occasional backups where two highways intersected. But in Miami, the highways were always crowded, and any slight problem could cause a huge delay.

It didn't help that periodically someone would shoot a gun from one car to another, or a semi-trailer would slam into a senior citizen's aged sedan, or that drivers eager to shave a minute or two from their trip by speeding or darting around other cars would cause a pileup.

We got onto I-95 as Katya hung up. "The detective investigating the case is named David Wells," she said. "He's out of the office right now but he's due back in an hour."

"That's about how long it will take us to get there." I looked over at her. "Is it a Russian thing to cut off hands?"

"Not particularly. I mean, long ago, yeah, they would cut off the hands of thieves. And the Islamic extremists still do that kind of thing, if you believe what you read in the media. But whoever killed Verenich could have cut off his hands so that he couldn't be identified by fingerprints."

Traffic was heavy, so I focused on driving. When we finally

reached the Palm Beach County line, the traffic eased and I turned to Katya. "Any reason why Russians have focused on Sunny Isles Beach?"

"It's like any immigrant community, such as Boston, where I grew up. Some people establish a beachhead, and others follow. And what's not to like about oceanfront real estate in a beautiful climate? Part of the problem we have in tracking these deals is that many of them are legitimate. When people come from Russia, they want to invest their money, and they don't trust the banks, so they pay in cash for the apartment."

"Nice to have that kind of cash on hand."

"Plus, Russians are paranoid about security," Katya continued. "They like gated islands and private communities with their own police forces, and all those big high-rises along the beach have outstanding protection. It's a negative for the Bureau. We have a harder time with surveillance when someone lives behind so many layers."

"Hasn't the volume of deals lessened because of the sanctions the United States placed against Russia after Putin sent troops into Ukraine?"

She shook her head. "Those sanctions only affect buyers from Russia, and not the wealthy Russian-Americans who are already established here in the States. And if the money is coming in illegally, the sanctions don't matter."

At the Okeechobee Boulevard exit we turned east, crossing over a broad lake edged by tall palms. You could almost smell the money in the air as we drove through downtown West Palm Beach—a cluster of high-rise towers and street-level restaurants and stores. "This is pretty," Katya said. "Very upscale."

I was busy watching the road signs so I didn't see much, but I agreed with her. We came out at a low bridge over the Intracoastal that led to Palm Beach, which was located on a barrier island like the one in Fort Lauderdale where Dorje was hanging out. A huge yacht drifted to our right, waiting for the bridge to open, and we made it across as the bells began ringing and the lights started to flash.

I drove slowly down Royal Palm Way, past a mansion turned museum and the offices of private banks. The island had an aura of wealth and privilege, and I thought how ironic it was that Alexei Verenich's body had washed up there. Rich people could only protect themselves from reality so much. Eventually it caught up to them.

We turned right onto South County Road. The Palm Beach Police Department was on our left a couple of blocks down. It was a three-story building painted a pale orange, with arched windows and the coral-tile roof that was everywhere. It could have been a shopping center or an office complex, and the only thing that said "police station" were the cruisers parked out front and a discreet sign over the entrance.

Detective David Wells looked like he played Santa at police Christmas parties—a shock of white hair over a friendly face. His smile and twinkly eyes probably disarmed criminals. "You say you have an ID on our floater?" he asked, when we were seated in an interview room.

"Not positive yet," I said. "We think it might be Alexei Verenich, a Russian-born attorney from Sunny Isles Beach." I handed him the screenshots from Verenich's website and from his fishing blog, and Wells nodded.

"Looks like our guy. You have a next of kin?" he asked.

"I've done some research on Verenich as part of my investigation," Katya said. "As far as I can tell, he has two ex-wives, no kids, a man in New York who may be a brother or a cousin, and an ex-girlfriend, Lyuba Sirko."

"I met her Friday evening and she told me that Verenich had a bad temper and a tendency to cheat clients." I looked at Wells. "What was the cause of death?"

"Two bullets from a nine-millimeter gun, applied directly to the back of the head," Wells said. "Coroner believes that the hands were cut off post-mortem, but can't be sure because of the water damage."

I was glad, if only because the thought of Verenich having his hands cut off while he was alive was pretty sickening.

"What's the Bureau's interest in Verenich?" Wells asked.

"He's part of an ongoing investigation," Katya said.

Wells snorted. "You Feebs are all the same. All take and no give."

"Excuse me, detective," I said. "This conversation began with us providing you with an identification for your John Doe, as well as information on his family and the name of his ex-girlfriend. I'd say that puts us in a cooperative position."

"Acknowledged."

"Is there anything else you can tell us about the body that hasn't been released to the media?" I asked.

He looked down at the desk as if he was considering what he could reveal. "The ME can't be a hundred percent sure, because of the time the body spent in the water and the fish that took some nibbles, but it looks like Verenich was tortured before he was killed."

"How?"

"The water did a number on the body, but the ME was able to identify burn marks on his upper thighs and the skin of his penis. He also extracted traces of nicotine, implying that someone applied lit cigarettes there."

He leaned forward. "You said he's part of an ongoing investigation. Any chance you tipped your hand and one of your suspects took him out?"

Katya shook her head. "Verenich is a collateral player in my case. I never spoke to him personally, or spoke about him to any of my sources. So if he was killed because of something the Bureau is working on, his killers didn't hear about it through me."

"You guys want to see the body?" Wells asked.

I looked at Katya, who didn't seem eager to visit the morgue, and I agreed with her. "Neither of us knew him before his death, so we can't ID him conclusively," I said. "And his murder is your investigation. We don't want to step on your toes."

"Appreciate it. Anything else you guys feel you can share with me?"

"There's a boat registered in Verenich's name, docked at the Sunny Isles Beach Marina," Katya said. "The *Bolshaya Ryba*. You'll want to check out the bloodstains on the transom."

Wells made a note of it, and I passed him my card. "If you find any fingerprints or other evidence on the boat, we'd appreciate being kept in the loop," I said.

"Always happy to cooperate with the Bureau," Wells said. "As long as it's a two-way street."

We said our goodbyes and walked back to where I'd parked. The sun was blasting overhead and the area had a sleepy feel, few tourists out on the streets, expensive cars moving sluggishly from one traffic light to the next.

"What do you think whoever tortured Verenich was after?" I asked.

"No idea. Maybe someone wanted to know who was behind the LLCs Verenich was fronting for, and he didn't want to say."

"He'd have to be extremely motivated to keep secrets if someone was sticking lit cigarettes onto his dick."

"If I'm right, Verenich was working for some very scary people," Katya said. "He could have been more frightened of what would happen if he told."

"But he didn't live to suffer the consequences," I said. "Could he have been caught between two rival Russian mobsters?"

"Sounds like he was stuck between the devil and the deep blue sea."

"And he ended up in the sea," I said.

• • •

The lights on the bridge from Palm Beach back to the mainland began to flash as we approached. I put the Mini Cooper in park and looked over at Katya. "Verenich was connected to both money laundering and underage porn," I said. "And if I'm correct, the LLC he fronted for may be distributing flakka, too. Anything else that you know of?"

"Nothing else has come up, but like I told Detective Wells, Verenich has been very peripheral to my case so I haven't paid much attention to him. Now that we've identified him, there should be something in the paper about his death, and that will give me an opening to talk to other agents and brokers about him."

She pulled out her phone and started to dictate questions she'd ask. "Who else did Verenich work for? Did he handle anything other than LLC work? Was he flashing a lot of money around?"

"Ask if anyone knows about that tattoo of his," I said. "The one about communism only producing victims."

She added that to her list. "What about you? What are you going to do?"

"I'll see if I can get a subpoena for Verenich's bank records and the records of the LLCs he was the agent for. And then I'll try and trace the flow of money."

"How are you going to get the subpoena?" she asked. "We have only the barest threads that connect him to either of our cases."

I stared ahead, watching as a big sport fishing boat like Verenich's moved under the open bridge and I began to put the pieces together.

"Verenich was an American citizen, right?" I asked, and Katya nodded. "It looks like his body was pushed north by the Gulf Stream, which is in international waters. If I can establish that Verenich's murder occurred on the high seas, then we have the authority to investigate."

"But you told Detective Wells we wouldn't interfere in his case."

"I have a master's in accounting, which gives me a leg-up on a homicide detective when it comes to examining financial records," I said. "I'm not trying to take over his case, just get the authority to do some research."

"I'd love to hear you explain that to him."

"Right now, Detective Wells is the last person I'm concerned about. I want to find those boys and the source of the flakka, and if I have to trample on Wells I'll do it."

# 16.
# DANCE CLASS

I stopped at Whole Foods on the way home and picked up a rosemary chicken breast and some grilled veggies for dinner. Jonas came home as I was eating. "Bitch of a day," he said as he walked in, his tie askew around his neck. "One of the verification systems went down and I had to stay late to get all the data entered once it came back up."

He shucked his sports jacket and undid his tie. "How was your day?"

"Tracked down a murder." I began to tell him about Verenich but he stopped me.

"How can you think about stuff like that while you're eating?"

I looked down at my plate. The grilled chicken didn't look anything like severed hands. "Don't know," I said.

"Sometimes you freak me out, Angus."

• • •

That night, I sat up in bed reading an article about the Russian mafia, trying to learn as much as I could in case the group—or someone involved with it—was behind the porn sites and the death of Alexei Verenich.

I was deep into the story of a crazy Russian nicknamed Tarzan when Shane McCoy called. "Have you made any progress on finding Ozzy?"

I didn't like the tone of voice he was using. I mean, yeah, I'm a public servant, but I wasn't Shane's servant. "Busy day at work." I explained about the connection between Verenich and the LLC that operated the porn site, and the way he'd ended up dead.

"Good for him," Shane said. "Fuckers like that deserve to die."

So much for Shane's good-guy attitude. I could have suggested that maybe Verenich had a troubled childhood, that he was as much of a victim as Ozzy or Dimetrie, but I resisted the impulse.

"Verenich's death means there's extra impetus to the investigation," I said. "I'm putting together a subpoena for all his records and there may be information there that will lead me to wherever Ozzy is."

"Bureaucracy," he said. "I hate it. You wouldn't believe all the paperwork I have to fill out in order to get the state to agree to let us help some of the kids we find. A bunch of paper pushers who care more about filling out forms than helping kids."

I hoped he wasn't throwing me into that group, but I was tired of his attitude. "Listen, I've got to get some rest. I'll be back in touch when I know something."

• • •

After a good night's sleep, I went to the gym early Tuesday morning. I worked my ass off and left with a pleasant sense of exhaustion, countered almost immediately by a grande mocha from a drive-through on my way home to shower and change for work.

As I drove south, I called Colin Hendricks and asked if I could stop by his office. A half-hour later I was there. "Any word on Brian Garcia?" I asked, as we sat down.

"His body temperature is normal, and it doesn't look like he suffered any significant organ damage. Doctors are slowly working to bring him out of his coma, but I've been warned that it could be a couple of days before his memory comes back."

He leaned back. "How about you? Find anything interesting?"

I told him about Verenich, and the possible connection to the

Russian mafia. "Not surprising," he said. "The Organizatsya has its tentacles all over the place."

"I'm working with an agent who's undercover, trying to trace money laundering," I said.

"I had a guy out at clubs, gay and straight, all weekend looking for flakka, but the supply seems to have dried up," Colin said. "I think the media reports on Brian Garcia have got people hesitant about buying it."

I promised to keep looking on my own, and then drove to work, where I began preparing the subpoena for Verenich's records. It was slow, tedious work, teasing out threads of information and putting them into a coherent format.

Most people think of a subpoena as a document that requires you to appear before a court, but there's a second kind, a subpoena *duces tecum*. It's a legal document that requires the recipient to produce documents or other tangible evidence. It would have to be prepared by the United States Attorney's office, but I needed to collect the raw materials for it.

To do that, I had to make a list of every kind of document that might help me track Verenich's income and expenditures. It was important to be thorough because we would only be given documents that fell under the scope of the subpoena.

I wrote out the full name and address of his law firm, requesting any and all documents relating to the LLCs he acted as agent for. That meant I had to list all of them in as much detail as I could. I asked for all bank records for Verenich's business and his personal accounts. For good measure, I threw in all records for his cell phone, his home phone, and his office phone.

Once again, I kept a window open on the webcam site, but every time I checked, Ozzy wasn't online.

I wanted to stay at work until I finished everything I needed for the subpoena, but I also wanted to show up at the conclusion of the four o'clock free dance class at Fort Lauderdale High that I thought Dimetrie Beauvoir might be attending.

On the way there, I wondered what I'd find. Maybe Dimetrie

had made those videos a while ago, left the porn house, and moved on with his life? That was the best possible outcome, provided he could also tell me how to find the operation so I could shut it down.

I had found only Ozzy in the ads for live webcams, not Dimetrie. And Dimetrie was going to age out of underage porn soon, too, so he might have already left.

What if he hadn't? What if I showed up and he refused to talk to me? After all, he was being paid for his work, enough to send regular money orders home to his sister, and he might resent having to go back to school and losing that income. And of course, it was possible he wasn't even taking this class or that he wasn't there tonight. There were a whole range of negative outcomes.

By the time I pulled into the big lot beside the school, I was thoroughly discouraged, and I hadn't even looked for Dimetrie yet. Most of the lot was empty, except for a cluster of cars at one side, so I parked near them and waited.

A few minutes after five, the side door popped open and a cluster of people spilled out. I set my digital camera on zoom and prepared to take pictures if anyone who looked like Dimetrie came out.

Four girls in their early teens wearing leotards and loose T-shirts, led the way, followed by two women wearing street clothes who were probably their moms. A pair of older women in tights, tank tops, and ballet flats followed. Then came three guys in their twenties. All of them were tall and skinny, and all walked with a curiously erect posture—the same way Dimetrie held his shoulders and head up in the video. They all carried shoulder bags and laughed and joked together.

The last of the three stopped to hold the door open, and a slender young man with dark skin followed. I focused on his face and shot a couple of pictures of him. I was pretty sure he was Dimetrie.

I was so focused on him, though, that it took me an extra moment to recognize the guy behind him. Eric, the guy from the gym that Jonas was crushing on.

I snapped a couple of photos of him to show Jonas, and I was surprised when he and Dimetrie walked to a new-looking Mustang together.

Was Eric taking dance classes, too? He was in great shape, but I'd never seen a ballet dancer who was so muscular.

I watched as Eric slid into the driver's seat, and Dimetrie got in beside him. I turned on my engine and joined the parade of vehicles leaving the parking lot, putting a couple of cars between me and the Mustang. Eric turned north toward the center of Wilton Manors, passing the old fifties-style Dairy Queen and rows of small stores.

It was easy to stay a few car-lengths behind them and my brain kept buzzing, trying to make connections between Eric and Dimetrie, but I didn't know either of them well enough to figure anything out. Were they boyfriends? Dance class friends? Did Eric know about Dimetrie's porn work? Was Eric acting in porn, too? He was too old and too masculine for the kind of stuff I'd seen, but it was possible that the powers behind Gay Guys LLC had different channels for different tastes. Jonas had said that Eric did odd jobs and had a weird schedule. Was that because he had to be online sometimes, jerking off for the camera?

It seemed like a huge coincidence that a guy my roommate had a crush on was friendly with someone involved in my case, but that was the nature of the small world of Wilton Manors. It was why I had told Colin Hendricks I couldn't go undercover at gay bars in town—there was too high of a chance that someone, even at a bar I'd never visited, would recognize me from Lazy Dick's and know I was a Federal Agent.

Wilton Manors was an extremely gay-friendly place, with openly gay elected officials, cops, and business owners, so it made sense that all kinds of homosexuals would gravitate there—from young guys like Jonas and me, to the older men I saw clustered around the bar at Lazy Dick's.

I was so caught up in those ideas, that I almost didn't notice Eric turning off Wilton Drive into a neighborhood of small single-family homes. I managed to turn in time to follow him, but he'd already slowed down, then stopped in front of a nondescript bungalow in need of a good paint job.

Rather than call attention to myself by stopping behind him, I passed as Dimetrie was getting out of the Mustang. I pulled into a driveway a few houses ahead and twisted around to watch. Dimetrie said something to Eric, then closed the door of the Mustang and walked over to the mailbox. He pulled out what looked like a stack of junk mail, then walked up to the front door of the house, leafing through it.

Eric gunned the Mustang and zoomed past me as Dimetrie went inside. I backed out of the driveway and cruised slowly past the bungalow, noting the street address. Was that where Dimetrie lived? It didn't look like he was being held prisoner there and being forced to perform, if he was able to go out for dance class.

I stopped across from the bungalow and took a couple of quick photos, then drove home. Before I jumped to conclusions, I needed to make sure that the two guys I'd seen coming out of the high school were Eric and Dimetrie.

• • •

At home, I downloaded an app for my computer that would let me compare pictures, and then cropped a good shot of Dimetrie's face taken outside the high school to the same dimensions as the screen capture from the porn video.

Though his hair was longer and he was facing more to the right side in one picture, it was clear that it was him.

It was harder to verify Eric's identity, though. I couldn't find the commercial for the car dealership online, and without Eric's last name, I couldn't look for photos of him. I tried uploading the photo I'd taken of him to Google's image search, but couldn't get a close enough match.

While I waited for Jonas to get home so I could show him the photos, I switched tactics and went to the Broward County

Property Appraiser's website. I plugged in the street address of the bungalow where Eric had dropped Dimetrie, and I wasn't surprised to discover that it was owned by an LLC.

Gay Guys LLC, to be exact.

I sat back in my chair. So the company that ran the webcam site owned the house where it appeared Dimetrie was living. Was Ozzy living there, too? How was Eric connected to this business? Was he selling the flakka? And most important, did I have enough evidence to justify a search warrant? Sadly, I knew the answer was still no. But I wasn't done yet.

# 17.
# IMMINENT DANGER

Jonas burst in the front door of the house like an over-excited golden retriever. He'd shucked his tie, and his shirt was open a couple of buttons, showing off his hairy pelt.

"He asked for my phone number!" he crowed as soon as he walked in.

"Who?"

"Eric! Who do you think?"

"Eric, the hunk from the gym? Why would he ask for your number?"

"Fuck you, Angus."

"I didn't mean that the way it came out," I said. "Where did you see him?"

"I was on my second happy hour margarita at Lazy Dick's when he walked in."

I looked at the clock. I'd seen someone who looked like Eric drop off Dimetrie about an hour before, so it was quite possible that Eric had gone directly from the porn house to the bar. "Did you see what kind of car he was driving?" I asked.

"I wasn't stalking him, if that's what you're suggesting," Jonas said. "He walked past me and I guess I had some Dutch courage from the tequila so I said hello. He smiled and said that he recognized me from the gym."

Jonas was glowing like a Halloween pumpkin. "I told him that anytime he needed a spot either before or after work, or on the weekends, he just had to call me."

"I'm impressed," I said. "You're putting yourself out there, and I think it's awesome. It's time you recognized you have a lot of good stuff going on."

He beamed. "So I gave him my number and he gave me his. We're probably going to work out together this weekend." He proudly showed me his phone, with a new contact for someone named Eric Morozov.

I meant what I said to Jonas—he'd been losing weight and taking more care of his appearance, and I was glad that he'd been gaining more self-confidence, too. But in my experience, hunks like Eric didn't have much use for ordinary guys like Jonas, and Eric's interest worried me.

"Funny, I think I saw Eric earlier today." I pulled up the photo on my phone. "This is him, isn't it?"

Jonas nodded eagerly. "Yeah, that's him," he said. "Where did you see him? And why were you taking his picture? *You're* not stalking him, are you?"

I explained about the dance class at Fort Lauderdale High, then following Eric as he dropped Dimetrie off.

"You think he's doing porn?" Jonas asked. "Sign me up!"

"This is serious, Jonas. That kid with him isn't even eighteen yet."

"But you don't know for sure that Eric is involved. He could have offered this kid a ride home from dance class."

"I know."

Part of me wanted to caution Jonas about getting too friendly with Eric, because I didn't trust Eric's friendship with Dimetrie and worried he might be more involved with the porn house than I could guess.

We agreed to heat up a big frozen pizza to share, and while it cooked, I looked up Eric Morozov in every database I had access to. He had no criminal record and little employment history that I could find. Several different addresses popped up, all of them around Wilton Manors, and I couldn't tell which was the most recent.

According to his Facebook profile he was from a small town

120

outside Jacksonville and he'd studied at the University of South Florida. His relationship status was single, and he liked bands called Tenement and Destruction Unit. Without "friending" him, that was as much as I could learn.

The oven dinged and Jonas and I shared the pizza. The computer verification system at work was still giving him trouble, and he'd spent most of the day working with the data entry operators he supervised to get around the issues. It was boring stuff but it kept us from talking about Eric.

After dinner I went back to my research, but I couldn't find anything more about Eric Morozov. If he was hanging around teenagers, though, maybe Shane or one of the kids at Lazarus Place had run across him.

I called Shane and told him that I'd spotted the other boy from the videos earlier that evening. "He was with a body builder named Eric Morozov," I said. "That sound familiar to you?"

"Nope. Another teenager?"

"This guy looks like he's in his late twenties. He was at a dance class with Dimetrie and dropped him off at a house in Wilton Manors. The address matches the one on record for the company that runs the porn site. It didn't look like he was being held captive there—he was pretty nonchalant about picking up the mail and going inside."

"Do you think Ozzy could be living there with this other kid?"

"I didn't see him."

"Give me the address," Shane said. "I'll go over and see if Ozzy's there."

"Hold off for a bit," I said. "We don't want to spook them."

"But what if they're hurting him? We have to stop it. And there could be other boys there, too. Can't you get a warrant or something and go in and arrest them?"

"All the evidence I have is circumstantial," I said. "I can't get a warrant until I have something concrete."

"You mean until one of those boys ends up in the emergency

room with a perforated bowel or an STD? Would that be concrete enough for you?"

"Shane. Calm down. I promise you, I'm pushing forward on this. We'll find out what's going on and get any boys there out and into someplace safe. I just need a little time."

"Give me the address. I promise you, I'll be discreet. I can pretend to be a Jehovah's Witness or something."

"Please. Let me do my job, OK? You focus on those kids at Lazarus Place. They need your full attention."

We argued for a while longer and I continued to refuse to tell him where the house was. Finally, he hung up.

There was something creepy about his insistence on rescuing the boys right away. Yeah, it wasn't a healthy environment for them, but I had no evidence that anyone was in imminent danger.

As long as they were smart enough to stay away from flakka.

# 18.
# ADDITIONAL EVIDENCE

I stayed up late that night, checking the webcam site, but still no Ozzy. The next morning at work I tracked down Roly as soon as I could. I explained about following Dimetrie back to the house and then discovering that it was owned by the same LLC that ran the website.

"Is that enough for a search warrant?" I asked. "Ozzy said in his e-mail that he got the flakka from the house where he was living. I can ID Dimetrie from the movie, and I can document that he's under eighteen."

"But you don't know that this kid Ozzy is living in the same house, so you can't connect the other boy to the flakka. And this dancer isn't being held prisoner at the house, right? You saw him come and go freely?"

"He wasn't on his own. What if the guy I saw with him was guarding him?"

"You're enthusiastic and that's great, but you can't let your imagination run away with you, not at this stage of the investigation. This Eric guy could be his friend, giving him a ride to his dance class." He leaned forward. "You still don't have enough to convince a judge. One more piece of evidence, something that clearly connects the property to underage sex or drug distribution and you've got it."

"Could I set up surveillance on the house? See who comes and goes? Maybe that way I can establish who's living there and what they're up to."

"Not without that one piece of information that would tie everything together. Go back to the materials you're collecting for the subpoena for the Russian agent's bank and phone records, and when you have it ready, show me."

I walked back to my office and called Colin Hendricks at the DEA. Maybe he'd be able to get a search warrant for the house when I couldn't. Unfortunately, he said the connection was still too tenuous—I didn't know for sure that Ozzy was in that house, and I had only his word in a private e-mail stating where he'd gotten the flakka.

It was frustrating, but I had to follow Roly's direction and go back to collecting material for the subpoena. After lunch, he read over all the supporting documentation and when he was finished, he nodded. "This is good work, Angus. Send it to the U.S. Attorney's office and see what they say."

• • •

While I waited for the attorneys to prepare the subpoena, I reviewed my list of all the LLCs that showed Alexei Verenich as registered agent. Many appeared to be named after the property that the LLC owned—18883 Collins LLC, for example. I found a couple of others with gay-sounding names, like Lambda Licenses and Pink Triangle Productions, and I set those aside for further research. There were another two dozen that I couldn't easily identify, entities like More Better Best, Over the Moon, and Changing Ways. My favorite was Little Lord Cheeses, LLC, which owned the building where a cheese shop with the same name was located.

I did a Google search for the gay-sounding companies and came up nearly blank, with nothing more than I had found in the Florida state database. Then I went through all the others, one at a time. Again, nothing interesting. There had to be thousands of these limited liability corporations in Florida and odds were most of them were either defunct or simply not indexed on the Internet.

Time for a different approach. I organized them chronologically and discovered that the first LLC Verenich served as an agent for had been formed eight years before for the purchase of The Isle of Capri, a motel on Collins Avenue south of the 163rd Street causeway. Though I was stepping over the bounds into Katya's case, I had an itch to follow the money.

As with the other paperwork, Verenich's name was the only one in the records. I went back to Google and searched for the property name. Most of the results were for a motel in North Wildwood, New Jersey, but I did find a squib from the *Herald's* real estate section that mentioned the sale of the motel in Sunny Isles Beach.

Verenich was quoted in the article, one of those bland comments that populated the business news. He announced that the purchasers intended to construct a condominium tower to be called Blue Heron Landing.

I followed that lead. The property's name had been changed twice, first to Heron Landing, then to Heron Beach Club. But none of those articles mentioned the names of the person or persons behind the LLC.

One of the last results on Heron Beach Club was an article from a monthly magazine called *Florida Russian*. It was a scan of an article from the printed paper in the Cyrillic alphabet.

I couldn't use automated translation tools because it was a picture, but I saved a copy of it and e-mailed it to Katya. Then I opened a Word document and painstakingly typed in the headline using the Cyrillic characters from the "insert symbol" feature.

Then I was able to translate it into something like: "Vadim Kurov to Build New Condo Tower."

I was pleased with my ingenuity, but I wasn't going to spend the next few hours copying the text character by character.

Google quickly informed that the tower had been built, and was popular with the Russian-American community. An ad for a condo for sale bragged that there was a Russian café in the lobby and that the concierge spoke all three of the main Russian dialects.

There was no mention of Kurov at the condominium's website, so I broadened my search. Finally, I got some results. Kurov was a colorful figure in the Russian community, outspoken in his anti-Soviet sentiments, a donor to charitable causes, and a frequent guest at community events.

He had no criminal record, and was frequently referred to as a wealthy real estate investor, though I could find no reference to actual buildings or properties he had developed beyond that single connection to Heron Beach Club.

It was time to check in with Detective Wells in Palm Beach. "It's Agent Green from the FBI," I said. "Were you able to get a search warrant for Verenich's boat?"

"I went over it yesterday with a couple of our best crime scene technicians. Picked up a bunch of fingerprints and two distinct blood samples. One of them is Verenich's."

"And the other?"

"Can't tell without something to compare to."

"How about the fingerprints? Able to match them to anyone?"

"Yeah. One of them is a real estate broker who says he often went out sport fishing with Verenich. He has an alibi for the day we think Verenich went out on his one-way boat trip. The other matches a New Yorker with a minor rap sheet. I'm trying to track him down now."

I thanked him and was about to hang up when he asked, "Any leads from your investigation that you'd care to share with me?"

"Honestly? Nothing yet. I have a request in to the U.S. Attorney's office for a subpoena on all Verenich's financial records, phone logs, and so on. If we find anything I can share with you, I'll let you know. But you do realize that under the Special Maritime and Territorial Jurisdiction section of the United States Criminal Code, we have authorization to investigate Verenich's murder in tandem with our case."

"I know that. But until someone tells me to halt my investigation, I'm going to keep looking."

"I understand that, and I have no intention of trying to stop you."

After I hung up, I sat there staring at my computer screen, until my phone buzzed with a text from Katya. "Need to talk to you ASAP. Can you come to SIB?"

I texted back that I could, and she suggested we meet at the Starbucks on Collins Avenue in Sunny Isles Beach in an hour.

That worked, I thought. I'd be closer to home by the end of the day.

• • •

After a long, slow drive I reached the shopping center, which held an international mix of stores—from a sushi restaurant to a Latin café to a clothing store with Cyrillic writing in the window.

Katya was by the window, talking on her phone, so I got a café mocha and joined her. As I sat down, she ended her call. "How come you're looking into Kurov?" she asked.

"I researched all the LLCs that Verenich fronted for and Kurov came up. You read the article?"

"It's from ten years ago, you know. About the development of a condominium tower called Heron Beach Club. A standard press release about how wonderful the property will be. It mentions Kurov, who is a big shot in the Russian community." She looked at me. "How did you find this article if you don't speak Russian?"

I told her the steps I'd gone through, including typing the headline out character by character. "You are a very determined guy, Angus," she said.

"So they say. But I'm still struggling to figure out how your case and mine are connected." I sat back in my chair. "Let me lay out a couple of facts. We have a pornographic video featuring two boys who are under eighteen. There's also a gay webcam site where one of the boys performs."

I took a sip of my coffee. The caffeine worked its magic on my bloodstream and I felt energized. "I tracked Dimetrie Beauvoir, one of the boys in that video, to a house in Wilton Manors. Because

Dimetrie performed with Ozzy Perez in that video, I'm drawing a dotted line that connects them and the house."

"Makes sense."

"Ozzy indicated in an e-mail that he got the flakka he gave to Brian Garcia from someone in the house where he's staying. So if we assume that Ozzy's in the same house as Dimetrie, then that's where the flakka came from."

"An assumption based on the connection between the two boys. But it's only an assumption until you can establish that Ozzy is in that house."

"I understand. But I think the connections are there. The house is owned by the same LLC that runs the webcam site, Gay Guys LLC. Verenich is the registered agent for that company."

"And Verenich is also the agent for a number of the LLCs that I think are laundering money for the Organizatsya."

"Do you think a Russian mobster is behind the porn sites? Maybe this guy Kurov?"

"It's too early to say. Yes, the Organizatsya has fingers in a lot of pies, and it's not surprising to find them involved in pornography, or in the distribution of flakka."

"There's a long history of connections between gay businesses and organized crime," I said. "At one time, a lot of the gay clubs were owned by the Mafia, or at least the clubs were paying protection to them."

"But that doesn't mean that Kurov is involved with the Organizatsya, or that he is behind the porn business."

"So what can we do?" I asked.

I was waiting for Katya's response when my phone rang and I recognized Shane's number. "I need to take this," I said. "It's one of my sources."

"He's at the thrift shop," he said as I answered. "I'm on my way there now."

"Hold on. Who's where? At what thrift shop?"

"Out of the Closet. The bright pink building on Sunrise Boulevard at US 1."

I shifted the phone away for a second and said, "I've got to go," to Katya. I grabbed the messenger bag I carried to and from work and kept talking as I walked out. "Who's there?"

"Ozzy Perez. Since you told me you thought he was in Wilton Manors, I've been looking for him, showing his picture to everybody I know. I left a copy with a clerk at the shop, and he just called and told me Ozzy's there with some big bodybuilder."

A bodybuilder? Eric Morozov?

"I'm in Sunny Isles Beach, so it's going to take me at least a half-hour. Don't do anything until I get there."

"Fine. But I'm not letting him get away from me."

I could have reminded him that he wasn't law enforcement, that he had no right to stop any other citizen from carrying out his own business, but I didn't want to get into that argument. I wanted him to avoid getting hurt, or getting Ozzy hurt.

# 19.
# UNDERSTANDING

I used all the tactical driving skills I'd learned at Quantico as I made my way up US 1, darting around slow-moving Canadian tourists and senior citizens so short their heads didn't show over their seat backs. The Mini Cooper was a front-wheel drive car, which meant my turning capabilities were more restricted, and it didn't have as much acceleration as the cars I'd driven in training, but I focused on the road looking for advantages I could exploit.

I didn't relax until I had to idle at the traffic light where US 1 veered right and merged with Sunrise Boulevard. I used that break to call Shane. "What's going on?"

"Ozzy's trying on clothes," Shane said. "I tell you Angus, that other guy isn't even a friend of his. Ozzy keeps showing him stuff and the guy doesn't care. He must be some kind of guard."

Eric had chauffeured Dimetrie to his dance lesson, and he'd mentioned to Jonas that he did odd jobs for the car dealer and his friends. Was he a driver? Or something more?

"I'm almost there," I said. "Listen, I don't want to engage Ozzy or this other guy in the thrift shop. I want to follow them when they leave. If they go to that house where I saw Dimetrie, then I've got concrete evidence that I can use to get a search warrant."

"You're going to let him go?"

"It's a free country. I have no cause to detain either of them."

"I need to talk to him. I want to make sure he's all right."

"Does he have any visible evidence that he's being abused? Broken arm, black eye, anything?"

"He looks OK," Shane admitted. "I haven't seen him up close. I'm hanging out in the office at the back of the store so that he can't see me."

"Hold on. I'll be there in a couple of minutes."

It felt like I could stop holding my breath when I pulled into the thrift store parking lot. As I walked in, I spotted Eric, and before I could turn away he recognized me. "Hey, you're Jonas' friend, right?" he asked. "I'm Eric."

"Angus." I shook his hand.

Out of the corner of my eye, I spotted Shane lurking at the back of the store, but I didn't want to approach him while Eric was watching me.

"You doing a little retail therapy?" I asked Eric. He looked like he'd come from the gym and was dressed in a tight tank top that emphasized his bulging pecs and biceps.

"Nah, just helping out a friend," he said.

The boy I recognized as Ozzy Perez came out of the dressing room, carrying an armload of T-shirts and skinny jeans. "I'm done," Ozzy said to Eric. "Can I have the money?"

Eric pulled a roll of bills out of the pocket of his jeans. "Ring him up," he said to the clerk.

That was my cue to get away from him. "Good to see you," I said to Eric.

"Yeah, say hi to Jonas for me."

"I will." I walked toward the back of the store where Shane met me behind a circular display of short-sleeve shirts.

I held my finger up to my lips. We watched the clerk ring up Ozzy's purchases and Eric hand over some cash. Ozzy looked happy and excited, not like someone being held hostage or being forced into anything. He grabbed his bags and followed Eric out of the store.

"I'll drive," I said to Shane.

He waved his thanks to the clerk as we hurried out behind Ozzy and Eric. "I want to talk to him," Shane said.

I grabbed his arm. "I told you, we have to wait."

"You're not my supervisor," Shane said, trying to break loose.

"No, I'm a Federal Agent investigating a case. And if you interfere, I have the authority to arrest you. Which is not going to do you, Ozzy, or those kids at Lazarus Place any good."

"You're bluffing."

I spotted Ozzy and Eric getting into Eric's Mustang. "Shut up, Shane, all right? Just get in the car with me."

We'd only been on one sort-of date, and here we were, squabbling like an old married couple. Not my idea of a fun relationship.

Fortunately, Eric didn't notice us in the parking lot, or recognize that we were following him. Since I already had a good idea where he was going, I was able to fall back, keeping several cars between us. Sure enough, he parked in front of the house where I'd seen him drop Dimetrie, and the two of them went inside.

"You're going to let them go in there?" Shane demanded, as I cruised past the house.

"I am." I pulled up along the curb. "Listen to me, Shane, because I'm only going to say this once. We have no proof—none at all—that anything bad is going on in that house."

He started to argue but I put my hand up.

"You and I may believe that someone in that house is forcing Ozzy and Dimetrie to perform in pornographic videos. But the law says we have to have reasonable proof that is happening before we go busting in."

"I can go up to the door and ask to speak to Ozzy."

"You could. But what if whoever is in charge freaks out and moves the kids and the video equipment out before I can get a warrant? Then we've lost the only lead we have and the kids are possibly worse off. I've seen Dimetrie go to dance class. We've seen Ozzy go shopping. We can reasonably assume neither of them are being chained up in a bedroom in fear for their lives."

Shane took a couple of deep breaths. "I hate to see anybody hurt like that," he said after a while. He turned to face me. "I need you to understand why this is so important to me. Can we go somewhere and talk?"

"Sure. Lazy Dick's?"

He shook his head. "No. Somewhere more private. Take me back to my car and then come to Lazarus Place with me."

I agreed, and neither of us spoke as I drove him back to Out of the Closet. It was after six by the time we reached Lazarus Place, and the smell of fast food burgers in the living room floated past us as we climbed to Shane's third-floor room.

He opened his door and walked in, then sat down on his bed, his legs crossed in front of him. "I don't tell many people this, but I feel like I can trust you," he said.

I sat on the chair across from him.

"I come from real white trash people," he said. "Born in West Virginia. You've heard of the Hatfields and the McCoys? My mom was a McCoy, and I grew up worried that somebody would come along and wipe out my family. My granddad used to take me out shooting squirrels, and then my grandma would cook them up for dinner."

Made my childhood sound idyllic.

"My mom was an alcoholic and never told me who my dad was. I figured she didn't know herself. When I was ten, she was driving drunk and caused an accident where an old lady was killed."

"That's awful," I said. "You weren't with her then, were you?"

"No, I was home by myself. I didn't know what happened until my aunt came over and told me I had to go home with her. Just like that, my whole world fell apart. I moved in with my aunt and uncle and my cousins. Had to share a twin bed with my cousin Derrick, who was fifteen and mean as sin."

He gulped. "He raped me a couple of times a week for nearly two years until I finally ran away."

"My god. I'm so sorry, Shane."

"Cops picked me up and took me back to my aunt's. When I tried to say what Derrick was doing, my uncle called me every kind of name in the book. Then, to punish me for lying, he took a strap and beat the living shit out of me."

I didn't know what to say. Sorry seemed so inadequate.

"That night, Derrick told me I was never going to get away from him, and he held me down on the bed and raped me again, harder and meaner than ever before. The next day, I tried to slit my wrists but my aunt found me before I could finish. She took me to the social service office and dropped me off."

He took a deep breath. "That was the best thing that ever happened to me. I jumped through a couple of foster families until I found a good one, where the people cared about me and pushed me to finish high school and go to community college. That professor I told you about recommended me to a therapist who helped me work out some of my issues and encouraged me to get my degree in social work."

When he looked at me, I saw he'd been crying silently. "That's why this matters so much to me," he said. "I can't stand by while some other kid goes through what I did."

I moved over to the bed and put my arm around him. "I know," I said.

He rested his head on my shoulder, and we sat there like that for a while.

# 20.
# A REASON FOR TORTURE

Shane's confession shook me, and I felt so terrible I couldn't eat dinner or focus on anything. I went out for a long walk around my darkened neighborhood, looking at the lit windows and wondering what was going on behind them. The sound of air conditioning compressors mixed with someone blasting the soundtrack to *Jesus Christ Superstar*. An elderly man passed me, walking a goofy-looking labradoodle, whose big head was too large for his long spindly legs.

The man said hello, and I answered him. In the glow of a streetlight, I saw how carefully he'd combed his hair, how neat his clothes were—even for walking his dog—and my gaydar pinged. What had it been like for him to be gay, back when homosexuality was the love that didn't dare speak its name?

As a teenager, for a long time, I felt like the world was conspiring against me. My dad was dead, and I was never going to have a happy life because I was gay and everyone would hate me if they knew. By the time I got to college, I began to realize how lucky I was, and that so many other kids had it a lot worse.

That feeling only accelerated after I joined the Bureau. Everyone whose arrest I participated in, seemed to have been a victim at some point who suffered some horror or loss that had doomed him or her to criminal action. I was fascinated by the background research I read as each time I tried to establish the turning point that had led to this activity.

I thought about taking some online courses in sociology, because I was so curious about the patterns I saw. I also began to understand myself more, recognizing my reaction to my dad's death and the responsibility of looking after Danny as my mom struggled to take care of us. I analyzed his behavior, too. Had I spoiled him? Had I doomed him to a life in which he expected someone else to make big decisions for him? And might that lead him to fall in with people who didn't have his best interests at heart?

My stomach finally stopped churning after I'd exhausted myself, and I ate a salad and went to bed.

• • •

Wednesday morning I felt better, but I was still haunted by Shane's story. It made me even more determined to rescue Ozzy and Dimetrie—to do for them what those good foster parents and college counselors had done for Shane.

When I got to work, on Wednesday morning I called Colin Hendricks at the DEA. I reminded him of how I'd seen Dimetrie go into that house in Wilton Manors, and that the evening before I'd seen Ozzy Perez there, too. "The best I can do is go to that address and talk to the guys there," he said. "You said the guy's a porn performer, so I don't trust anything he wrote in an e-mail. And we have no evidence that there are drugs on the premises at this time."

I groaned. Following the letter of the law was frustrating. "Don't go there yet," I said. "I'll keep gathering information."

I sent a text to Shane reminding him that I was on the case, and that if he contacted Ozzy he'd jeopardize my investigation. Short of locking him up, that was the most I could do to keep him from spooking Ozzy and whoever was with him.

A couple of hours later I received an e-mail from the Assistant U.S. Attorney who had prepared the subpoena. It had been delivered to Verenich's secretary, who had spent the day before organizing and photocopying his business checkbooks and the other records we had asked for. They had been delivered to the attorney's office that morning, and would be sent to me shortly.

Verenich's secretary had also downloaded PDF files of his bank records, and attached them to the e-mail. I separated the records by account and created spreadsheets to track the flow of money. I loved that kind of mindless work—at least in small doses. I got into the zone, shutting out everything else and focusing on the numbers in front of me. Interesting patterns began to develop.

Each LLC that Verenich managed was initiated with a large deposit from an offshore account. Some were from the Cayman Islands, others from Switzerland, a few from the Bahamas, and Bermuda. In each case, all I had was an account number where the money had come from. I knew it would be very difficult to identify who owned the account or where the money in it had come from because of bank secrecy regulations in those countries.

Verenich took a percentage off the top of the deposit as his fee and transferred that money to his business bank account. Then, each quarter, each of the LLC accounts were charged administrative costs. I didn't know much about the operation of an LLC, but it seemed like he was charging quite a lot for a guy with a small office and only one secretary.

I matched up the debits from the accounts to the property acquisitions and I was surprised to find that each of the LLC accounts still retained a cash balance in the form of CDs or money market funds after the sale was consummated. Of course, Verenich charged a fee for each transaction.

A lot of cash had been parked in those LLC accounts, though they were being drained each quarter by Verenich's charges, which were greater than the balance's accumulated interest.

I met up with Roly and explained what I'd found so far. "This is good stuff," he said, when I'd shown him all my spreadsheets. "Do you think this is what got Verenich killed?"

"I can't tell yet if one person or organization is behind all these LLCs," I said. "It could be that Verenich had a bunch of different clients. But if there was one individual…if it was me, I'd get pretty pissed off if I realized my accounts were being plundered like this.

And if there's a connection to the Russian mafia, you'd have an angry guy who's accustomed to using violence."

Roly nodded. "That would be a good reason for someone to torture Verenich, too. To punish him, as well as to get him to return the money. Make sure you get this information to Agent Gordieva."

"I will."

As I walked back to my office, I wondered who was going to take over as the agent for the LLCs now that Verenich was dead. Had he left a succession plan behind? Or would the owners of the LLCs have to come forward and claim them? From what I understood of LLCs, all someone had to do was keep filing annual reports. And almost anyone could do that. Was there anything, anywhere in the data that would lead me to another human being, one who could also be involved with the porn house and the flakka distribution?

# 21.
# CRUISE CONTROL

I went back to the data. It appeared that Verenich managed—or advised—some legitimate businesses as well. There were a dozen individual accounts at Florida Southern Bank & Trust, a local bank with a branch in Sunny Isles Beach. Each of them had a name that probably meant something to the owners but nothing to me—combinations of numbers and words that might have referred to addresses, or family members, or perhaps nothing at all.

A couple of checks on Verenich's office account had been written to Eric Morozov. I knew that he had been chauffeuring Dimetrie and Ozzy around. Was Verenich paying him to watch the guys at the house? Or for something else?

I called Verenich's office, hoping to ask the secretary about Eric, but I got a recording saying that the office was permanently closed and all inquiries should be directed to the Florida Bar Association.

That was pretty quick, wasn't it? She had assembled those materials for the U.S. Attorney the day before. I called the attorney who had prepared the subpoena and he said he hadn't been in touch with her since she called to let him know the courier could pick up the materials.

He had no way to contact the woman other than through the office phone number, but he did give me her name: Zinaida Afanasyev. I found a phone number for Boris Afanasyev in Sunny Isles Beach, and called it.

"Mrs. Afanasyev? Mrs. Zinaida Afanasyev?" I asked the woman who answered.

"Yes. Who is this?" I recognized the heavy Russian accent of the woman who'd answered the phone at Verenich's office.

"Agent Angus Green of the FBI," I said. "I'm investigating Mr. Verenich's murder and I have some questions to ask you."

"I'm about to liff for a cruise," she said, flattening her hard e's the way I was coming to recognize with Russian speakers. "I haff no time."

"You're leaving from Port Everglades?" I asked.

When she agreed, I said that I could meet her at the port. "You'll have to wait in line to check in," I said. "We can talk then."

In the background, I heard a man's voice in Russian, and she turned away to speak with him in that language. When she came back to the phone she said, "The boat is Ecstasy of Seas. We are there in about one hour. But I only speak for few minutes."

I said that was all the time I needed, and I got her husband's cell phone number so that I could connect with them at the port. Then I called Katya. "I might need some translation help," I said. "And your ability to persuade in Russian."

She agreed to meet me at the port. On the way there, my brain was buzzing as I tried to make connections. Jonas had said that Eric did odd jobs for the owner of the car dealership and his friends. Did those friends include the people behind the LLCs—and whoever had killed Verenich?

Could Zinaida Afanasyev tell us what Eric Morozov had done for Verenich? Could we convince her to tell us who was behind the LLCs? Did she know anything about the porn house? There had to be money coming in from that—where was it going?

I showed my badge to the guard at the entrance to the port, and drove to the garage closest to berth 23, where the Ecstasy was docked. As I walked out, I spotted Katya, and when we met up, I had her call Boris's cell phone.

She spoke to him for a minute and then hung up. "They just got here, and they're in line to check their bags."

We hurried across the busy street to the dock. The Ecstasy was a huge ship, one of the newest designs, and a long line of people waited to check in. Half of them were still in their northern-climate clothes and had sweaters and coats hung over their arms as they sweated in the Florida heat. The smarter group was already wearing shorts and T-shirts, though they looked as uncomfortable.

Zinaida Afanasyev was a short, plump woman in her fifties, her husband of similar stature and build. Katya began the conversation in Russian, introducing herself and me, and after some handshaking, Zinaida asked, "What you want to know?"

"Who is Eric Morozov?"

She looked surprised. "Eric? He is a man Mr. Verenich knows. Knew."

The line moved forward quickly, and I helped Mr. Afanasyev with the bags. "How did Mr. Verenich know Eric?" I asked.

She shrugged. "We are Russians. We know each other."

I had the same connection to gay men in Wilton Manors. We knew each other, too.

"Do you know what Morozov did for Mr. Verenich?"

"Whatever Mr. Verenich ask. Clean boat, deliver papers. He is big, strong man, so he do all kinds of work." She leaned forward. "Sometimes, when one of Mr. Verenich's clients want to buy a property and the owners are not to sell, he send Eric to speak with them."

I looked at Katya and could see she thought the same thing I did. Eric Morozov was some kind of enforcer.

The ship's horn sounded, reverberating around us, and the Afanasyevs were only a few parties behind the check-in desk.

I chose not to ask Zinaida about flakka distribution. I was pretty sure she'd say she had no idea what that was. "Who is taking over Verenich's work now that he's gone?"

Zinaida shrugged. "Is up to Mr. Kurov. He was Mr. Verenich's big client, and is one who tell me to shut down office."

"Vadim Kurov, the real estate developer?" I asked.

Zinaida nodded. "I am lucky—his company run contest to win this cruise, and I don't know he enter my name until he tell me I won." She beamed. "Eleven days, through Panama Canal. Is first time we have had such vacation."

"What can you tell me about the house in Wilton Manors?" I gave her the address.

She shook her head. "Mr. Verenich represent many property owners. I had no contact with them."

"What about a company called Gay Guys LLC? There must have been money coming into that operation."

"Mr. Verenich, he handle all money. Me, I am answering phones and sending faxes."

The check-in clerk called them forward. Katya and I told them to have a good trip, and we stepped back.

"Isn't that convenient?" I said. "Zinaida and her husband won an eleven day cruise a short time after Verenich's murder. You think someone wants to get her out of the way?"

The Afanasyevs checked in and waved to us as they moved forward in the snaking line to board the ship.

"At least no one is killing her," Katya said. "Though I hope she stays away from the railing on this cruise."

# 22.
# EXOTIC IMPORTS

"Who is this Morozov guy you asked about?" Katya asked, as we walked back to the garage. "I haven't heard that name before."

"He keeps popping up." I explained how Jonas had noticed him at the gym. "And then I saw him pick up one of the boys from the videos at a dance class on Tuesday night. He drove him to the house in Wilton Manors owned by Gay Guys LLC. Yesterday, I saw him chauffeuring around the first boy, the one who was e-mailing with Brian Garcia."

"He works for the company producing the porn?"

"Not clear. Verenich paid him for something, but it could have been enforcer work, based on what Mrs. Afanasyev said. Maybe he's friendly with the guys at the porn house and doing some favors. Though that's unlikely."

"Could he have killed Verenich?" Katya asked.

"What motive would Morozov have to kill the guy who was paying him?"

"Maybe Verenich owed him money?" Katya asked.

"Not likely," I said. "There was plenty of money in Verenich's accounts, and all the checks to Morozov were no more than a few thousand dollars each. Not worth killing someone over."

"How about roid rage?" Katya asked. "The guy I dated in New York was a bodybuilder too, and he took steroids that made him crazy sometimes."

"Eric Morozov looks like the kind of guy who takes steroids," I admitted. "Yeah, he might have gotten angry with Verenich. But torture him? Shoot him? That's doesn't fit. It's more likely that he was the muscle to hold Verenich down while someone else tortured him."

"Vadim Kurov?" Katya asked. "We already know he's behind at least one of the LLCs that Verenich was bleeding cash from. From what I've heard of him he wouldn't take kindly to being ripped off."

"Makes sense," I said. "Maybe that's what Verenich was tortured for, the information on where he put the money he took from Kurov."

As we reached my car Katya said, "I have some stuff to show you about Kurov. But I'll need internet access. There's a Starbucks around the corner, on the 17th Street Causeway. I'll meet you over there."

It was slow leaving the port, a jam of cars, taxis, and buses, and I had to pay attention to avoid an accident. As I crept past one of the big ocean liners, I wondered if Eric Morozov was in danger. Or would he leave town quickly like Verenich's secretary? How long did I have before the porn house and its flakka connection would shift operations?

At the coffee shop, Katya opened her laptop and initiated her VPN software. She pulled up her research report on Vadim Kurov and I shifted so I could look at it with her.

*Kurov, Vadim Artemovich. Born August 1, 1955 in St. Petersburg, Russian Soviet Federative Socialist Republic to Artem Vadimovich and Valeria Denisovna Kurova. Received his certificate of secondary education in 1973 and enrolled in St. Petersburg Technikum.*

*Though the family did not identify as Jewish, Artem Kurov established Jewish descent through a grandmother, and his family was allowed to immigrate to Israel in 1974. Vadim dropped out of the Technikum at this point and never resumed formal education.*

*His family remained in Israel for only nine months*

until relatives sponsored them to immigrate to the United States, where they settled in with the Russian community in Brighton Beach. Vadim began as a construction laborer, but quickly ascended to the position of superintendent. By the time he was twenty-five he owned a small apartment building on Coney Island Avenue.

At about this time, his name began to come up in investigations of the Organizatsya in New York. Kurov was suspected of laundering money for Russian mobsters in the purchase of properties for cash. He would then renovate them and sell the properties, turning criminal proceeds into legitimate income.

In 1985 he married Alla Alekseyevna Golubkina, who bore him two daughters: Diana and Irina. In 1995 the family moved to Sunny Isles Beach, where it is common knowledge that he is a real estate developer, yet it is very hard to attach his name to any projects, built or in the process of development. Agent Green discovered that Kurov was behind the development of a condominium tower called the Heron Beach Club. Word of mouth among real estate agents and brokers in the area is that funding was provided by Organizatsya members but I have been unable to establish concrete proof as of yet.

Kurov maintains a fairly low social profile and most of his personal connections remain in the New York area. Both his daughters graduated from a private high school and the University of Florida. Diana is unmarried and teaches fourth grade at an elementary school in Gainesville. Irina married Leo Mitkin in 2013 and lives in Manhattan.

Kurov's passion is expensive foreign sports cars, and he owns a Porsche Cabriolet convertible, a Ferrari Testarossa, a Bentley Mulsanne, and a Lamborghini Aventador.

The list of expensive vehicles sparked something in my brain. "How'd you find out about these cars?" I asked. "DMV records?"

She shook her head. "Kurov doesn't have any cars registered to his name. A source told me about them."

"You didn't happen to get their license plate numbers, did you?" I asked.

"I did. Why?"

"That commercial I told you about, the one with Eric Morozov in the background? It was for a dealership in Fort Lauderdale that sells expensive cars, called Exotic Imports."

"I can pull up the sales records from the DMV," Katya said.

"While you do that, I'm going to research the dealership." I turned to my own laptop, and did a quick search. Exotic Imports was the only one in Florida that sold the Aventador.

I brought up the company's website, and the "about us" page. Antonio Cruz, the man from the TV commercial, was listed as owner. In the photo above his name, his white mane appeared to be a toupee, and the skin of his face was so tight and flat that he looked like a victim of bad plastic surgery. His bio bragged that he had been in the luxury car business for nearly forty years, first in his native country of Venezuela, then in South Florida since 1995.

Cruz looked familiar, and I wondered if that was because I'd seen his commercials on TV. Or had I seen him in person?

On a hunch, I started Googling his name in conjunction with gay charity events in Fort Lauderdale over the past year. I found Cruz in several shots taken at fund-raising events for various LGBT causes in south Florida—the Stonewall Archives and Library, a non-profit focused on archiving and lending out LGBT literature; The Gay Men's Chorus of Fort Lauderdale; and Lazarus Place.

Exotic Imports was a few blocks to the left of the library's location on Sunrise Boulevard, and the Publix where Dimetrie Beauvoir bought his money orders was right across the street. The thrift shop where I'd spotted Ozzy Perez in company with Eric Morozov was a few blocks farther east.

Did Cruz hang around bars like Lazy Dick's? Was that how he met Eric Morozov? Did Cruz's tastes run to young boys? Was that why he supported Lazarus Place?

"I found a connection," Katya said, and I looked up. I'd forgotten she was there.

"I went into the DMV records to see who sold him the cars and I discovered that yes, they came from Exotic Imports." She shifted her screen around so I could see. "But there's something more. Each car was bought by a different LLC."

"All cash sales, I'm sure," I said.

"Most likely. And here's what's most interesting. Verenich was the registered agent for each of these LLCs. That's a direct connection between Verenich, Kurov, and the LLCs."

"Was one of them bought by Gay Guys LLC? Maybe with profits from drug dealing or porn?"

She shook her head. "Nope. All real estate operations."

I sat back in my chair and we began to outline all the connections. "We have a nexus of activity focusing on Wilton Manors," I said. "The porn house, the Publix, the thrift shop, the library, the dance class at Lauderdale High, and Exotic Imports. And Eric Morozov is right in the middle of that."

She nodded. "Morozov is also connected to Verenich through the checks Verenich wrote him, and what Mrs. Afanasyev told us. Kurov connects to Verenich through the LLCs, which invested in property in Sunny Isles Beach. Those transactions appear to be money laundering with a connection to the Organizatsya."

"Well, we've been thinking that your case and mine were connected somehow," I said. "Looks like more connections than we thought."

I showed her what I found on Cruz. "I wouldn't be surprised if he met Eric at a bar and hired him to be eye candy for his dealership ad, then gave him other odd jobs to do. He could have in turn introduced Eric to Kurov."

"Or the other way around," Katya said. "Maybe Eric knew Kurov through the Russian community, and Kurov introduced him to Cruz, knowing Cruz was gay."

"It's like a Venn diagram," I said. "Where the gay circle and the Russian circle intersect." It reminded me once again of what a small world it was, where a Russian mobster by the beach could be connected to a gay bodybuilder and a porn house.

My brain was firing on all cylinders but there wasn't much more I could search for online. I needed to get to a bar. "It's four o'clock," I said. "Happy hour in Wilton Manors. I'm going to see what the gay grapevine has to say about Antonio Cruz."

# 23.
# SEXUAL TENSION

I'd been avoiding Eclipse, a gay bar on the outskirts of Wilton Manors, since I broke up with Lester, the bouncer there. But it was the closest bar to the Exotic Imports showroom and I knew I'd have to get there eventually to look for information on Antonio Cruz.

I ripped off the metaphorical bandage as I parked in the lot. I hoped Lester would be on the late shift, as he usually was, and I'd be long gone before he showed up to work. If he was even still employed there. Bar staff in Wilton Manors tended to move around at the drop of a jockstrap.

The parking lot was half-empty, which meant I'd have a good chance to speak to the bartenders and servers and show them Cruz's photo. I stripped off my tie and suit jacket and left them folded on the seat beside me. I pulled the tails of my shirt out to cover my belt holster and opened a couple of buttons on my shirt.

Unexpectedly, Lester was a few feet inside the door sitting on a bar stool. He was a dark-haired, muscle-bound hunk, six-foot-four with an oval face, and a small goatee at his chin. "Of all the gin joints in all the world, he walks into mine," he said as I stopped in front of him.

So Lester was a fan of old movies. I hadn't known that about him. But then, we'd only gone out on a couple of dates, and most of the time we were in bed together.

"How's it going, Lester?"

"Same old, same old," he said. "The guy who works the day shift quit so I'm pulling a double."

He scanned me. "You look good."

"Thanks." I looked down and toed the floor like a nervous pony. "Listen, I'm sorry I blew you off," I said. "Getting shot rocked my world, and it wasn't fair to keep you hanging on if I couldn't even face getting out of bed."

"Must be feeling better now if you're hitting the bars."

Was there a note of resentment in his voice? Should I have called him more recently? I knew what it felt like to be dumped and I hated to have put him through that.

"I'm here on a case." I pulled out a screenshot of Antonio Cruz.

Lester got off the stool and took the picture from me, then turned so he could see it in the light. "Yeah, I know him. Chicken hawk," he said. Chicken hawk was an old-fashioned gay-slang term for older men who liked younger boys.

"We card everybody here," Lester said as he handed the photo back to me. "You're not twenty-one, you can go find some other bar to hang around. Cruz has to settle for legal twinks here."

"He comes around often?"

"He's a Saturday night special. Once or twice a month he shows up at two or three in the morning when the lights are low and the boys are nervous. He can usually persuade someone to go down on him or go home with him."

"He been here lately?"

"Couldn't say. I haven't worked the late-late shift in a while." He lounged against the wall.

I noticed how his tight shorts pulled against his body when he leaned back, and I remembered what kind of weapon he had there.

Did I want to get back together with Lester? He was a sweet guy underneath all those muscles, and he made me feel safe and protected when I was with him. Like I could forget I had a gun and a badge and just be a guy. My brief flirtation with Shane McCoy had reminded me what it could be like to be with someone else.

Focus, Angus. I pulled out the photos of Dimetrie, Ozzy, and the guy Dorje had called Frank. "Recognize any of these?"

"This is turning into a regular interrogation," Lester said, but he took the pictures and looked at each one carefully.

He handed back the photo of Ozzy. "No." Then the one of Dimetrie. "No."

He looked at the one of Frank for a while, then finally gave it to me. "Maybe. Hard to say because he looks like a lot of other guys. But if he has been here, he hasn't been in often enough to make an impression."

Lester stood there staring at me, and I couldn't read his expression. Was he angry at me? Still interested? All I knew was that his stare was getting me hard, but I had investigating to do.

"Anything else I can help you with?" Lester asked, with his arms crossed over his massive chest.

"Is there any bar in Fort Lauderdale that isn't so careful about IDs?" I asked. "Some place that might be more to Antonio Cruz's liking?"

The shaft of light that illuminated Lester's face showed his strong jawline and deep, dark eyes that were part of what attracted me to him. "I wouldn't know."

I stood there for a moment, my eyes locked on him. The sexual tension was zinging in the air between us. I sure as hell felt it, and I was sure Lester did, too.

"Check with the bartender," he said finally. "Tony. He's worked at every gay bar in town, usually in short stints. He might know."

I wondered about the "short stints" comment, but I thanked Lester and walked over to the bar. Tony was a skinny, balding guy in his late fifties or early sixties, wearing a Hawaiian shirt patterned with palm trees and surfer boys.

"What'll it be?" he asked.

Eclipse had the same frozen drink machines as Lazy Dick's, so I knew the margarita would be weak, and I ordered one. I watched as Tony worked; his movements were quick and rabbity, like someone very hyper or on uppers.

"I'm Angus," I said, when he brought the drink back. I reached out to shake his hand, which was cold and clammy.

"Tony. Saw you talking to the bouncer. He's a hunk, isn't he?"

"He sure is. He's a friend."

He eyed me appraisingly. "Nice to have friends like that."

I nodded, then pulled my badge out of my wallet and showed it to Tony. "He can vouch that I'm a good guy," I said, though I wasn't sure what Lester would say about me. "I'm investigating a case right now where some teenage boys are being exploited for porn."

"Whoa. I don't know nothing about that. My interests are strictly age-appropriate."

"No worries, I'm just nosing around trying to find places where guys might be taking advantage of underage boys. Lester said you know every bar in town."

"I do," Tony said, nodding proudly.

"So which bars aren't so careful about checking IDs?" I asked.

"I always do my job," he said. "Most places I work there's a bouncer who cards everybody when they walk in."

"And the places that don't?"

He stared at me and curled his lip. Then he leaned in close. "You didn't hear it from me, but there's a dump on Flagler Drive south of Sunrise called Second Star. No signs out front—just two neon stars above the door."

Someone called to Tony from the other end of the bar. "You get there in about an hour, you'll hit the primetime," he said, then he walked away.

As I expected, the margarita was watery and tasteless. I pushed it away, pulled out a ten-dollar bill for the drink and tip, then walked back to Lester. I waited while he IDed a couple of guys who looked barely old enough to drink.

"Tony able to help you?" he asked, when they were gone.

"He suggested a bar called Second Star on Flagler Street. You ever heard of it?"

He shook his head.

"Second star to the right and straight on 'til morning?" I

asked. If he knew the *Casablanca* quote he might know the one from *Peter Pan*, too.

But he cocked his head slightly. "Huh?"

"It's how you get to Neverland, where Peter Pan and the Lost Boys live," I said.

"Well, that's creepy." He leaned in close. "Be careful out there, G-Man."

"I will be."

At that moment, a busboy dropped a tray of plates and glasses on the concrete floor with a sharp bang, and my whole body tensed. I reached for my gun as Lester put his arm around me and pulled me close to him.

My pulse raced and my body shook. I stayed in his embrace for an extra couple of beats until I pulled away. "I guess I'm not fully recovered," I said. "But don't tell the Bureau shrink or she'll pull my leash."

"You're OK with me," Lester said. There were a lot of different ways to take that statement but I shelved considering them until later. He stepped back a couple of paces so that there was more distance between us. But that sexual tension continued to zing.

# 24.
# SECOND STAR

When I walked outside, I called Shane. "Do you know a guy named Antonio Cruz?"

"Name sounds familiar. One of our donors, maybe?"

"Yup. You ever met him?"

"Not that I can recall. Why?"

"Something I'm looking into. You ever hear of a bar in Fort Lauderdale called Second Star?"

"No. Another thing you're looking into?"

"You got it. Can you ask the boys about Cruz and the bar and then call me back?"

While I sat in the parking lot and waited, I pulled up a map of the area on my phone. The Florida East Coast railroad tracks ran through the center of the neighborhood, with low industrial buildings on either side.

A couple of minutes later, Shane called back. "Nobody recognized the name Antonio Cruz. I looked him up online and he looks vaguely familiar but I can't say where I recognize him from."

"How about the bar, Second Star?"

"It took some arm-twisting but Yunior admitted he's been there before."

I remembered Yunior, the fey young kid with coffee-colored skin and shoulder-length hair. "I need to talk to him about the place. Can I come over now?"

He agreed, and I asked, "Pizza to sweeten the boys up for information?"

"Always. But what's this about?"

I explained that I'd heard a rumor that Second Star attracted chicken hawks and wanted to find out what I could about it.

"I've heard there are places like that but nobody's ever fessed up to going to one," he said. "It's amazing what a weird underworld there is out there." I agreed with him, then called in an order for pizza.

• • •

When I arrived at Lazarus Place, carrying two boxes of pizza, Yunior met me at the door and squealed with delight. "Hey, sugar!" He took the pizzas from me and then kissed me on the cheek. "We love it when you come visit."

I followed him into the living room, where a half-dozen kids dove into the pizza and the two half-gallons of soda I'd brought. "They're going to be wild on the caffeine," Shane grumbled, but he took a big glass for himself.

After I'd devoured a slice of pizza dripping with cheese and oily pepperoni, I wiped my mouth with a napkin and said, "Shane told you guys I'm interested in a bar called Second Star, right?"

"What you want to go there for, sugar?" Yunior asked. He was sprawled elegantly on the couch, in denim shorts and a skin-tight tank top that showed off all his assets—from his long, tanned legs to his basket and booty. Everything I could see of his body was hairless except for his head, which was topped with an exuberant mop of gelled hair. "You're too old to cause a stir and you're too young to fit in with those wrinklies."

"I'm not looking to pick anyone up or get picked up. But I'm worried that it might be a place where boys like you all can get into trouble."

"Ozzy went there," River said, looking down at the ground and speaking softly.

"You didn't tell me that before," Shane said. "You said he met a guy by the beach."

"He didn't want you to know what he was doing."

"It's OK, I'm not mad," Shane said, though he sure looked angry to me. "I want you guys to know you can trust me. With anything."

There was a mumbled assent from the crowd.

"You can trust me, too," I said. "I know you guys don't know me, and sometimes the suit and the badge can throw you off, but I'm on your side. It wasn't that long ago that I was your age and I guarantee you I was as confused and scared as you."

"I ain't scared of nothing," the heavyset boy I remembered as DeAndre said.

"You should be scared," I said. "There's a shitload of people out there who want to hurt you, because you are who you are. Because you dare to be honest, to look and talk and act like you do. Bible-thumpers and closeted assholes and drunks with two-by-fours. Not to mention homicidal maniacs and people who think they can text at the same time as they drive. Fear is good. It strengthens your senses and makes you pay attention to the world around you. Don't let it hold you back, but don't ignore it either."

I sat back. "Sorry for the sermon, but in my job, you see a lot of bad shit."

The room was quiet for a moment. "I am scared of my step-dad," DeAndre said. "He's a mean mother and he has guns. Reason why I left."

"Thank you for being honest." I waited a beat. "Now, back to Second Star. Anything?"

"Like I told Shane, I been there," Yunior said. "It's a dump. Creepy old guys who look like they want to eat you up."

"You have a fake ID?"

"Like duh," Yunior said. "But don't matter. Bartender can't see it in the light. And if you ain't got money, you just got to look around and one of them guys will pay."

We went around the room and no one had anything more to add. "Thanks guys," I said. "I'm going to go over there myself and see what it's like."

"You can't go in there looking like you do," Yunior said. "You too young." He stood up. "Come with me. Yunior fix you up right."

I looked at Shane, who shrugged. I followed Yunior down the hall and he stopped at the bathroom. "You go in there and take that pretty shirt off," he said. "You don't want to get makeup on it."

"Makeup?"

He made a shooing motion. "Go on."

I took off my shirt and white undershirt, then wrapped it around my waist to cover my holster. I looked at my chest in the mirror. I was nowhere near as built as Lester, but I was proud of my muscles. No scars from the bullets that had hit my vest, and the purple bruises over my fractured rib had faded, but when I touched the area I still winced.

Yunior came in and I quickly plastered a smile on my face. He carried a hard plastic case covered with sixties-style decals of brightly colored flowers and butterflies. When he opened it, I realized it was filled with makeup and brushes. "Now usually we do this so we don't look like we just walked out of middle school," he said as he dipped his index finger into a jar of cream. "But the idea's the same for you. And the bar is dark so you have to make an impression."

I stood there patiently as he smoothed some of the cream over my face, then dipped a brush into something darker and drew a couple of lines across my forehead and under my eyes. "That tickles," I said, as I squirmed.

"Hold still, sugar." Yunior put his finger under my chin and shifted my face. I had a powerful moment of wanting it to be Lester who touched me that way.

Yunior blended the colors in for a couple of minutes. When he was finished, he turned me to the mirror so I could see myself. "What do you think?"

"Holy crap. I look like my grandfather," I said.

"Yeah, you do. But your chest is way too fine for an old guy."

"I can handle that," I said. "I've got my Kevlar vest in my trunk."

"Oh, I love it when you go all FBI on us," Yunior said. "I'd give you a kiss but I don't want to smudge your makeup."

I waited for Yunior to leave before I put on my tee and shirt because I didn't want him to see my gun. Then I walked back to the living room. "Holy cow," Shane said. "You look twenty years older."

"Yeah, not a look I'm going to practice when I go out clubbing."

I thanked Shane, Yunior, and the rest of the kids and when I got to my car I took off my shirt, and put my vest on over my tee. The vest was a new one, issued to replace the one with the bullet holes in it. Since getting shot, I kept it with me all the time as a good luck charm. By the time I slipped my shirt on over it, I looked and felt bulky. Protected, but also weighted down.

Even with the air conditioning on high, I sweated profusely in the car as I drove the few blocks to the bar. I parked in the lot of the dry cleaners next to Second Star. As Tony the bartender at Eclipse had said, there was no sign outside the bar, just a pair of neon stars. The windows had been blacked over and so had the glass door.

There was no bouncer at the door and I walked unchecked into the small room, which was lit only by a couple of neon beer signs and some dim bulbs hanging on wires overhead. The two high stools on the left side of the bar were taken by middle-age men, who turned to look at me as I walked in. When they realized I was over the age of majority, they went back to their drinks.

I walked past five small round tables. Only one was occupied, by a grizzled-looking man and woman who were probably neighborhood regulars who didn't care what went on around them. No one around appeared to be underage.

The bartender was a bald-bear type in a T-shirt that stretched across his ample belly. Behind him was a scant rack of bottles I recognized as cheap, well brands because of the years I'd spent behind the bar while I was in college. "Gin martini, rocks," I said, leaning against the bar on the other side from the two men. "Two olives, if you've got 'em."

He poured the drink without any particular grace and slid it across the bar to me. "Seven-fifty," he said.

I pulled a twenty out of my wallet and laid it on the bar. "Slow night?" I asked. "Or things get busier later?"

"You want action, there's plenty of bars downtown," he said. "This is a neighborhood place. And there ain't no later for us. We close at midnight."

He smiled, revealing a chipped front tooth. "Got to get my beauty rest, don't I?"

The door opened and I sensed the attention of the bar shift in that direction. A young guy in a polo shirt and skinny jeans hesitated on the threshold, and one of the men at the bar said, "Come on in, we won't bite."

The man next to him added, "Unless you want us to," and both of them laughed.

That invitation seemed to clinch it for the guy in the doorway, and he walked in. As he passed me, a shaft of overhead light showed that he was a lot younger than he appeared at first. He walked with the coltish awkwardness I remembered of my own teen years, soon after my growth spurt, when my arms and legs were so much longer and I didn't know what to do with them.

He stepped up to the bar between me and the two men. "A Bud Light draft," he said to the bartender.

"You have an ID?" the bartender asked.

He pulled a plastic card out of the back pocket of his tight jeans. It had to be a fake; there was no way this kid was even eighteen, no less twenty-one. I watched his Adam's apple pulse as the bartender glanced at the card, then handed it back. He pulled the beer, handed it to the kid. "Five bucks."

The older man closest to the boy said, "Put it on my tab." He turned to the boy. "Haven't seen you here before."

Though they were talking quietly, there was no music on and I could hear everything they said.

The boy sipped his beer. "My first time."

"A virgin!" the man crowed, and the boy blushed.

"Ah, he's just kidding you," the man's friend said. "I'm Virgil and this is Flip."

"K—Kyle," the boy said, stuttering a bit, and I wondered if that was his real name.

"Come on over here between us," Virgil said, and they scooted their stools apart. Virgil pulled a third stool between the two and Kyle joined them.

I sat at the bar by myself, listening to their conversation, laden with humor and sexual innuendo, and I fought against the instinct to pull my badge out and drag Kyle away. But if I did, I'd lose any chance of learning something that might lead me to Ozzy and Dimetrie.

Kyle didn't look like he was being forced into anything he didn't want. His posture had relaxed and he was laughing along with the two men, though I was reminded of the way lions circled a single gazelle on the savannah.

The door opened and closed a couple of times as patrons came and went. A skinny guy who looked like he might be homeless got a plastic tumbler of water from the bartender and was then shooed away. Another pair of older men came in, ordered drinks, and sat at a table after eyeing Kyle with Virgil and Flip.

I sipped my watery martini slowly. I was considering another when the door opened again and a single middle-aged man walked in.

He went up to the bar and greeted the bartender, Virgil, and Flip. "Nothing for me, can't stay," he said to the bartender. "Just stopped in to check out the scene."

He turned to Virgil and Flip. "Who's your new friend?"

"This is Kyle," Flip said. "Kyle, you stay away from Frank here. He's too old for you."

Frank.

A common name, of course, but was he the Frank I was looking for?

"Ha!" Frank said. "I was still in short pants when Flip started sucking dick."

Virgil laughed. "Yeah, but you were sucking right along with him."

Kyle kept looking back and forth nervously, and Flip put his arms around the boy's shoulders. "Don't you worry, they're just messing around." He licked his lips.

Yeah, and he and his buddy would be messing with Kyle before the night was out. But if I said anything, did anything, I'd spook this guy I thought was Frank. The more I looked at him, the more I thought he resembled the man in the porn videos.

"Anyway, I got shit to do," Frank said. "Later, losers." He turned and strode toward the front door.

I left two singles for the bartender and grabbed the rest of the cash, waited a beat or two, then followed Frank out.

When I got outside and I was relieved to see Frank's back was to me as he walked to his car. I stayed in the shadows and watched him get into a Japanese convertible and let the top down. I wasn't about to tail him in the dark and on my own, but as he backed out of the spot, I got a good look at his license plate number, which I memorized. Once he'd driven away, I pulled out my phone and dictated a note to myself with the plate, color, and make.

I was about to get into my car when the door to the bar slammed open and Kyle rushed out. Virgil was right behind him. "Come on, Kyle, we was kidding," he said. "Come on back in the bar, have another beer."

"I gotta get home," Kyle said, scurrying through the parking lot like a frightened mouse.

"Ah, fuck you, you little faggot," Virgil called, then went back into the bar.

I watched as Kyle reached the street. He stopped and looked left, then right, as if unsure which way to go.

"Kyle, my name's Angus," I called to him. He turned to look at me. "I'm going to hold up my ID in the light here. You can come over and look at it if you want. I'm a Federal Agent."

He looked at me but didn't say anything.

"If you stay there, I'll come over and show you my ID. I don't want to hurt you or take advantage of you."

He waited, and I walked slowly over to him.

He stepped into the light of a street lamp and I showed him my ID. He looked at it, then at my face. "You look a lot older than this picture."

"It's makeup," I said as I grabbed a tissue from my pocket and wiped at the lines Yunior had drawn into my forehead. "See?"

"What were you doing in there?"

"I'm undercover," I said. "Looking for places where older men prey on young boys." I paused. "Like you."

"I can't stay here. I have to get home."

"I'm happy to give you a ride, wherever you want to go," I said. "Look, I'm twenty-eight. I was your age not that long ago, and I was scared and confused about being gay and I did a lot of stupid things, but I was lucky nothing turned bad. Let me help you."

He crossed his arms over his chest. "I'm not gay."

"What you are or aren't isn't my business." I held up my keys. "My car's the Mini Cooper over there."

His posture relaxed a bit. "Cool car."

I beeped the doors open and slid into the driver's seat. Kyle got in beside me as I turned the engine on.

I took a deep breath and tried to remember what it was like when I was still a virgin, as I was starting to put a name to my feelings. How did I know, after all? Was it as simple as getting a boner in the locker room? Crushing on some other guy and wanting him to be my friend?

"Are you gay?" Kyle asked.

I put the car in gear and backed out of the space. "Yup."

"How do you know?"

"When I was about fourteen, I found some porn magazines. They were real hardcore, not *Playboy* or anything. Lots of men and women having all kinds of sex."

I remembered it well. One day I was home sick from school, all alone in the house, and I got nosey—snooping around in my stepfather's drawers. I found this stash of porn magazines in the bottom. I saw stuff there I'd never seen before. I was fascinated by the variety in male dicks. One was short and stubby, another long and skinny. I peered at the uncircumcised one for a while, comparing it to mine.

"The naked women didn't do anything for me. But there were a couple of photos of naked men with hard-ons, standing by the women, and those really floated my boat."

"So that makes you gay? Getting turned on by dicks?"

"It didn't make me gay," I said. "It made me realize that I was gay. It was a couple of years later before I had the chance to try anything out."

I turned south on Flagler Street, heading toward downtown Fort Lauderdale. Something about Kyle said "suburban" to me and I figured he'd want me to drop him at the bus terminal on Broward Boulevard.

"I was at the beach with my family," Kyle suddenly said. "I had to go pee so I went to the men's room and this guy was there. This older guy, like my dad's age."

We stopped at a traffic light, and in the glow of a street lamp I saw Kyle's face, caught up in the memory.

"He was peeing at the urinal next to me, and I saw him looking down, and I felt, like I don't know what. I got hard and I had to pull my trunks up fast."

He looked over at me. "He was really nice. We were the only two guys in the bathroom then, and he said not to worry, that it happened to him all the time—getting hard when he peed. He even showed me he was hard himself."

The light turned green and I moved forward.

"I went to wash my hands and he said something like he remembered what it was like getting hard all the time when he was my age. He said he jerked off like three or four times a day and asked me if I did too."

"What did you say?"

"I said yeah, I did, too. And then he said that sometimes a

buddy helped him out, and that felt good, and asked if I wanted to be his buddy?"

I realized that I didn't want to hear anything more about what had happened in that bathroom, even if Kyle needed to tell someone about it.

"How'd you end up at Second Star?" I asked.

"He told me that if I ever got a fake ID and wanted to go somewhere to meet nice guys like him, I should go there. We have a laminator in our computer classroom and a friend of mine showed me how to make an ID."

"Are there other gay kids at your school?"

He looked down at his lap. "A couple. But kids make fun of them and call them names. I don't want to be like that."

I remembered Tommy Carlton.

"There's all different ways to be," I said. "You don't have to be out at your school if that makes you uncomfortable. But you could, you know, reach out to one of those other boys, on the side. Not necessarily to be your buddy, if you know what I mean. But to kind of, keep you out of trouble."

"Keep me from going to bars, you mean?"

"Yeah. Gay kids are going to prom with their boyfriends now. When you get to college, there'll be gay clubs you can join so you won't feel alone. And someday, you'll find a boyfriend, somebody special."

I remembered Lester then. He was special to me. Had I screwed things up completely? Or was there a chance he and I could get back together?

"Hey, there's the bus station," Kyle said. "Can you drop me here?"

"Sure." I turned into the parking lot and pulled up. I got a card from my wallet and handed it to Kyle. "If you ever want to talk to somebody, give me a call," I said. "You ever heard of Lazarus Place?"

He shook his head.

"Look it up. It's not far from here. It's a shelter for LGBT kids, but you don't have to be homeless to go there and hang out. A lot better place for you than Second Star."

He took the card from me. "Thanks, Angus. You're sweet."

"I try." He got out of the car and I watched him walk up to a waiting bus and get on.

One lost boy rescued from Neverland, I thought, and then I went home.

# 25.
# REWARDS

Jonas was in the living room when I walked in. "Holy shit! What happened to you?"

It took me a moment to remember the makeup Yunior had put on me. I struck a pose and asked, "You don't like my new look?"

Jonas covered his face. "Please, make it stop."

I went into the bathroom and stared at my reflection in the mirror. In the bright light it was easy to tell it was makeup, but if I narrowed my eyes and stepped back I could see that Yunior had done a good job of making me look like I was in my forties. Especially bulked up by the vest under my shirt, I made a convincing older guy.

I took a long shower, partly to get rid of the makeup and partly to wash away any trace of Second Star. What an awful place, I thought. Somebody needed to shut it down.

Not me, though. An underage boy had showed a fake ID, and two older men had said something to him that got him scared enough to run. But it was not a case for the FBI.

I could make a complaint to the Florida Division of Alcoholic Beverage and Tobacco. They'd have to open an investigation and send operatives undercover. But if I shut down Frank's operation, that would probably scare the guys away from Second Star anyway. Rats tend to scurry away any time you shine light on them.

The word would spread, and kids wouldn't go to Second Star anymore either. Maybe that boy, Kyle or whatever his name was, would be motivated to find sex among more age-appropriate guys, and he'd tell everyone what a scummy place the bar was, and abuse of teens would go on a downward slide.

Yeah. Soon I'd be clapping my hands to save Tinkerbell and all the other fairies, too.

• • •

Friday morning I went to the gym before Jonas woke up, and I was at my desk by eight. I pulled up the notes I'd made the night before, with the color, make, and plate number from the car in the Second Star parking lot. I put the information into the system and crossed my fingers.

A moment later, I learned the plate was registered to a Frank Cardone at the same address as the house where I'd seen Dimetrie Beauvoir and Ozzy Perez go in with Eric Morozov.

I opened a new FD302 and started typing my notes. Frank Cardone had a police record—two misdemeanor arrests for exposure of sexual organs under the terms of section 800.03. According to what I read, charges for the first were dropped, and he received a fine and hours of community service for the second.

I added that information to my FD302 then went to see Roly and fill him in on what I'd discovered the night before.

"It's like a lot of small pieces of a big puzzle," I said. "But I'm not seeing the whole picture yet. Frank Cardone's car is registered to the house where I think two of the runaway boys are living. But I haven't made any connection to the flakka yet."

"And you can't get inside without a search warrant," Roly said. "You don't have enough to get one yet, do you?"

"Nope. Alexei Verenich's murder took place on his boat, and my only connection between Verenich and the property is that he was the agent for the LLC that owns the house. So I couldn't include the house in the subpoena materials I prepared."

"Then all you can do is what you've been doing. Keep picking at threads and see where they lead you."

I leaned forward in my chair. "Could I put Cardone under surveillance?" I asked.

"Why?"

"I've heard that he recruits underage boys on Fort Lauderdale Beach. If I watch him this weekend, maybe I'll see him make contact with a boy and bring him back to the house."

"That's a shaky premise," Roly said. "Do you have any reason to believe that he will go to that place, this weekend, for that purpose?"

I shook my head.

"The only video you've seen was filmed in a locker room, right? Do you have anything that you could link to the house?"

"I e-mailed you the photo of Ozzy that's being used on the webcam site to advertise his services. The picture was taken indoors."

He opened the picture I'd sent, and looked at it, then he shook his head. "There's nothing here that connects the picture to that address."

I felt like a small child being chastised by the principal.

"So even watching the exterior of his house would be a fishing operation," Roly said. "Review the Fourth Amendment, Angus. People have the right to be secure in their homes against unreasonable search and seizure."

"I know. And I need probable cause supported by oath or affirmation in order to get a warrant."

"I'm not trying to bust your chops, Angus. You're eager and dedicated, and you know the rules. But you need to learn how to operate effectively within them."

He looked at the clock, then pushed back his chair. "It's close enough to quitting time. You know where the Fort Lauderdale police department is on Sunrise Boulevard?"

"Sure. I drive past there all the time on my way to work."

"I'll meet you there and we'll scope out the neighborhood around your house together. You can leave your car in the police department lot."

• • •

We met there about forty-five minutes later. My Mini Cooper was not exactly a surveillance vehicle. I'd chosen the British Racing Green paint job because, well, my name was Green. And I thought it looked good with my red hair and pale skin. But it stood out, and Roly's big black SUV didn't.

"Where am I going?" Roly asked, as I got in.

I gave him the address of the house. "What are we looking for?" I asked.

"The screenshot from the webcam you sent me included a pair of sliding glass doors that looks out to a patio, right?" he asked.

"Yup."

"So I wonder whose backyard looks out at that patio. And whether you can see inside this house from the neighbor's."

"You think maybe we could watch some porn being filmed?"

"I don't know. If we can see into the living room, we might be able to take some photographs and match them to the furniture in the webcam screenshot. Or maybe we'll see lights and cameras set up. That would be unusual in an ordinary house."

"Maybe one of the neighbors has seen something," I said.

"There you go," Roly said.

We turned off Wilton Drive as I had when I was following Eric Morozov the other day. "That's the one," I said, pointing ahead of us. "That one-story with the faded gray paint."

"OK." He continued down the street, looking around, then turned left and made a complete circle around the block. When we got back to the house, he asked, "What did you see?"

"Lots of mature trees," I said. "Privacy."

"Good. What else?"

I leaned forward and looked out through the windshield. "There's a two-story apartment house over there," I said. "I wonder if any of the apartments there look out at the house."

"Describe the building for me."

Why did he want me to describe it when he could look right at it?

"Looks maybe fifty years old," I said. "Two stories, like I said. Flat roof. Parking lot."

"How do you get to the second floor?"

"Exterior staircase to a catwalk. Oh." I realized what he was trying to show me. Anybody climbing the stairs to the second floor, or hanging out on the catwalk, might have gotten a glimpse of the house.

"You know what you have to do now?" Roly asked.

"Yup. Come back here this evening and knock on doors."

Roly dropped me at the police department parking lot, and I called Katya. "You busy this evening?" I asked.

"Nothing I can't get out of easily. What's up?"

I asked if she could help me with the surveillance. It was a big building and I wanted to cover as many apartments as I could as quickly as possible.

"Tell you what," Katya said. "I'll help you tonight, and even tomorrow, if we can't get any answers, and then you come with me to Krasotka tomorrow night."

"Sure. I can talk to Lyuba again, see if she's heard anything about Verenich's murder. Have you been able to find out any more about Kurov?"

"He's been very careful to keep his name out of any public records," she said. "A lot of people I spoke to say it's common knowledge, for example, that he's the developer behind the Valentina, a big triangle-shaped building at the north end of Sunny Isles Beach. But I can't find his name on any of the paperwork."

"Maybe we'll learn some more tomorrow night."

We made plans for her to come to my house around five this evening so that we could be in place for folks coming home from work, as well as catching those who might be working a late shift.

I had about an hour to kill, and I drove around the neighborhood a couple more times, looking for anything I might have missed. If I did get to set up surveillance on Frank Cardone, where could I park? If my car was too visible, where could I position myself?

Eventually, I went home, changed into something more casual, and met Katya at the front door when she rang the bell. "Very boys-just-out-of-college," she said, surveying the living room.

"Hey, it's a rental," I said. She wore a loose coral-colored top over a pair of jeans, with espadrilles and a shoulder bag in the same color. She followed me back out to my car.

We drove past the porn house first, and since there were no cars in the driveway and there was less chance we'd be spotted, we decided to begin with a canvas of the surrounding houses. I parked at the far end of the street and Katya took one side, while I took the other.

There was no one home at about half the houses on my side of the street, and the people I spoke with had little to contribute. No one had noticed anything unusual at the house. "What are you looking for?" one older gay man asked me.

"A routine investigation," I said. "Nothing to worry about."

It was that story over and over again until I reached the last house. "There was one thing," the man who answered the door said. He was in his early thirties, tall and skinny, with a shaved head. "A couple of weeks ago, I was coming home after work and I saw two people arguing in the front yard."

"Do you mind if I record this conversation?" I asked. The guy said it was OK, and I set my phone to record.

His name was Daniel Lambert, and he consented to the interview. "It was a couple of weeks before Christmas," he said. "I remember because lots of houses were decorated and the whole street looked neon. Maybe about seven-thirty or eight o'clock at night, though I could be off by an hour or so."

"What did you see?"

"This older white guy was outside, arguing with a skinny black kid. It seemed odd, you know? I thought, at the time, it was a trick gone bad. That maybe the kid was a hustler and the guy in the house didn't want to pay him."

"Could you hear what they were saying?"

He shook his head, and I had to ask him to answer verbally for the recording.

"No, I couldn't hear. I passed the house, drove into my garage, and that was it. But it gave me an impression, you know? That the guy in the house was the kind to bring tricks home."

"You ever see him any other time?"

"No. But I have seen a couple of kids going in and out. Teenagers, black and white. I thought maybe I was wrong the first time, that the guy in the house was a foster parent."

"Did the kids ever look like they were being forced to be there?"

"You mean like sex slaves or something?" he asked.

I didn't answer his question because I didn't want to prejudice his comments in any way. "Were they able to come and go freely?"

"As far as I could tell. They were always with somebody else though, getting in and out of cars. I never actually saw any kids come out of the house by themselves."

That was all he could tell me. I thanked him and then met Katya back at the car. "I got nothing," she said. "Most houses nobody was home, and the ones who were there didn't see anything."

I told her what I'd discovered. "That's good," she said. "Still not enough to get a search warrant, but it's one more piece."

We drove around to the apartment building and parked in the lot. We climbed the exterior staircase and looked back toward the house. The tree cover was so full I couldn't even tell which one it was. So there was no chance anyone at the building could have looked over and seen the backyard, or into the house.

"It was a good try," Katya said. "You want me to come back tomorrow and help you canvass the street again?"

"I think I'm good. Help me make a list of all the houses we covered."

We drove slowly down the street and Katya marked down the house numbers and whether we'd been able to speak to anyone. Then I drove us back to my house, with a promise to meet Katya the next night at Krasotka.

• • •

Jonas got home about a half hour later. "Do I smell pizza?" I asked him when he walked in. "Did you bring a pie home?"

"I had to do Eric a favor," he said.

"Eric? What kind of favor?"

"He called me about an hour ago and asked me to pick up some pizzas for him. He was working at this place and his car is in the shop, so he'd ordered takeout. But then the delivery guy got in a wreck after Eric had already ordered and paid."

I told him the address of the porn house, and he verified that was where he'd taken the pizza. So the whole time we'd been walking up and down the street, Eric had been inside. And he knew me, for sure—he recognized me at the thrift shop.

"I wish you had called me," I said. "I would have come to the house with you. I'd love to see what's going on inside."

"He didn't ask me in," Jonas said, and he looked sad. "I thought at least he'd offer me a slice but he thanked me and closed the door."

"He didn't pay you?"

"He'd already paid for the pizza. And it wasn't like I was expecting a tip or anything."

Jonas sat down on the sofa. "By then I was jonesing for pizza, so I ordered a pie for us and went back and picked it up. Did I do something wrong?"

"Not at all. But if he calls you again, please let me know. And if he asks you anything about me, tell him I'm an accountant. Don't let him know I work for the FBI."

Eric's involvement with the runaway boys was looking more and more like bad trouble. Was he guarding them?

I remembered how I'd rewarded the kids at Lazarus Place with pizza. Was Eric getting more than information from them? Rewarding them for some acting? How was he involved with Frank Cardone?

And had he noticed me canvassing his neighbors?

# 26.
# BE MY BACKUP

I couldn't go back to canvass the rest of the neighbors on Saturday because Eric might still be at the house and I didn't want him to see me. So I worked out at the gym and read more about the Russian mafia before I had to meet Katya at a coffee shop a few blocks from Krasotka. It was a cool evening and we sat outside under a green umbrella, the Saturday night traffic slow and noisy on Collins Avenue beside us.

"I wanted to give you some background before we go in." She picked up the paper cup with her cappuccino in it but she didn't drink. "My grandfather taught me to play poker when I was a kid. He used to sit around drinking tea from a glass and playing poker with these other old men from his hometown in Russia."

She took a sip. "I financed part of my degree with periodic trips to Atlantic City and Vegas. I never played a big tournament or anything, but I could walk away from a table with a few grand in my pocket."

"My dad's mother played bingo," I said. "When I was little I used to go to the bingo parlor with her and she'd let me mark the numbers. No money in it for me, though."

She laughed. "It was a natural matchup for me when I joined the Bureau to get involved in the investigation of the Organizatsya," she said. "My background, my language skills. When the SAC discovered I played poker, he asked if I'd be willing to go undercover."

I sipped my café mocha and waited for her to continue.

"I thought it was very glamorous," she said. "I got a cover job with a real estate broker in Brighton Beach, right in the middle of all the Russians. Within a couple of weeks I was a regular at a poker game at a social hall on Brighton Beach Boulevard."

The keening wail of a police siren rose above the susurrus of traffic, the red and blue lights flashing off the lobby windows of the high-rise across from us. The car dodged and darted around traffic and we had to wait for the siren to fade until we could talk again.

Katya toyed with the paper wrapper around her cup. "Around the time I wanted to leave New York, the Bureau got a tip that the Organizatsya was moving a lot of money through some cash-only businesses here in Sunny Isles Beach, and it seemed like a good place to send me."

I noticed the way she'd skipped over the details of whatever case she was working on in New York, but I didn't press her. I'd accepted early on that so much of the information at the Bureau was on a need-to-know basis and, as the new guy, I didn't need to know anything more than my superiors chose to tell me.

"Is Krasotka one of the businesses you're investigating?" I asked. I knew from my bartending years how much cash passed over bar counters and inside leatherette folders.

She nodded. "I've been trying to find out who owns the bar, but it's like a *matryoshka*—you know, the peasant woman doll with a bunch of smaller ones nested inside."

"Yeah. I've seen those."

"It took me a couple of months but I finally got invited to join an occasional poker game in the back room at the bar." She looked at her watch. "There's one starting in about fifteen minutes. And I've been told there will be a couple of 'special guests.'"

She used her fingers for the air quotes. "Berdichev, the guy I think is laundering money through his various businesses. Vadim Kurov, who keeps coming up in the investigation of the LLCs. And Doroshenko, the guy from New York who flew in last week. If that's true, this could be my chance to pull in all three of them on gambling charges. Then we pressure Berdichev into giving us the goods on Kurov and Doroshenko and trigger a formal investigation into their finances."

"You think Berdichev will flip?"

"He's small potatoes compared to the other two. It's the best chance we've had to get anything on Doroshenko."

I sipped the last of my coffee, then put the cup down on the table. "What about your ex, the one who you thought was Doroshenko's bodyguard last weekend. What are you going to do at this game if he sees you?"

"He doesn't know that I work for the Bureau, but he does know that I play poker. So if he's there, I can finesse him."

I nodded. "What can I do to help you?"

"Be my backup. As long as everything's going well, I'll text you every half hour. Give me your phone."

I handed it to her.

"I'm putting in the number for a cheap disposable I'm using so that in case anyone gets hold of it there's no incriminating information."

"What do I do if you don't text me? Go looking for you in the back room?"

"No. I'm putting another number in your phone. It belongs to the agent I've been working with on the Russian Task Force. Just tell him that your comrade is in trouble. He'll know what to do."

"My comrade? I can't use your name to someone from the Bureau?"

"You don't know who'll be listening around you."

"OK. In the meantime I'll look for Lyuba and see if she knows anything about Verenich's murder."

"Just keep an eye on your phone."

It was close to nine o'clock as we walked toward Krasotka. Tall sodium vapor lights overhead lit the parking lot which was filled with expensive cars and SUVs.

Katya walked up to the front door of the bar and I followed a few steps behind. The bouncer nodded hello to her, but stopped me and asked for ID. He looked me up and down and said something in Russian. I wasn't sure if he was going to let me in or not, but then I saw Lyuba in the background behind him and called to her.

She spotted me and came to the door. "Hey, you came back!" She smiled and put her arm through mine, and we walked past the bouncer.

The music was as loud as I remembered, the lights even hotter. Lyuba didn't even give me time to get a drink—she dragged me out to the dance floor, put her arms around me and started to sway to the music. They were playing Rihanna again, a different song but the same hard-driving beat.

We danced for a while, and then my phone buzzed in my pocket. I pulled away from Lyuba for a moment to check it. The single letter K appeared on the screen.

Was that her signal? Her initial? Or shorthand for OK?

I slipped the phone back in my pocket as Lyuba leaned back. "Who's that?"

"My roommate," I said. "He's on a blind date and I promised to call him if he gives me the right signal."

"You boys," Lyuba said, and pushed playfully at my chest.

By then I was sweaty and my throat was parched. "I need a drink. Can I get you one?"

"Stoli on the rocks," she said. "I go powder my nose while you get the drinks."

Funny expression, especially for a young woman with a strong Russian accent, which implied she hadn't been born in the United States. But how did any of us learn those phrases anyway? From watching old movies. A good way to learn English as well.

From my bartending days, I knew the best drink to order when you wanted to pretend to be drinking alcohol was a plain tonic with lime. It was hard for anyone to tell there was no vodka in it. If anyone challenged me, I could always blame the bartender for pouring light.

To add to my story, when I was facing away from the crowd I poured a few drops of Lyuba's Stoli onto my index finger and smeared it around the edge of my glass.

Lyuba returned from the bathroom and I handed her the Stoli. "I'm glad I saw you tonight," I said. "I've been trying to get in touch with our mutual friend, Alexei, and I can't reach him."

She frowned. "You don't know? He is dead."

"Dead? My God. What happened?"

She shrugged. "No one know. Or no one say, which is same thing." She tossed back the rest of her Stoli. "Now we dance."

I finished my tonic and put both glasses down on a table by the wall, and let Lyuba lead me back to the dance floor. The beat was much faster by then, and Lyuba couldn't hold me so close.

How far would I have to go that night? Lyuba was going to expect more from me pretty soon. First base, second base? Did I even know what to do with a girl? Sure, I'd watched enough movies, and even some straight porn, so I knew the basics. But would I seem like a clumsy fool? A virgin? Or would she figure out I was gay and wonder what I was doing with her?

It was foolish to be frightened of being embarrassed by a woman I hardly knew. But even so I was scared—and not just of being found out by Lyuba. Katya had put herself in danger, leaving me as her backup.

I pulled out my phone. Had fifteen minutes passed? What if I'd missed my cue and Katya was in trouble?

Fortunately, as I held the phone out, a second text came through.

"I take phone away so you pay attention to me," Lyuba said. Before I knew what she was doing, she'd grabbed the phone and slipped it under the strap of her bra.

It seems silly to admit my first reaction was yuck. My phone and her breast. But I needed that phone back, and grabbing it from her right away would make a scene.

So instead I pulled her close and leaned down to her ear. "I'll pay attention to you," I said. And I did what I'd have done with a guy who pulled that move—I ground my dick against her, letting her know that she turned me on.

I held Lyuba tight, shimmying my hips in time to the music,

and her face flushed red in the shimmering lights. "You know how to treat girl, Andy," Lyuba said.

"You don't know the half of it," I said.

We danced for a while longer and I managed to get a glimpse of my watch. Nearly fifteen minutes had passed since my last text from Katya. If my phone vibrated against Lyuba's chest, would I be able to tell?

I leaned down against the left side of her neck, on the other side from where she'd stowed my phone. I nipped at her flesh, surprised by its softness, and she shivered with pleasure. Then with my other hand I retrieved my phone.

"Ooh," she said, startled by my hand.

I glanced at the phone's display. No text.

"I've got to go to the men's room," I said.

"Your friend needs rescuing?" Lyuba asked.

"You could say that."

I hurried across the floor and into the men's room, which smelled of chemical cleaners and the faint tang of old urine. I locked myself into a stall and checked my phone again. Still no text from Katya, and it had been twenty minutes.

Should I try to text her? Phone her Bureau contact? But what if I was wrong and I screwed things up?

I took a deep breath. Stick to the plan. Katya was very clear: if she didn't text me every fifteen minutes, call the number she gave me. My fingers trembled as I pressed the button to dial the number she'd put in my phone.

When a man answered, I said, "My comrade is in trouble."

"Are you somewhere you can talk?"

"Men's room at Krasotka. I'm alone."

"Good. Your comrade should be in a room at the back of the bar. You'll recognize the door because there'll be a goon in front of it. Don't try to go inside, just keep an eye out for whoever spills out."

Then he ended the call and I stared at the phone for a

moment. This was definitely not the way I'd expected this evening to turn out.

Someone came into the men's room, and I turned to face the toilet and emptied my bladder. I flushed and when I walked out of the stall there were two big bruisers speaking to each other in Russian. They stopped talking while I washed my hands.

Before I walked back out to the dance floor, I checked my phone one last time. Still no text from Katya. I hoped I'd done the right thing, and that she was OK.

# 27.
# POPSICLE STAND

Lyuba was waiting for me. "I think maybe you fall in," she said.

Was that another American expression she'd picked up from the movies? There was something not quite right about Lyuba, though I couldn't figure out what it was.

"No more dancing," she said, lacing her arm in mine. "Come, I live close."

I couldn't walk out then, not when I had been told to watch the door to the back room. "One more dance." I tugged her toward the floor.

She came along, though she wasn't happy. She rubbed her hand over my groin and my dick stiffened again. "You don't want dance," she said to me. "You want play."

I pulled her hand away. "You don't want me to play in my pants." I backed away a few inches and began dancing faster, moving my arms and swaying my hips. Lyuba had no choice but to dance with me.

Fortunately, the DJ was playing some endless house music. I shifted around so that I had a good view of the door behind the bar and one of the bruisers from the men's room next to it. As I was watching, the door popped open and a man dashed out. Through the open door I saw bright fluorescent lights and heard loud voices under the music.

As the man hurried past me, I recognized him as Antonio Cruz—the exotic car dealer—and I managed to stick my leg into his path, causing him to crash against Lyuba, and then fall to the floor.

I leaned down to grab his arm. "So sorry," I said. "Are you all right? Here, let me help you up."

I wasn't trying to help him, though. I just wanted to keep him immobilized.

A moment later, a guy in an FBI windbreaker came through the door, and I waved him over.

"What's going on?" Lyuba asked.

"Just being a good citizen," I said. I stepped back as the agent, who I didn't recognize, approached.

The music stopped and the dancers around us moved into a circle, leaving me, Lyuba, and Cruz in the center. The agent broke through, leaned down, and cuffed Cruz, then helped him to his feet.

There were more agents at the front door, and I realized that Katya's operation was much more sophisticated than I'd imagined. The lights came up, and an announcement was made on the PA system—first in Russian, then in English—instructing us to leave the premises in an orderly fashion.

I saw an agent I recognized from the Miami office. I slipped away from Lyuba and showed him my badge. "Can I do anything to help?"

"No, we're good," he said. "Thanks for your help."

I looked around for Lyuba but she had disappeared. As I waited in a line of people leaving the club, I texted Katya. "You OK? Need anything?"

I didn't realize I'd been holding my breath until I got a text back. "All good. Thanks."

I hurried down Collins Avenue to where I'd left my car, grateful I'd managed to elude Lyuba, wherever she was. I drove south on Collins and then turned east on the 163rd Street causeway toward I-95. By the time I'd reached the highway I knew where I was going.

About twenty minutes later I pulled up in front of Eclipse. My second bar of the night—but the one where I'd belonged all along.

It was close to one o'clock in the morning, and the parking lot was hopping with guys going into the bar on their own and coming out in pairs. I took a moment to look at myself in the rearview mirror. I ran my fingers through my hair, licked my lips, and realized I was stalling so I got out.

Lester was holding a tiny flashlight over the driver's license of a guy in front of me when I walked up to the door. He didn't see me until he'd handed the license back to the guy and looked up.

"G-Man," he said. "Still working your case?"

"Off duty now," I said. "How about you? When do you get off?"

"Why are you asking?"

My heart was thudding against my chest. "I know I shouldn't have shut you out after I got shot," I said. "But I was scared. Not just of getting hurt again. But because if being an agent could put me in danger, and by extension anyone else, how could I have friends, a boyfriend?"

Lester didn't say anything, just stood there with his arms crossed over his chest.

"Will you give me another chance?" I asked. "I know that I hurt you, but I promise I didn't do it intentionally."

"Intentional or not, how do I know you won't do it again?"

"Life is risky. You take a chance on anybody you date, right? A stranger can turn out to be an asshole as easily as the love of your life. Or anywhere in between."

"True."

"You already know I'm not an asshole. At least I think you do. And I know you're a good guy. Even if you feel you can't trust me, I know I can trust you, and I want to prove to you that I'm worth the risk."

He shifted his head to the side. "There's guys behind you who want to get in," he said. "My shift ends at two."

"I'll be waiting," I said.

• • •

A few minutes after two, Lester found me sitting at a table on the outdoor deck. It was quieter out there—if you counted the noise of traffic passing, the undercurrent of conversation, and the low buzz of music from the bar as quieter.

I'd gulped down a vodka tonic and had a second half-finished in front of me. He turned the chair across from me around and straddled it.

"I wanted to go see you when you were laid up," he said. "But I was waiting for an invitation. I even cruised past your house once or twice but I felt too stalker-ish to go up and ring the bell."

"I was in bad shape," I admitted. "I was on sick leave for a few days, and then they put me on this crap assignment going around to colleges, and I had way too much time to obsess over everything that happened. I was scared that I'd blown it with you and I didn't know what to say."

"So what changed?"

"A lot." I told him about investigating the missing boys. "I realized how lucky I've been, but also how quickly things can change." I hesitated. "And then tonight, I had this work thing, and it could have been dangerous, and I realized that I've been stupid and scared. If anything does happen to me I don't want to regret anything. And I regret letting you go and I want to try again."

I felt that same fear as earlier that night, a gnawing at my intestines. But this fear had a more personal meaning. I was with Lester, where I wanted to be, and I wanted him to want me, too.

If he said no? I'd try and be graceful. I'd wish him well and walk away. But I knew it would hurt like hell.

"I can't deny it," Lester said. "There's something about you that floats my boat, G-Man. You've got a rocking body, but lots of guys do. And you're smart and tough. But sometimes I can see into you, and I see you're as vulnerable as I am. And I think maybe you're the right kind of guy for me."

I couldn't help grinning like an idiot.

He stood up. "Come on, let's blow this popsicle stand."

I was happy to agree.

• • •

Sunday morning I woke to unfamiliar sunlight streaming through a big window. Lester lived in a new apartment complex on Sunrise Boulevard, on the edge of Wilton Manors, and his bedroom faced east.

I groaned and put my hand over my eyes. "Make the light go away," I said.

"It's ten-thirty," Lester said. "That's late. Don't you get up early for work?"

"Not on Sundays." I sat up and let the covers fall to my waist. "Especially not if I've had a late Saturday night."

Lester was standing in front of the bed. The T-shirt that stretched taut over his massive chest advertised a new brand of premium vodka. It was tucked into bright orange nylon shorts. "We were back here by two-fifteen," Lester said. "That's not late."

"But we didn't sleep for a long time after that," I said.

He gently kicked my foot. "Come on, I want to get to the gym. See what kind of shape you're in."

"I thought you saw that last night," I said, but I got up and used the bathroom.

When I returned, Lester had laid out a pair of faded gym shorts from the University of Kentucky, where he'd gotten his undergraduate degree. "Those shorts ought to fit you," Lester said. "And the T-shirt will be loose but you can manage."

I leaned down and picked up the jock strap that was on top of the shorts. "And this?"

"Somebody left it behind one day," he said. "Don't worry, I washed it."

At least the jock strap was the right size. The shorts were baggy and so was the T-shirt. I'd worn a pair of Nikes to Krasotka the night before, anticipating an evening on my feet, so with Lester's gear I was ready to go.

Lester got me into his gym on a guest pass, and we began with stretching exercises. I was a lot slimmer than he was and nowhere near as muscular, but I had flexibility on my side. When I worked out with Jonas, we spent more time talking than exercising, but Lester kept me focused—critiquing my form, occasionally gently repositioning me on a machine.

We lifted weights and used the elliptical, then jogged around the indoor track for a couple of laps. "What's on your schedule for today?" Lester asked, when we were ready to head back to his place.

"Nothing urgent. How about you?"

"My shift at Eclipse starts at four. You want to go to the art show on Las Olas?"

The idea of big, muscular Lester as an art aficionado surprised me, but I didn't let on. "Sure. Sounds like fun."

We stopped at my house, where I took a quick shower and changed into a polo shirt and cargo shorts, then drove to Lester's so he could clean up himself. While I waited for him to finish, I looked around his apartment.

I'd been there before but I'd always been so focused on him that I hadn't paid much attention. Now I noticed the little touches he had added to make the apartment his home. A short bookcase was stacked with books, mostly about anatomy and exercise, but interspersed with a couple of gay mystery and romance novels.

A pair of hand-carved wooden candlesticks sat on the coffee table, and the two decorative pillows on the sofa looked like Indian silk. I was peering at a photo of a tropical beach when Lester joined me in the living room. "I love this photo. Did you take it?"

"Nah. Bought it at an art fair. I'm hoping to find that guy again, maybe get another one today."

Lester continued to intrigue me. He'd majored in physical education in college, then taught high school gym and worked as an assistant football coach for a while until he'd followed the sun to Fort Lauderdale. I'd never thought of him as an art collector.

We drove over to the fair, and had a great time on the shady street at the center of Fort Lauderdale, which had been closed to traffic so that artists and other exhibitors could set up tents and tables in the road. The street had a whole different vibe from the evening when I'd walked it with Shane—but maybe the vibe was different because the guy was.

I fell in love with a painting of a palm-lined beach with gorgeous blue-green water. For fifty bucks I had my first piece of original artwork, and I felt like a real grown up.

Lester found the photographer he liked and bought another picture. We slurped frozen lemonade and ate soft pretzels. I saw a couple of kids I recognized from Lazarus Place, accompanied by the handsome Dominican kid, Yunior, and I hailed him over.

"Hey, sugar," he said. I introduced the three of them to Lester, and told him that I'd met them at Lazarus Place.

"You guys ever work out?" Lester asked Yunior.

"Depends on what you mean by working out," Yunior said, licking his lips lasciviously.

Lester dropped to the ground and did five quick pushups, then hopped up and did five jumping jacks. The boys stared at him in awe.

"That's what I mean," Lester said. "You guys gonna be out on your own, you need to be able to take care of yourselves."

"You want to be our coach?" Yunior said.

"I can show you some moves," Lester said.

I offered to put Lester in touch with Shane, and the boys wandered off.

"Who's Shane?" Lester asked as we walked back to where he parked.

"Social worker I met through my case. He runs the shelter."

As we drove back to his place, where I'd left my car, I told him what I could about the investigation. "It would be great if you help out at Lazarus Place. Those kids need good gay role models, as well as the physical training."

"I'd like to do that," he said.

When we pulled up in the parking lot for his building, we kissed goodbye and promised to talk during the week. "Be careful out there, G-Man," he said. "Don't want you to get screwed up again."

"I'll do my best," I said.

On my way home my head was buzzing. I'd enjoyed my weekend with Lester, but I was still worried that the dangers in my job would pull us apart again. I wasn't sure I was fully recovered from the trauma of getting shot, and I was afraid that I'd do something to push him away again.

Instead, I tried to focus on work. I was full of curiosity about what had gone down on Saturday night at Krasotka, but I'd only discover what I was authorized to hear.

Antonio Cruz had been at the poker game with a bunch of guys Katya had connections to in the Russian mafia. Cruz knew Eric Morozov, who was somehow entangled with the porn house. Was Cruz involved in my case, too? Would his arrest trigger some information?

Katya knew what I was working on. Could she try and leverage him for something that would help me shut down the flakka distribution and the porn operation and rescue those boys who were being taken advantage of?

# 28.
# FLORIDA SOUTHERN

I was at my desk in Miramar by eight-thirty Monday morning, ready to jump back into the case of the lost boys. In my master's year at Penn State, one of my forensic accounting professors had a favorite refrain: follow the money. It was estimated that Americans spent over a million dollars a year on porn, and some of that had to be going to the videos Frank produced and the web chats Ozzy did.

Was there a financial trail that would lead to rescuing Ozzy and Dimetrie from the porn house? Since I already knew that Verenich managed the accounts for Gay Guys LLC, I pulled out the records from Florida Southern Bank that Verenich's secretary had provided to the United States Attorney.

I thought about Katya's case. Money laundering required the cooperation of a banking entity, and a small one like Florida Southern was a good option. It was based in Fort Lauderdale, and had grown in recent years by buying up other small banks. It currently had about two billion dollars in assets, and about a billion and a half in outstanding loans, making it the fourth largest locally based bank in the state.

The Board of Directors was composed of area business leaders such as attorneys, accountants, and small business owners. One name jumped out: Antonio Cruz, owner, Exotic Imports Ltd.

That could not be a coincidence. Did Cruz own the LLC behind the porn house? Was one of the accounts Verenich managed a cover for Cruz's business? I went back to the list and tried to decipher each one.

1814North1 LLC owned a property on Federal Highway, also known as U.S. 1, in Fort Lauderdale. SCLP2 was a limited partnership that owned a small shopping plaza called Sunset Center at the corner of Sunrise Boulevard and Sunset Strip.

I resisted the urge to sing the song from *Fiddler on the Roof.*

TXXXF owned a business called The XXX Factor, an erotic bookstore on Dixie Highway in Wilton Manors—down the road from Exotic Imports. Every Monday, a cash deposit was made at the First Southern branch in Fort Lauderdale. It varied from a few hundred to a few thousand dollars.

It appeared that Verenich made monthly transfers from that account, to one for Florida Commercial Assets LLC, one of the real estate companies Verenich managed. I did some cross-referencing and discovered that FCA owned the building where The XXX Factor was located, as well as a number of small buildings in run-down neighborhoods around Fort Lauderdale.

Verenich paid the utility bills for the property from the XXX Factor account, and wrote checks for a few hundred dollars to a variety of individuals, probably the staff. He also paid for what appeared to be inventory from a number of different video distribution companies as well as manufacturers of "novelty specialties," which I assumed meant stuff like dildos and lube.

Most of the checks had been signed by Verenich himself, but a number of them had been signed in a scribble. The first name began with F, the last name with C. Frank Cardone? Was the XXX Factor account being used to pay for the porn house?

● ● ●

Late in the afternoon, Katya came by my office. "Thanks for your help Saturday night," she said. "Sorry to spring it on you at the last minute, but we didn't know for sure the poker game was going to happen, or that there'd be enough money there to make busting it worthwhile."

"And there was?"

She nodded. "I had to play for a quite a while before I could say for certain."

"That was Antonio Cruz, wasn't it?" I asked. "The guy who owns Exotic Imports?"

"Yeah. We were playing casino hold 'em, which is a game against the house, and he was losing big. He threw a marker into the game and said that he'd skip his commission the next time Vadim Kurov bought a car, if Kurov would cover him. I was wearing a wire and was able to get enough evidence from the conversations between Kurov and Cruz to make a raid worthwhile."

"I understand. So does this mean you're going back to New York?"

"My cover is blown down here, so I won't be able to be under-cover anymore, at least not out of this office. For now I'm giving up the real estate business and working here in Miramar putting the case together against Kurov, Cruz, and some of their buddies."

"We'll have to hang out sometime," I said. "When there's no danger of getting involved in another raid."

"I'll take you up on that," she said.

"In the meantime, though, I need your help." I explained what I'd discovered about Florida Southern Bank & Trust. "Has that bank come up in any of your investigations?"

"A couple of times. But we've never had anything specific to pin on them."

"Look at these transactions with me," I said. "This is as far as I've gotten with this X-rated bookstore."

"I assume you've been into a store like that once or twice," Katya said. "You know there are two parts, the front room and the back room."

I nodded. "The front room is where the merchandise is sold, and the peep show machines are in the back."

"Exactly. The income from the front room goes to pay for the store's operation—rent, utilities, staff, and stock."

"Yeah, I was able to track those transactions." I showed her the checks written on the account and the electronic transfers.

"The money from the back is in cash," Katya said. "Quarters, dollar bills. It's a good way to throw in extra cash from poker games and other illicit operations."

"There are regular cash deposits every Monday. Although the amounts vary a lot."

"Could be based on traffic. Or someone's skimming cash from the deposit."

"There's usually a transfer to an offshore bank within the next day or two," I said. "That's as far as I can trace the money."

"Welcome to my world. Once it's gone to Bermuda or Luxembourg or somewhere, it's almost impossible to follow."

We split up the accounts and reviewed them, looking for irregularities and connections. "I've got one," I said, after an hour or so. "I have a bunch of checks here with the same signature as some of the checks on the bookstore account. The first name F and the last name C. For a company called Triple Lambda LLC."

"The gay symbol," she said.

"Exactly. Triple Lambda has both a merchant account and a checking account with Florida Southern." A merchant account was set up to accept payments from credit card companies, with the cash then transferred to the checking account.

"Lots of volume of small transactions—ten and twenty dollars," I continued. "Which is consistent with sales of online porn."

"And which add up to big numbers," Katya said.

Most of the money from Triple Lambda's checking account was transferred regularly to an offshore account, but FC wrote weekly checks to Frank Cardone on that account, always for $1,500. "You think that's his salary for managing the porn house?" I asked.

"Nice work if you can get it," she said.

We worked for another hour, and then compared notes. "We have at least two businesses connected to Frank Cardone, the man who manages the porn house," I said. "One runs the X-rated bookstore, the other the website that sells the movies made in the house."

"I'll feed this information into my investigation and see if it's enough to get a search warrant on the house," Katya said. "If you find any other connections to Kurov, let me know."

I didn't like passing off my investigation to Katya, but if it got me the warrant I wanted I was willing to deal.

• • •

That night, I exchanged a couple of texts with Lester. He had contacted Shane McCoy and arranged to go over to Lazarus Place the next night and give the kids some quick self-defense lessons and maybe get a bunch of them interested in working out regularly.

I answered the last message with a couple of hearts and a ZZZ emoticon. It felt good to have that connection with Lester again.

• • •

Tuesday morning I left for work early but still got caught in a traffic jam on Sunrise Boulevard while an accident was being cleared at the entrance to I-95. While I waited, I read the local news headlines on my phone. One short article jumped out.

The headline was "Unidentified man found dead at Fort Lauderdale Beach construction site," and it gave me the creeps. I checked to see that the flashing lights were still ahead of me and when no one was moving, I clicked through to read the whole article.

> Friday morning workmen renovating a 1960s era apartment building on Fort Lauderdale beach discovered the body of an unidentified man.
> The man, in his early twenties and of Asian descent, was believed to be camping out in the building, according to police spokesperson Carolyn Braider-Hare. Anyone with information is encouraged to call Crime Stoppers at 954-493-TIPS.

Early twenties, Asian descent, camping in an apartment building under renovation? That had to be Dorje, didn't it?

# 29.
# ENLIGHTENMENT

I managed to inch forward enough at the traffic light so that I could make a U-turn, swinging in behind an old Jeep plastered with alt-rock decals and a roof surfboard rack. The jerk chicken stands and check-cashing operations gave way to the yuppie stores on the outskirts of Wilton Manors, and I passed the Exotic Imports showroom. I took Sunrise Boulevard all the way to the beach, then turned south on A1A.

Without Shane's directions, I had to circle around the neighborhood between the ocean and the Intracoastal until I found the Morningstar Apartments where he and I had met Dorje. I wasn't surprised to see crime scene tape surrounding it.

There were no cops in the area, and no construction vehicles in front of the building. I parked in one of the spots with a faded yellow bollard that read "reserved." The only tenant in the building was dead, and wouldn't be needing the parking space.

I stood there trying to get a feel for the place, as sunshine filtered through the clouds. Poor Dorje, he was just trying to get by. Had someone followed him back to his hideout over the weekend? Had he picked up a trick who'd gotten violent?

Living rough was always risky, especially for young kids, which was why there was such a need for shelters like Lazarus Place. There were too many dangers out there in the world. It was a shame Dorje had run into one of them.

Or was there something more going on? Dorje was the second person on the periphery of my investigation who ended up dead.

Was there a chance that the same person killed both Dorje and Alexei Verenich?

It was too early to do much speculation. I didn't even know how Dorje had died.

A skinny, elderly man approached, carrying a small Chihuahua in his arms. Not the way I'd consider walking a dog, but what did I know? He walked with a slant, leaning to his left, as if he'd had a stroke or some other physical damage.

"Hell of a thing," he said to me as he passed, nodding toward the building. "You work there?"

I showed him my badge. "You probably know what goes on around here. I'll bet you're out with the dog a lot. You ever see anybody coming or going after hours?"

"A couple of damn kids," he said. "Camping out in the building. Probably doing drugs. This used to be a nice neighborhood before all this construction."

"The boy in the building," I said. "You ever see him?"

"Don't know which one it was. There were a few of them, thought they were slick because they only went in and out after dark and before dawn. But I'd see them."

"Anyone else besides boys?"

The man thought for a moment. "Yeah. Last week a middle age guy went in, must have been six o'clock or so, because it was right after Buster's dinner. Saw him trying to climb over the dumpster and he fell right on his fat ass. Serves him right, hanging around with them kids."

Could that have been Frank Cardone? "You remember what day it was?"

"Nah. The days all blend into each other, you know?"

The dog mewled in the man's arms and the man said, "All right, we're going home."

I thanked him and he resumed his march, but he stopped a moment later and turned back to me. "There was one other guy, now I remember," he said. "Maybe thirty, skinny, with a T-shirt cut off at the shoulders to show off his muscles. He didn't have no trouble getting up over the dumpster, though. Almost like he was in the Olympics or something the way he sprinted over it."

"When was that?"

"Saturday morning," he said. "I remember because Buster had diarrhea. I was out a half-dozen times that day, but I only saw the sprinter once, right after dawn."

"The police are going to want to talk to you," I said. He gave me his name and address as Buster wriggled in his arms, and finally he put the dog down on the ground and it peed copiously.

After they left, I looked around for a couple of minutes but I didn't want to cross the police tape. I didn't know anybody in the Fort Lauderdale Police Department, but I had met Dr. Maria Fleitas, assistant coroner at the ME's office, on a previous case. I figured she was the best place to start. I hoped she'd be on duty, and I was lucky that when I called the office I was able to reach her.

"Sure, come on over," she said. "I finished the autopsy yesterday evening but we don't have an ID or next of kin so I haven't had any request to release the body."

It was only a couple of miles from the beach to the Medical Examiner's Office, but it felt like a whole world away. To get there you had to go past the industrial buildings, around the airport, the animal shelter, and row after row of manufactured homes that were a stark contrast to the palatial homes off Las Olas.

The ME's compound was unimpressive, a collection of single-story buildings and trailers. A couple of guys in uniforms swarmed around a bomb truck in the driveway of the sheriff's station next door, and then the truck backed out and drove away.

The morgue was busy and I had to wait until the sheriff's deputy ahead of me got the forms he needed before the receptionist could call Dr. Fleitas for me.

She was a short Latina with funky red-framed glasses and shoulder-length dark hair with bangs. She wore light-green scrubs and lab coat with her name embroidered on the left breast. "Agent Green," she said. "You're developing a habit of identifying my John Does."

"Anything I can do to help," I said, as I shook her hand.

"You have a photo this time?"

I shook my head. "If it's the guy I think it is, I met him myself a few days ago."

As we walked down the hallway to the refrigerated room, I explained how I'd been introduced to Dorje at the apartment building by the beach. "Very beautiful young man, long dark hair, half-Caucasian and half-Tibetan," I said.

"Sounds like him. Though his face isn't very pretty anymore."

I shuddered as we ducked out the backdoor and hurried across to a refrigerated trailer. The sun was bright as a knife and I was glad to get into the cool air, even though the smell of death inside was harsh and visceral. She handed me a tub of Vicks VapoRub and I rubbed a bit on my upper lip—something I'd learned the last time I'd been at the morgue.

I followed her into an operating room and watched as she opened the door of a cooler. She bent down to check the ID on a bed-like shelf. Then she slid the shelf with the body out and pulled down the sheet covering the face.

My stomach lurched as I recognized Dorje. Someone had swiped a knife down his face in several sharp lines, tearing through his perfect skin. Had he survived the attack, he would have never been beautiful again.

"Is this your guy?"

I nodded, though I couldn't speak for a moment, worried that the muffin I'd had for breakfast was going to come up and spatter Dorje's corpse.

"I was told his name is Dorje," I said.

She grabbed her clipboard and I spelled the name for her.

"No last name?" she asked.

"Not that I know. No fingerprint match in the database?"

"Nope." As she pulled on a pair of rubber gloves, she said, "A number of things happened to Mr. Dorje and I haven't been able to put the timeline together yet."

I took a deep breath. Mistake. I choked for a moment, then said, "Tell me."

She pointed at the lines on his face. "These were done before he was killed. Lots of blood, probably very painful. There are bruises around his wrists and ankles consistent with being forcibly restrained with a nylon fiber rope, though the person, or persons, responsible removed the ropes from the crime scene."

"Cause of death?" My throat was dry and scratchy.

"Two bullets to the brain," she said. "Fired from the rear, probably while the victim was restrained and lying flat on the floor."

I thought of Alexei Verenich, who was killed the same way. Would the bullets match? "Who's the homicide detective handling this case?"

"Ana Cespedes. You'll like her. She's smart." I copied down Detective Cespedes's name and phone number. Then I took a couple of photos of Dorje's face, even though the slash wounds gave me the creeps.

From my car, I called Detective Cespedes and left my name and number. I didn't want to drive all the way to Miramar while I waited for her to return my call, so I found a coffee shop nearby, set up the VPL, and did some searching on Dorje.

It was hard to find anything without a last name. Dorje was a common given name among Tibetan men. It meant "the thunderbolt of enlightenment." A dorje was also a ritual object that lamas used in religious ceremonies, a short rod with decorated balls on either end. And it was the name of a British rock group.

I found a bunch of men named Dorje on Facebook but none of them matched. I was clicking random links by the time I found a page belonging to a girl named Yonten Brewer, who posted a photo of herself and her brother Dorje.

She was almost as beautiful as he was, but her dark hair was wild and frizzy, while his was slick and shoulder-length. She was from Mountain View, California but attending the University of California at Santa Cruz.

Dorje Brewer had no online profile, but I was able to find an address and phone number for a Richard and Dohna Brewer in Mountain View. I wasn't going to be the one to call and break the news, though. I'd leave that task to Ana Cespedes.

I answered a few e-mails and did some personal surfing until I got a call back from Cespedes and agreed to meet her at the Fort Lauderdale Police Station where Roly and I had rendezvoused a few days before.

She met me in the lobby. She was a petite woman with a heart-shaped face and dark hair in ringlets. Three earrings in each ear, a mix of gold balls and stars. She appeared to be under thirty, so I was impressed she'd made detective so young.

"You said you have an ID on the John Doe from the beach?" she asked as she led me up to her desk on the second floor of the building.

"I do." I handed her a piece of paper on which I'd written Dorje's name, along with the information on his parents. I pronounced the name for her, too.

"Tell me about your interactions with this kid," she said, as we sat down at her desk. "How did you find him?"

"Let me start at the beginning," I said. "So you can see how Dorje fits into my case."

I explained about the connection between the face-eating zombie, the flakka distribution, the porn house and the lost boys. "I got a lead on the boys from a guy named Shane McCoy, a counselor at Lazarus Place."

"I'm familiar with Mr. McCoy. He's been pestering me for a while about a boy who disappeared from his operation. And you found him?"

"I did. His name is Ozzy Perez, he's fifteen, and I believe he's acting in gay porn, either voluntarily or because he has no place else to go."

She made a couple of notes.

"I met with the kids living at Lazarus Place and in the course of speaking with them, one of the boys told us that Dorje knew the guy who was making the movies."

She turned to her computer and began making notes. "Was this boy Dorje living there too?"

"No. Shane had heard that he was squatting at a construction site on Fort Lauderdale beach, so he took me over there."

"Mr. McCoy was familiar with Dorje?"

"It was my understanding he'd tried to convince Dorje to come live at Lazarus Place, but had been unsuccessful."

She nodded and made more notes. "What happened when you met with Dorje?"

I explained about climbing over the dumpster and talking with Dorje. "I showed him a screen capture from the video and he identified the man in it as someone who'd asked him to participate in porn videos." I remembered Dorje saying that the boys had to be very handsome, and how proud he'd been of his own appearance, and I shuddered at the way his face had been marred.

"Did he give you a name for the man?"

"Just Frank. Later I spotted the man at a gay bar called Second Star, and followed him to his car. The registration told me his last name is Cardone."

"Second Star? I don't know that one. Where is it?"

"It's a low-key operation," I said. "With a reputation for fixing up underage boys with older men. Your vice department probably knows about it."

"Never assume," she said.

"It makes an ass of you and me," I said, and she looked at me curiously. "Sorry, it's something my mother's husband says. The bar's on Flagler Street south of Sunrise—no sign out front, just two neon stars."

She made some more notes. "So you identified this Frank Cardone as participating in porn videos featuring underage boys. Why haven't you arrested him?"

"Not enough evidence yet." I gave her the address of the porn house. "If you can get a warrant to search the premises I'd like to be included. I want to see if it's where the porn videos are being filmed, and if there are underage boys participating, I want to help them get somewhere safe. I also want to see if someone in the house is distributing flakka."

She typed more information into her computer, then turned back to me. "Getting back to my case," she said. "When you spoke with Dorje, did he appear frightened?"

"Not at all. More like arrogant."

"Didn't mention anyone with a grievance against him?"

I shook my head.

"How was he able to live at that building unnoticed?" she asked.

"Shane told me he'd heard a rumor that Dorje was trading favors with the construction superintendent. He may be able to give you more information, and I'd suggest you interview the kids at Lazarus Place. One of them might have been in closer contact with Dorje."

"You think one of those kids might have been involved in his death?"

I shook my head. "This was a pretty violent situation," I said. "My experience is limited, of course, but this looks like the work of an adult rather than a teenager."

"Any idea who that adult might be? This Mr. McCoy?"

"Shane seems to be a good guy who cares about runaway kids. I don't know him that well, but I haven't seen any indication in his behavior that he'd be capable of such a violent act."

Then I recalled Shane's obsession with finding and speaking with Ozzy. That wasn't violent, it was protective. But then, if Shane ran across whoever had been victimizing Ozzy, would that obsession turn into violence? That wasn't a matter for Detective Cespedes, though.

I waited until she finished making notes to ask, "Did you pick up any prints from the site?"

"Yes. It looks like Mr. Dorje had a lot of company in the room where he was staying."

"Cardone has a record for a couple of misdemeanors, so his prints ought to be in the system."

"But without a connection to the body or the instruments of death, there's no guarantee that even if his prints appear I'll be able to pin him as the murderer. He could say he was a visitor like you."

"A search warrant might turn up the rope he used, for example. Or the gun."

"Absolutely. But you know as well as I do that I have to have sufficient evidence in order to get the warrant."

And there I was again. Not enough concrete evidence to justify the invasion of a citizen's privacy. "You'll want to contact Detective David Wells in Palm Beach," I said. I pulled out my phone and read her the number. "I think there's going to be a connection to the death of a Russian-American real estate attorney from Sunny Isles Beach named Alexei Verenich. The method of death is the same in both cases, and maybe the ballistics from both murders will match."

"You're making this into a very interesting case, Agent Green," she said.

"I do my best."

# 30.
# TAKE IT SLOW

By the time I left the Fort Lauderdale police department, the day had turned hot and sunny and my car burned like a furnace. I opened the windows and turned the air conditioning on high as I made my way back to the highway.

My brain buzzed with what I'd learned that day. Both Alexei Verenich and Dorje Brewer had been killed by gunshots to the back of the head. From the same gun? I'd have to wait for the ballistics results to know.

Who was at the intersection of those two individuals? The easy answer was Frank Cardone. He worked for Verenich, or at least Verenich wrote him periodic checks. And Cardone knew Dorje. But was Cardone the kind of stone-cold killer who could shoot two men in the back of the head?

I couldn't come up with anymore connections between the two victims. When I got to Miramar, I wrote up yet another FD302 about my conversations with Maria Fleitas and Ana Cespedes. I reviewed everything I knew, and it was frustrating to have so much information and yet still not enough.

After I made it home, I went for a long, sweaty run around my neighborhood, then took a shower to cool off. I began to feel better, and a call from Lester helped.

"I went over to Lazarus Place this afternoon," he said. "Those kids are way tougher than I expected. Even the really femmy ones already know how to take care of themselves."

"They have to be, to survive on the street," I said. "What did you do with them?"

"I showed them holds I use when I have to drag guys out of the bar, and then they practiced how they could get out of them if someone used one on them. It was fun."

"You going back?"

"I think so. They need some good role models, you know?"

That was Lester in a nutshell. Big and tough and able to toss jerks out of the bar, but with a sweet heart beating in his chest.

"So what's up with you and that Shane guy?" he asked.

My heart skipped a beat or two. "What do you mean?"

"He kept asking me questions about how I knew you, were we friends or dating. You fool around with him?"

"Nothing more than a kiss and a hug," I said. "Honestly? He's got some baggage."

"Baggage? Honey, he's got a matched set of luggage to carry around everything that's wrong with him."

Lester had pitched his voice an octave higher than normal, and I had to laugh, even though I knew he was right. "How can you tell?"

"Working in a bar you get a keen insight into human nature," he said. "But you know that already. How many years did you say you tended bar? All through college?"

"I started as a server, but I was able to get behind the bar about a year later because I worked in a restaurant and the rules in Pennsylvania were you only had to be eighteen." It struck me that our common experience in nightlife was another connection that Lester and I shared, though I hadn't seen that before.

"Anyway, I made it clear that you and I are back together," Lester said. "That's what we are, right?"

"We are as together as peanut butter and jelly," I said. "And sometimes just as sticky."

He laughed. "I dig you, G-Man."

"I dig you too," I said.

We compared our schedules, and for the next couple of days

he was starting at Eclipse as I was ending my day at the Bureau. "I might be able to get Saturday night off," he said. "You think you'd be free?"

"I will make it my business to be."

After I hung up, I sat back in my chair and thought about the men in my life. First, of course, was my brother Danny. I was tied to him by blood and by our shared upbringing. I knew that no matter what happened, I'd have his back, and he'd have mine. That was a good feeling.

Then there was Jonas. Nothing romantic between us, and I wasn't going to have even the most casual sex with him while I was dating Lester. Not the way I rolled.

I honestly doubted I'd continue to see Shane McCoy after the case was over. He was a nice guy, and cute in a hipster way, but the darkness was gnawing away at him, and I saw enough of that kind of personality through my job. On my off time I wanted someone whose heart was lighter—like Lester.

His body rocked—he was a walking anatomy textbook, with bulging pecs and a narrow waist. When he held me I felt safe in his arms, and when we were naked together—well, that was pretty awesome. But beyond the physical, Lester and I clicked somehow. I was a few steps ahead of him when it came to discovering my life's work—I knew he wasn't going to be a bouncer forever, and that he was struggling to find something he could do that would engage him. Maybe he'd end up at the Bureau like me. Wouldn't that be wild—not just a single gay agent in a field office but a married couple?

I was getting ahead of myself, though. Like the sign on the locker room wall in the racetrack video said, I had to take it slow.

# 31.
# INNOCENCE LOST

Wednesday morning I worked out with Jonas, but we didn't see Eric Morozov. "What if he left town?" Jonas asked. "Just as I was getting to know him."

"Cool your jets," I said. "You hardly know the guy. And just because he's not at the gym at the exact time we're here, doesn't mean he's moved away."

As I drove to work, I realized that Jonas' fear wasn't completely unfounded. I hadn't told him all the connections I'd found to Eric, so I wouldn't be surprised if Eric disappeared. After all, he'd worked for Alexei Verenich, who was dead. Had he known Dorje, too? If he had, then Dorje's death might be a motivator to run as well.

I remembered Eric's bulging muscles. Had he been involved somehow in the deaths of Dorje and Verenich? Either as killer or security?

Or was he dead, too?

OK, I was starting to fantasize like Jonas. Sure, there was a chance that Eric was dead because he'd associated with some unsavory characters. But until I got some hard evidence, I was assuming he was alive and well and somewhere in Fort Lauderdale.

When I got to the office I called Detective Wells in Palm Beach. "Any progress on Verenich's death?" I asked.

"The Lauderdale detective who called me is waiting for ballistics reports to see if the same gun was used in both murders. Same caliber, so there's a good chance they'll match."

"I think they might, too." I looked at my notes. "You said

there was another guy whose fingerprints were on Verenich's boat. Have you been able to track him down yet?"

"Yeah, I had a detective in New York interview him and he swears he was on the boat with Verenich a few days before his death. He says he has an alibi for the last day Verenich left the marina but I haven't been able to confirm it yet. He has a record that stretches from my office out to the ocean, so I don't trust anything he says."

"What's his name?"

"Nicholas Geier." He spelled the name for me and I wrote it down on a Post-it note.

Wells said he'd keep me in the loop, and hung up. I was adding that information to my paperwork when Ana Cespedes called.

"The prints we found at the site of Dorje Brewer's murder match Frank Cardone," she said. "I'm going to head over to his house and interview him. You want to join me?"

"I'd love to," I said.

I was excited. Finally, some progress. I was sure we were going to find video equipment at the house, and hopefully both Ozzy and Dimetrie. Maybe even other boys who were being exploited. I was going to crack the case open and rescue them. And then we'd be able to grill Cardone about the distribution of flakka.

An hour later, I pulled up at the house behind a Fort Lauderdale Police cruiser. Cespedes was standing beside it talking to two uniformed officers. Eric Morozov's Mustang was in the driveway, but there was no sign of the sedan registered to Frank Cardone.

"You have an arrest warrant for Cardone?" I asked as the four of us walked up to the front door.

"No. I don't have enough evidence yet for a warrant. I just want to talk to him."

I stood back with the two uniforms as Cespedes rapped sharply on the front door.

Someone spoke to her from the other side of the door, and she announced her name and rank, and that she wanted to speak with Frank Cardone. Then the door opened and Eric Morozov stepped out. He was wearing a baggy pair of board shorts and a sleeveless T-shirt that showed off his guns.

"Frank Cardone?" Cespedes asked, before I could say anything.

Eric shook his head. "He's gone." He saw me and said, "Hey, I know you. Jonas's roommate. What's going on?"

"Does Frank Cardone live here?" I asked.

"He used to. He took off yesterday with Ozzy and I got stuck keeping an eye on things. As if I didn't have enough to do already."

"Do you mind if I come in and check the premises, to verify that Mr. Cardone isn't here?" Cespedes asked.

"You don't want to," Eric said. "At least not until I get Felix under control."

Was he another one of the boys being filmed? Maybe Felix was on a webcam at that very moment. I might be able to stop this whole operation.

"Who is Felix?" Cespedes asked.

"A cat," Eric said. "But not an ordinary house cat. He's a cheetah."

As soon as he said it, I made the connection. He was cat-sitting for the car dealer. "Antonio Cruz is in jail," I said.

Eric nodded. "He was denied bail."

"Slow down," Cespedes said. "You're saying there's a wild animal in the house?"

"He's not exactly wild," Eric said. "He isn't comfortable around strangers. I have to get his leash and collar on him before I can let you inside."

Cespedes looked at me.

"Antonio Cruz owns Exotic Imports, the car dealership," I said. "Maybe you've seen his ads on TV? He walks his pet cheetah on a leash. He was arrested at an illegal poker game on Saturday night."

She glared at me. "You might have mentioned that before."

"Didn't know it was relevant."

"Fine. Get the cat on a leash," she said to Eric, who went back inside and shut the door. Then she turned to me. "You know that guy?"

"His name is Eric Morozov. He does odd jobs for a couple of different people, including Antonio Cruz. And he used to work for the victim you spoke to Detective Wells about, Alexei Verenich."

She shook her head. Then she directed the two officers to go around the back of the house to watch any rear exits. "Are all your cases this crazy?" she asked me.

Since I'd only been responsible for one big case before, I had to say yes.

It took a couple of minutes for Eric to come back to the front door, this time walking the cheetah on a very short leash. It was a magnificent animal, the size of a German shepherd, with a tan coat and black spots. Its short ears were erect and its expression wary.

"It's OK, Felix," Eric said, stroking the cheetah's head.

"Is anyone else in the building?" Cespedes asked. "Any other humans or wildlife?"

"Only Dimetrie," he said. "And he's pretty harmless."

Cespedes looked at me.

"Runaway teenager," I said. "I've never met him but I've seen his work."

Eric laughed. "If you can call it that." He skirted around us, holding on tight to Felix's leash. "Try to make it quick, will you? I don't know how long I can keep him outside."

Cespedes handed me a pair of rubber gloves. "Observe, don't touch," she said. "Remember, we don't have a warrant to search the premises. We're just verifying that Cardone isn't here."

We walked in the house, and my first reaction was how ordinary it was. The living room looked a lot like the one Jonas and I shared, with beat-up armchairs around an old coffee table and chairs, a worn terrazzo floor, a nearly empty bookcase, and a tall floor lamp in the corner. Sliding glass doors like the ones I'd seen in the screenshot of Ozzy from the webcam led out to an empty patio.

I walked over to the bookcase, where I saw a stack of DVDs in plastic cases on the top shelf. Beside them was a clear container like the kind we stored rice in at my house, with a small pile of whitish rocks in it. They looked like the rock candy I ate as a kid, but this was something more deadly. It was the flakka I'd been looking for.

I called her over and pointed it out to her. "Holy shit," she said. "That's a lot of gravel." There was also a stack of small, plastic zipper bags beside the box, along with a small electronic scale.

"I'm going to call my contact at the DEA, who's been looking for the supplier of this stuff. You OK with that?"

"I have my hands full with a murder case," she said. "You want to pass this on to the DEA, be my guest."

I called Colin Hendricks and told him what I'd found. "You want me to confiscate the drugs? We don't have a search warrant, but the person in charge of the house let us in, and the flakka is in plain sight, so I can bag them up for you."

"No, I'm coming over. This situation is complicated and I want to check the scene myself."

When I hung up the phone, I realized that the case I was officially investigating was over. By finding the flakka on the bookcase, I'd followed the thread from Brian Garcia's e-mail chain with Ozzy Perez. I wasn't responsible for the murders of Alexei Verenich or Dorje Brewer.

I couldn't walk away knowing that Ozzy was out there with the man who'd been forcing him to have sex on camera. To my right was a sophisticated video setup—a couple of cameras on tripods and some studio lights. All the equipment was shut down.

Could I take on shutting down the porn operation as my case? I knew that both Ozzy and Dimetrie were under the age of consent, so the FBI had jurisdiction under the Innocence Lost National Initiative. The program had been operating for twelve years, with seventy-three dedicated task forces and working groups involving federal, state, and local law enforcement agencies working in tandem with U.S. Attorney's Offices.

We did not have an active group working those cases in our office, so if I could convince Roly to let me follow the evidence, I could jump in and use my investigation to find Ozzy.

I was excited. The Bureau had rescued nearly five thousand

children and convicted more than two thousand pimps, madams, and their associates, resulting in lengthy sentences and the seizure of real property, vehicles, and monetary assets. It was a thrill to be able to add to that list.

If Roly would only agree.

# 32.
# WHAT LOVE IS

I stood next to the equipment as I called Roly and brought him up to date. "I have all the evidence right here," I said. "I've turned the flakka investigation over to Colin Hendricks so I want to run with this. Find this missing kid and make sure that this operation gets shut down completely."

Roly was silent for a moment, and I worried he was going to turn me down. He'd already told me a couple of times that the porn operation wasn't my case.

"I knew you wouldn't give up on this missing boy," Roly said eventually. "Once you get your teeth into something, you don't let go. But you've got to do this by the book. Get a search warrant, log all the evidence. If the boy is with this man who you believe is making the movies, then you'll find him. But keep your focus on the business operation."

My pulse raced as I realized that I was finally able to investigate the case I had wanted to all along. "Will do," I said.

I ended the call and looked at the equipment. Without a warrant, I couldn't start snooping into footage in the camera or look on the computer's hard drive. If I could get Dimetrie to confirm what was going on, I'd have no problem getting the warrant I needed from even the most conservative judge.

"Dimetrie?" I called. "You here?"

The lithe teenager I'd seen in the video with Ozzy walked out wearing only a bright red thong. His skin shimmered and I wondered if he'd been oiled up for an online session. "Who are you?" he asked.

Cespedes introduced herself and me.

"Can you and I have a chat?" I asked Dimetrie.

He shrugged. Cespedes continued to look through the rest of the house to verify that Cardone wasn't there, and I followed Dimetrie to his bedroom. The only furniture was a narrow twin bed and a small dresser, and the floor was littered with books, magazines, and computer equipment. He'd hung posters of male dancers on the walls, and as he sat on the bed, I walked over to one of the posters—a dancer in flight. "Beautiful," I said. "Can you do this kind of thing?"

"I wish," he said. "So what's the FBI doing here? You going to arrest me?"

He lounged on the bed, his long legs splayed out and his hand resting beside the tiny red pouch that did little to conceal his erection.

"Tell me what's been going on," I said. "I saw you coming home from dance class, so I'm assuming you aren't a prisoner."

"You've been stalking me?" He stroked his dick through the pouch. "That could be kind of sexy."

"Cut the crap, Dimetrie." I'd had the idea I was there to rescue him, but it didn't look like he was interested in that. So plan B. "You get paid for your work?"

"You know what I do?"

I leaned against the wall. "I know a lot, but I don't know it all. I know your grandmother kicked you out. I've been told you're a very talented dancer, and I know it's illegal to film boys under eighteen in sexual scenarios. Why don't you fill in the blanks for me?"

"Frank took me in," Dimetrie said. "He gave me a place to live and put food on my plate. He pays me, and I get to hang out all day and fool around. Sometimes I have sex with him or with other guys he brings in, and he makes a movie out of it. Other times I sit in front of the camera and play with myself. It's all good."

"Who else lives here with you?" I'd noticed only one other bedroom on my way to Dimetrie's room.

"Frank and Ozzy. But they booked yesterday."

"You know where they went?"

"Nah. Frank was freaked out about something but he wouldn't say what, least not to me. He packed up his stuff and Ozzy trailed off behind him."

"Of his own free will?"

"Ozzy's a loser, man. He thinks Frank loves him."

There was something almost sleepy about his demeanor. "You're high, aren't you?"

"What's it to you?"

"Getting high makes it easy to handle the pain, doesn't it?" I asked. "How'd you like to live where you don't have to feel that pain, and you don't have to numb it?"

"What are you? A social worker?"

"No. But I know a guy who runs a shelter for boys like you. A place you can get back to dancing, kick off your career. Nobody will make you do anything like this."

He shrugged. "Eric says I can stay here for awhile until his boss figures out what to do with me. Keep performing, make some money."

"Is that what you want? Don't you want to be somebody Lucie can be proud of?"

He was quiet for a moment. "You know my sister?"

"I talked to her a couple of days ago. She's worried about you."

He hesitated.

"Lucie believes in you, Dimetrie. So does your teacher at the New World School, Mr. Arristaga. You could have the career you want as a dancer. But you have to be willing to give this up and get to work."

"You spoke to my teacher, too?"

"I did. And the dancer who substituted for him when he was sick. Everybody I talked to said how talented you are. Mr. Arristaga said he can put you in touch with people who could help you get back on your feet." Then I played my last card. "You go back to school, go someplace safe, maybe Lucie can join you, get away from your grandmother and all her negativity."

He nodded, then stood up. "I gotta put some clothes on and pack up my stuff."

I walked back out to the living room where I called Katya and explained the situation to her. "Can you put together a search warrant for me?" I asked. "The detective from Lauderdale will get one, but she's only looking for evidence connected to the murder of this kid on Lauderdale Beach. To collect what I need I'll have to have my own warrant."

"Sure. You have something I can get started with?"

"I have a couple of FD302s with all the details. I printed them out and they're in a folder on my desk."

She agreed to get them and put together the information for the warrant.

Cespedes was in the kitchen. "I found some nylon rope under the sink. I'll have the ME see if it matches the marks on Dorje's arms and legs," she said. "The boy tell you anything useful?"

"He verified that Frank and Ozzy left together. He says Ozzy's in love with Frank."

She shook her head. "These poor kids. They don't know what love is."

I agreed with that. I was having a hard enough time figuring out my feelings toward Lester, and I was older and hopefully more mature than Ozzy and Dimetrie.

We heard the front door open and found Eric and the cheetah back in the living room. "You guys done yet?" he asked. "I've got an operation to run here."

"Not anymore," I said. "Dimetrie's coming with me."

"No fucking way. Dimetrie works here."

The cheetah sat on the floor beside Eric and bared its teeth.

"You his boss?" I asked. "Because there's a Florida statute against lewd and lascivious offenses committed against persons less than sixteen years of age. And if you're running this operation that puts you behind bars ASAP."

"Tough shit, Sherlock. Dimetrie's seventeen. And he's here of his own free will."

"No more," Dimetrie said, walking into the living room toting a plastic trash bag full of stuff. "I'm going with the FBI dude."

"You are not," Eric said.

"Stand down, Mr. Morozov," Cespedes said. "I am not finished with my search of the premises, and you're interfering. And you have no authority to prevent this young man from leaving with Agent Green, if that's his choice."

Eric dropped the cheetah's leash and the big cat leapt at Detective Cespedes. I pulled my gun and shot by instinct, hitting the cat in its hind leg. He snarled and turned to me. "Call him off!" I said, but when I looked toward the front door I realized that Eric Morozov was gone.

The cat leapt at me as I fired again. The force of the shot sent him backwards toward the bedrooms.

"Out of here!" Cespedes said. "Now!"

Cespedes, Dimetrie, and I rushed out of the house and Cespedes slammed the door behind us. She pulled out her phone. "Good shooting," she said to me, her voice shaky. "I owe you one."

"Eric's the only one who can control that cat," Dimetrie said.

We heard the cheetah making chirping sounds inside the house as Cespedes called animal control. "Yup, a cheetah," she said. "With at least two bullet wounds. Not having a good day."

When she ended the call she said, "They'll be here soon with a tranquilizer gun."

"Will they be able to treat the cheetah? I didn't want to kill it."

"Sometimes you gotta do what you gotta do," she said.

# 33.
# LA DI DAH

Cespedes and the two uniformed officers were going to wait at the house for animal control. While I waited for Colin Hendricks to show up, and for Katya to get the search warrant I needed, I focused on getting Dimetrie settled at Lazarus Place. I called Shane and arranged to meet him there.

Dimetrie tossed his trash bag of belongings in the back of my Mini and then folded his long legs into the front seat. He spent most of the trip texting on his cell phone. When we pulled up in front of Lazarus Place, he said, "This is it? Doesn't look any better than the house where I was."

"Yeah, but here nobody's going to force you to have sex."

"Nobody gonna pay me, either," he grumbled, but he got out of the car.

Before we went inside, I asked, "You have any idea where Frank and Ozzy might have gone? Frank say anything at all?"

"I know Frank had some bucks," he said. "A whole bag of coins and bills."

The erotic bookstore. If I was right, Frank had made his regular Monday pickup from the XXX Factor, and he had the cash from the register and the back rooms.

"Anything else? Anything he said to Ozzy?"

"Frank said he was gonna go somewhere and lie low for a while, some la-di-dah type place. He didn't want Ozzy to go with him but Ozzy begged and pleaded. Dumb ass."

Shane opened the door and I introduced him to Dimetrie. "Come on in," he said. "Let me show you around."

While Shane took Dimetrie upstairs to the boys' dorm, I saw Yunior playing a video game with one of the other boys. "Hey, sugar," he said to me, in that exaggerated voice of his. "You can't stay away from us, can you?"

"Can I talk to you for a minute?"

He handed the controller for the game to another boy. "Don't lose this for me," he said. Then he turned to me. "What's up, sugar?"

"I have some bad news. Dorje's dead."

"Oh shit," he said. "I liked that dude. What happened to him?"

I explained that he'd been murdered in the building where he was squatting, but I left out the gory parts. "You know anybody who had beef with him?"

He shook his head. "He was a very sharp dude, always working the angles. I saw him a couple of days ago on Las Olas, and he said he had a deal cooking that was going to get him enough cash to launch his modeling career. Head shots, plane ticket to New York or Paris, the whole thing."

"Any idea what kind of deal it was?"

"He wouldn't say. It was all on the down-low. I figured he had hooked some sugar daddy who was going to front him the money."

Or he had decided to take what he knew about Frank, or Eric, or whoever, and use it to leverage himself into a cash bonus. And instead of walking the runway in Paris, he was lying on a slab at the morgue.

I thanked Yunior and he reclaimed his place at the video game. Shane was waiting for me. "Dimetrie told me that Ozzy ran off with the guy running the porn house. This is your fault. If you'd let me talk to him when we knew where he was he'd be safe now."

"You don't know that, Shane. Dimetrie says that Ozzy's in love with Frank, so he might have blown you off." I took a deep breath. "Listen, Shane, I've got some bad news." I motioned to the front door and he walked outside with me. I told him about

Dorje's death, but this time I included all the details. "You know any reason why someone would want to hurt him that way?"

"It's a rough world out there," he said. "Lots of bad people who want to take advantage of kids. Dorje probably picked up a trick who got mad at him."

I doubted that Dorje had been killed by a trick and I wondered why Shane had latched onto that idea. "Mad enough to kill him?"

He shrugged. "You never know. Anyway, thanks for bringing Dimetrie by. I'm going to try and get him into the performing arts program at Dillard High so he can get his diploma. And he thinks he might be able to get some part-time work teaching dance to kids through a program he went through himself."

"That's awesome. Let me know if you hear anything more about Dorje, all right?"

He agreed, and I got back into my car. In the brief time it had been locked up, the temperature inside had skyrocketed and I had to turn the air on full blast. I sat there for a moment with my face against the vents, thinking of what I ought to do next.

As I fanned myself, Katya called. "I filled in the warrant request for you and I'm on my way to the judge's office to get it signed. I can meet you at the house in about an hour, assuming the judge signs off."

"Excellent. Can you get one of the computer guys to meet us there, too? Ask Wagon. He knows me." Wagon was a Chinese-American guy I'd worked with on my previous case.

She agreed, and I checked back with Cespedes, who told me that animal control had arrived. "I'm going to get a search warrant for the house, but I can't do anything about the video equipment."

"I've already got an agent putting together my own warrant. Can you have a uniform wait at the house until she and I get there? Could be an hour or more."

Cespedes said she could, and while I waited for Katya and Wagon to get organized, I made a detour to The XXX Factor. It was a single-story building in an industrial neighborhood down the street from Second Star, the bar where I'd gone with Yunior.

The windows and glass door were all blacked out but there were neon signs advertising what the store had to sell.

The store was empty except for a bored clerk at the register, hunched over a video game system. I'd been in a couple of places like this in my life. Like the others, it was an ordinary room with fluorescent lights and wire racks—a K-Mart of porn. Next to the register was a flat open display case filled with dildos and cock rings and various kind of anal massagers. Straight material was in the front—books and magazines and movies displayed face-out. I figured the gay stuff was in the back.

I walked up to the clerk, introduced myself, and showed him my badge. "You know a guy named Frank Cardone?"

When he nodded, I asked, "He here now?"

The clerk shook his head. "He only comes by on Mondays to pick up the cash and credit card slips," he said. "Or if there's an emergency."

"When was the last time he was here?"

"Monday like always. He left the paychecks for the staff and he took all the cash from the register, as well as the coins and bills from the machines. Pain in my ass because I didn't have anything to make change with."

"He say anything to you about where he might be going?"

"Nah. But the new manager might know."

"New manager? Who's that?"

"This Russian guy came by yesterday. Introduced himself, said he was going to be taking over for Frank."

I found a photo of Eric Morozov on my laptop and showed it to the clerk. "Was this the guy?"

He shook his head. "Nah, the guy who came here had bushy black hair and a scar along his chin line."

Someone else who'd gotten cut on his face like Dorje had? Was there a connection? "Did he give you a way to get in touch with him?"

"Nah. He said he'd be back next week. I was like, but what if something goes wrong? Who do I call? He was like, deal with it yourself. Yeah right."

I thanked the clerk and left him my card. If I had to, I'd come back to the porn store the following Monday and hang out until this new manager showed up.

As I was leaving, I wondered where Frank could have gone. What had Dimetrie said—that Frank was going to some la-di-dah place? Did that mean something fancy? Somehow I couldn't imagine Frank Cardone and his boy-toy checking into a high-class hotel—although maybe that was a good move, because I wouldn't ordinarily think to look for Frank anywhere elegant.

Did he know that the FBI was after him? Or was he running from someone else—perhaps the same person who had killed Dorje and maybe even Alexei Verenich?

I didn't think Frank would stay in Lauderdale—it would be too easy for him to run into someone who knew him. But which way would he go—north or south? Since I had my laptop with me, I decided to spend the rest of the time waiting for Katya and Wagon by doing something productive.

At a nearby coffee shop, I ordered a grande café mocha and plugged in the VPN software. Then I went online and started researching high-end resorts, beginning in Palm Beach and working my way north.

After a half-hour, no hotel or resort had jumped out at me, and I realized that I had no idea what Frank Cardone would consider a la-di-dah place anyway.

Was that even a term he'd use? My mother had called one of the women she worked with 'la-di-dah,' meaning she was the kind of person who thought she was better than everyone else. But that didn't sound like something a guy like Frank would say. Could it be that La-di-dah was a specific place, not a generic phrase?

I went back to Google. But there were too many results for the phrase, and even when I added "gay" to my search, I got over four million hits. I hit pay dirt, though, when I added "Florida" to my terms.

The first link that popped up was to a hotel-restaurant-bar in Key West called La Te Da. The name came from La Terraza de Marti, a Spanish reference to the Cuban patriot Jose Marti. From the rainbow flags out front, to the mention of an adjacent bar, it looked like the place for Frank and Ozzy.

I called the hotel's reservation line and asked to speak to the manager. I identified myself as an FBI Special Agent, and asked if he could tell me if he had a guest staying there by the name of Frank Cardone.

He came back on the line a moment later. "He hasn't checked in yet, but he has a reservation for Sunday," he said. "We're booked up until then."

I thanked him and hung up. The net was closing around Frank Cardone. It was up to me to make sure that I was in the right place to pull it up.

# 34.
# PREDATORS

When I got back to the porn house, Cespedes was gone, but the two uniformed officers were still there. One of them verified that Animal Control had subdued, and taken away the cheetah. "Still alive?" I asked.

"And very unhappy about being shot," the officer said.

I called Cespedes and she agreed that the two officers could stay outside the house until my search was complete. "I put out a BOLO for Cardone's license plate," she said. "And the one registered to Eric Morozov, too."

Colin Hendricks arrived a few minutes later with his own search warrant for materials related to the production and distribution of illegal substances. "Nobody to show it to," I said. "The owner of the house is an LLC and the registered agent is dead. All three of the guys who were living here are gone now."

"But you have their names and contact information?"

"I do. But I don't have any evidence that implicates any of them in the flakka—just that one of the boys gave some to Brian Garcia."

"I'll work on that." I showed him where I'd spotted the white crystals and he peered at the plastic container. "Sure looks like it, but I won't be able to say for sure until I have it tested."

"You can't do field tests?" I asked.

"I have a kit back at the office, but it involves a respirator and eye protection so I'd rather do my testing in a controlled environment. This is powerful stuff and exposure to even a tiny bit can have very negative effects."

Katya arrived as Colin was packing up the materials. She'd brought evidence bags and rubber gloves for both of us. As Colin began his search, we stood by the front door.

"When I went into your office to pick up the FD302s, I saw a Post-it note on your computer," Katya said. "With Nicholas Geier's name on it."

"You know him?"

"He's the guy I told you about—the one I was seeing in New York as part of my cover for the poker games. The one I got in too deep with."

"His fingerprints were on Verenich's boat."

Her face paled.

"Could he have been involved in Verenich's death?" I asked.

"That's what I'm afraid of."

I heard a car pull up outside. "Hold that thought." I walked out and saw Wagon getting out of one of the Bureau vans. He was a dark-haired guy in his early thirties in jeans and an FBI polo shirt, with a white lab coat over his arm.

He was towing a hard-sided suitcase I knew was full of his specialized equipment. "Hey, Angus. What have you got?"

I led him inside and showed him the photo equipment and the computer console beside it. "I'm looking for any evidence of the production and distribution of pornographic materials involving underage individuals."

"Looks like I've got some work to do," he said. I introduced him to Colin Hendricks, who had completed his search by then, and Wagon offered to share any fingerprints he found in the area with the DEA.

Colin left and Katya and I began our search, looking for evidence that the porn videos were made at the house as well as information on how they were produced and distributed. I also hoped we'd find something that would tie the house further into Katya's case, like business records of money laundering.

We began with the living room, going over everything. In a cabinet near the front door, I found what looked like a purple and white jockey's uniform—what Ozzy had been wearing in the racetrack video. We also found a lot of sex toys, and bagged and tagged each one.

We skirted around the area where Wagon had spread black fingerprint powder over all the video and computer equipment. "You have any prints I'll need to match to these?" Wagon asked.

"I'll get you a list," I said.

He raised an eyebrow. "That many?"

"There's an older man who was living here and was in the videos himself," I said. "I don't know if someone else was working the camera while he was performing, and I don't know if he's the one who did all the video work as well. Two teenagers were living here. One of them is at a shelter in Fort Lauderdale, so I can get his prints for comparison and elimination. Then there are a number of other characters who've been floating around the periphery of the case, and I'd like to see if any of them have had their fingers on the equipment."

Katya and I went into the kitchen to continue our search. "You think Nicky Geier was involved here?" she asked.

"I don't know. Right now we know that he has been on Verenich's boat, though he told Detective Wells that he'd been on it before Verenich was killed, and that he was in New York that weekend."

I hesitated, then asked, "Does Nicky have a scar on his chin?"

She traced a line across hers. "Like this. Why?"

"I think he's taken over as the manager of The XXX Factor from Frank Cardone."

Katya shook her head. "Nicky, Nicky."

We worked our way around the kitchen and found nothing useful. Dimetrie had cleared out the bedroom where he'd been staying, and the one where Frank and Ozzy had been sleeping was equally empty. There were a couple of bottles of lube in the bathroom but nothing else worth taking in. Disappointingly, there weren't any business records in the house at all. I hoped there would be some spreadsheets or other material on the computer attached to the video equipment.

By the time we were done, Wagon had packed up all the hardware to take back to the lab for further evaluation. Katya and I helped him carry it all out to the Bureau van he'd arrived in. By then it was after six o'clock. We put a padlock on the front door and crisscrossed it with crime scene tape.

When we were finished, Katya said, "I should tell you more about New York."

"Sounds like a conversation we should have over dinner." I took all the evidence bags and arranged to meet her at a French restaurant on US 1 that would be quiet enough for our talk.

We met in the parking lot outside the restaurant. The sun had already gone down but it was still hot and humid, and Katya said, "I don't know if I can ever get accustomed to this weather."

"It's growing on me," I said. "Particularly this time of year when I look at how cold it is up north. My brother has been complaining that even his leather gloves don't keep his hands warm enough."

We went into the restaurant and each ordered a glass of wine. Katya dithered over the menu and I got the sense she was stalling, but she finally ordered a chicken crepe, and I got the mussels in garlic and white wine. When the server left, I said, "So… New York."

"Like I told you, I was able to get into a regular poker game in Brighton Beach. Then one of the men I played poker with introduced me to Nicky. He's very handsome—very sexy—in a bad boy way. Leather jacket, motorcycle, too much product in his hair. He was a personal trainer at a Russian gym."

"A hard to resist combination," I said.

"You got it. I fell for him hard. It took a long time for me to realize we were both lying to each other."

Our food arrived, the rich scent of garlic, wine, and ocean rose up in waves from my overflowing bowl of glistening black mussel shells. Katya's crepe took up the whole dinner plate, a creamy mix of chicken, mushrooms, and cream oozing out the far end.

We told the server that everything looked delicious, and we started to eat.

"How long did you and Nicky date?" I asked.

"About a year," she said. "But it only took me a month to discover that the job at the gym was a cover for his real job, as an enforcer for the Organizatsya."

"Wow."

"Yeah. Wow. I should have broken up with him as soon as I found out, but then, you know, I became a valuable asset. The Bureau wanted all the details of our pillow talk. Who did I meet through Nicky? What did I learn?"

"That must have been incredibly stressful," I said.

"It got worse and worse. Everyday I was worried Nicky would find out about me and I'd be in big trouble. The Bureau was collecting evidence and preparing subpoenas and warrants, and I had to hold on until they were ready to pounce."

She finished her wine and signaled the server for another glass. I declined a refill myself.

"Then one day Nicky disappeared. None of his friends knew where he'd gone. One of them told me that he quit the job at the gym and rode off on his motorcycle. Of course I didn't believe him. I thought someone had killed Nicky and I was going to be next."

I could see why talking about the incident made Katya so nervous. "What happened?"

"The Bureau triggered the warrants and subpoenas and pulled in a lot of big guys from the Organizatsya. A couple of the agents were suspicious that I had warned Nicky, and that's why he had disappeared. It made for a tough working relationship, let me tell you."

The server returned with Katya's second glass of wine, and she took a long gulp. "By the time I finished all my depositions I was ready for a nervous breakdown. The department shrink advised me to take a long vacation. I took some time off, but I kept looking for Nicky. I was sure he was dead and that I owed it to him to find out what had happened."

"But obviously he didn't die."

"No, he didn't. I didn't know that, though, until I saw him at Krasotka. You probably noticed that I freaked—I hadn't seen him since the day he walked out."

"But he must have surfaced at some point. Detective Wells from Palm Beach spoke to him."

"I didn't know. But after I saw his name on the Post-it note in your office, I called a couple of people in New York. The word on the street was that he said he'd taken off for a few weeks to clear his head, and he's back at the gym."

"He was never arrested in your investigation?"

"There was no direct evidence against him."

I considered that statement as the server removed our plates. Had Katya deliberately covered up evidence that might have incriminated her boyfriend? Or was he smart enough to keep a low profile? Even if I asked, there was no guarantee Katya would tell me the truth.

"It seems pretty likely that Nicky's managing the porn shop. You think he's doing it for Vadim Kurov?" I asked.

"It's possible. There isn't much action in Brighton Beach while the prosecution goes forward."

"Can you get in touch with him?"

I could see in her face that she knew this moment was going to arrive. "I'll have to, won't I?" she asked. "If he killed Verenich then he deserves to go to jail."

"And it's possible he killed Dorje Brewer, too," I said. "And that right now he's on the hunt for Frank Cardone, like we are."

She nodded. "Make no mistake, he's a predator."

Like the cheetah. I hoped I wouldn't have to shoot Nicky Geier, too.

# 35.
# RUSSIAN DUDE

I spent Thursday morning cataloging the physical evidence I had collected at the house the day before. I took screen captures from the video that showed each toy and made sure that each item was properly tagged with where and when I'd found it, and how it connected to the photos from the videos. Then I checked it all into the evidence locker. Brian Garcia's tumbler and his laptop were still there, and I wondered when they'd get turned over to whichever agency would prosecute him for his attack on that innocent woman.

Wagon called me down to the lab late in the morning. I found him in his white coat standing at the fingerprint screen. "These are the prints I was able to lift from the video camera," he said, pointing at one set. "And these are Frank Cardone's." He pointed out the loops, whorls, and arches that matched.

"How about the prints from Alexei Verenich's boat? Any of those come up on the equipment?"

He shook his head. So Nicholas Geier probably wasn't involved in making the porn movies. The scar on his chin, which the porn store clerk mentioned and Katya verified, made it likely that Geier was the Russian guy that had taken over from Cardone, but I'd have to go over there and show him a photo array to confirm.

Wagon had the computer from the house set up in a corner of his lab, and I pulled up a bar-height stool and started reviewing the contents of the hard drive. In a folder called "Contracts" I found a PDF of a simple employment agreement. It stated that

"Employer" (Gay Guys LLC) desired to obtain the services of "Employee" (Frank Cardone). Frank's position title was "Executive Producer" and his duties included hiring and supervising staff as well as producing films for distribution.

Nothing about the type of film, though. His compensation of $1,500 per week matched the paychecks I had found. Everything else was boilerplate—vacation, health benefits, and so on. I skimmed to the end where I found Cardone's name and signature. Beneath it were lines for Employer Rep and Employer Rep's signature.

The rep's signature was an unreadable scrawl, but his name was clear: Antonio Cruz.

It was the link I needed. Either Cruz was the owner of the LLC, or he could lead us to that person. Vadim Kurov? Perhaps.

I spent a couple of hours looking through the contents of the hard drive, but I didn't find anything else that connected Cruz to the LLC, or the names of any other individuals who might be involved.

Lester texted me that he had to switch shifts with another bouncer, so he was free that night for dinner. Was I? I texted back that I was, and that I'd confirm time and place later in the day.

Then Ana Cespedes called. "A couple of uniforms picked up Eric Morozov early this morning," she said. "I met with him and he's willing to talk about what was going on at that porn house, though he insists he didn't do anything illegal."

I agreed to meet her at the Broward County Jail in downtown Fort Lauderdale. "I'm going to need some caffeine for this," I said. "Can I get you something on my way?"

"You must have already sampled the coffee at the jail," she said. "Sure, I'd love a green tea latte."

"And in return…" I said.

"Yes?"

"You must have Morozov's prints by now, right? Can you get them sent over to our lab so my tech can compare them to ones from the video equipment?"

I gave her Wagon's e-mail address and she said she'd get the prints to him. Before I left the office I put together a photo array including a head shot of Nicholas Geier that I could show to the video store clerk.

It took about a half hour to get downtown from Miramar. I got my grande mocha, along with the latte for Cespedes, and met her in front of the jail. It was a modern eight-story facility on the bank of the New River, adjacent to the county courthouse. It was ironic that many of the neighboring buildings were fancy high-rises with water views. Not much luxury for prisoners, though.

"What's Morozov charged with?" I asked, as we walked inside.

"Battery on a Police Officer—he set that cheetah loose on us. And he was found in the house where I have a reasonable suspicion child abuse was occurring." She sipped her latte. "I met with him very briefly this morning after he was processed. I asked him if he knew where Frank Cardone was, and he said he doesn't know. He denied that he knew anything about the pornography, that he was there watching the house because Cardone had booked."

"Who asked him to do that?"

"That's where he got cagey. He said he has information that would get him a free pass, but he insisted that you be present for the interrogation."

"I'm certainly interested to hear what he has to say."

We went through security and the sergeant in charge of the holding cells had Eric brought to an interview room. He had handcuffs around his wrists and he looked a whole lot less sure of himself than he did when he was working out at the gym.

Cespedes got out a pocket recorder and established our location, our identities, and Eric's permission to have the interview recorded.

"Let's start with the house in Wilton Manors," she said. "Please explain what you were doing there when we arrived yesterday to look for Frank Cardone."

"I do odd jobs and favors for a couple of different people," he said. "A couple of times I've house-sat for Antonio Cruz, watching Felix for him."

"Felix is the cheetah you had in your possession when we arrived?"

He nodded.

"Please say all your answers for the recording," Cespedes said.

"Yes. I was staying at Antonio's house with Felix."

"Does the property in Wilton Manors where we found you belong to Antonio Cruz?"

"No. It belongs to some corporation owned by a friend of his."

"Who's the friend?"

"I never knew his name. Antonio introduced me to Frank Cardone, who needed some help now and then."

"What kind of help?"

"I ran errands for him. Nothing illegal. I took Dimetrie to his dance lessons. I'd do the grocery shopping. That kind of thing."

"Were you aware of the activities going on at the house?"

He hesitated, licked his lips. "I knew they were making movies," he said. "But I never knew that Dimetrie or Ozzy were under eighteen."

"Yet you told me yourself that Dimetrie was seventeen," I said.

"I didn't know that until the day before," he said. "Frank told me they were both over eighteen. That he made them shave and use that hair removal stuff so that their skin would be soft and they'd look like they had barely reached puberty. I thought it was a scam for the people who bought the videos."

"Did you ever participate in the videos?" I asked.

"No." He was pretty emphatic. "Frank said that I looked too muscular and too old, anyway."

"How about in the operation of the business," I asked. "Did you ever help in making the movies?"

"No."

"Distributing them?"

"No."

"How did you get paid for your work?" I was hoping that he'd say that Alexei Verenich wrote him checks, so that I could ask more about his relationship with Verenich.

"Cash. It was a pain in the neck sometimes. Frank would give me a whole bag of coins and I'd have to take them to the Publix to convert them to bills."

Probably money from the Triple X bookstore. So no lead there.

"What was Antonio Cruz's involvement with the porn house?" I asked.

Eric shrugged. "Never saw him there."

Cespedes said, "In Florida, Battery on a Police Officer is a third degree felony and carries penalties of up to five years in prison. Even if it's your first offense, judges come down pretty hard. So you better have some information to trade. Or else you're wasting our time."

Eric was sweating. "I swear, I didn't do anything. And Felix getting loose, that was an accident. I was freaked out, man. I had to get away."

Cespedes leaned toward the recorder. "This concludes our interview with Eric Morozov," she said.

"Wait!" he said.

She looked up at him. "Mr. Morozov has something else to add. Yes?"

"Talk to Mr. Cruz. He'll tell you I'm a good guy. I do my jobs, I don't complain."

"Let's go at this from a different angle," I said. "You were present while the videos were being made, weren't you?"

"No, man, I swear I wasn't."

Though I hadn't heard from Wagon yet, I took a gamble. "Then how come your fingerprints are all over the cameras and the lighting equipment?"

Eric gulped and his eyes widened. "I might have…I might have helped Frank out with the filming sometimes," he said. "But I swear, I didn't know the boys weren't legal." He started to cry. "You've got to believe me."

"I wish I could, Eric," I said.

Cespedes' phone rang, and she stopped the recording, then stepped outside.

"Please, Angus," Eric said, still crying. "You've got to help me. I can't go to prison."

"You're a tough guy," I said. "You'll manage."

I crossed my arms and stared at him until Cespedes returned to the room. She started the recording again. "New evidence has come in against you, Eric, and I have to say it doesn't look good."

"Wh…what?"

"Tell me about the Morningstar Apartments," she said.

He looked blank. "I don't know what you mean."

I didn't either, but I was curious to see where her questions were going.

"Sure you do. Two-story apartment building on Fort Lauderdale Beach. A friend of yours was camping out there, wasn't he?"

It took him a moment. "Oh, yeah. I never knew the name of the building. Where that Asian dude was staying, right?"

I ran through what I remembered of the investigation into Dorje Brewer's death. Did Eric know him? Well, Frank did, so it was possible that Frank had introduced them.

"That's correct. Did you know Dorje Brewer?"

Eric looked around the room like a caged animal. "I met him once or twice."

"At his residence at the Morningstar Apartments?"

"Why?"

"Because your fingerprints were found there," Cespedes said. "And because that's where he was murdered."

She leaned forward and stared directly at Eric. "Did you kill Dorje Brewer, Eric? Was that one of the odd jobs you did for Frank Cardone? Because this is the time to man up."

"No! I didn't kill him. I swear. It wasn't me. It was this other guy, this Russian dude. I wasn't even inside the building when it happened. I drove the guy over there, and pointed out the building. Then when he came out I dropped him at the airport."

"A Russian dude?" Cespedes asked. "You sure that's not you shifting the blame to some imaginary friend?"

"This Russian dude," I said. "You get his name?"

He swallowed hard. "Just his first name," he said. "Nicky."

# 36.
# INTERESTING LIVES

I looked at Cespedes and nodded my head toward the door. She ended the interview and told Eric we would be back in touch with him.

"I presume you know someone named Nicky," she said, when we were out in the hallway.

"The name has come up in another Bureau investigation."

"You know where I can find him?"

I could give her Nicholas Geier's name, and let her track him down and interview him. But that might screw up Katya's case. I knew she was trying to get hold of Geier and I wanted to give her that leeway. But what if Geier ran again, as he'd done when he left New York? It was a tough decision, but finally I said, "No, I don't. But we're on his trail."

"You realize that Morozov has implicated this Nicky in the murder case I'm investigating. I need to be able to follow up."

"When we find him I'll let you know."

I called Katya, but she didn't answer. I left her a message that I needed to speak with her urgently. On my way back to the office, I stopped at The XXX Factor and showed the clerk the photos. He made a positive ID of Nicky Geier.

Geier was showing up in too many places to be a coincidence. His prints were on Verenich's boat, he was connected to the local branch of the Organizatsya, and now he was moving into the operation of the porn store. Would he take over the filming operations soon, too?

I gave the clerk my card. "If he comes in again, call me. But be careful. He's a dangerous guy."

As I was leaving the store, Katya called. "I got in touch with Nicky. Surprise, surprise, he's here in Florida. I'm having dinner with him tonight."

"I have a date tonight," I said. "Why don't he and I have dinner in the same place you guys will be? Then I'll be there in case you need backup."

"That would be good," she said.

Nicholas Geier wanted to meet her at a steakhouse on US 1 at seven o'clock, and I said I'd be there. "Are you going to wear a wire?"

She shook her head. "Nicky's too smart to say anything incriminating, and I don't want to tip my hand by asking him specific questions."

"But weren't you IDed at the poker game? Will he know that you work for the Bureau?"

"That's part of what I want to find out. If he knows about me, then it's clear he's connected to Kurov somehow."

"This sounds like a dangerous game, Katya."

"That's why we're meeting in a public place. And I'll have you in the background in case he tries anything."

I checked with Lester and he was free to meet me at the restaurant at six-thirty—I wanted to get there early enough to stage the scene properly.

I got there before Lester did and I went inside. I showed my badge to the hostess and said, "I'd like to ask you a favor. A couple's going to come in at seven, and I'd like to be seated close enough to watch them, but not on top of them."

She had to get the manager, a middle-age Korean man in a sharp business suit. I explained the situation again. "There isn't going to be any risk to other customers, is there?" he asked.

"Not at all. This is a training exercise—another agent believes that she's meeting with an informant, and I'm here to observe how she acts."

That wasn't quite a lie, right? Katya was another agent, and she believed that Nick Geier had some information.

The manager agreed, and when Lester got there we were seated in a booth along one wall. "What's going on?" he asked, after the hostess had left us.

I explained about Katya and Nicky. "They're going to be seated at that empty table across from us," I said. "I'm just here to keep an eye out in case there's trouble."

"You lead an interesting life, G-Man," he said.

"And you're part of what makes it interesting." I smiled at him. "You're free all evening, right?"

He smiled back at me, and I thought for a moment about what a nice, open face he had. "I am indeed."

We dawdled over drinks and appetizers, waiting for Katya and Nick to show up. They walked in right at seven and were immediately ushered to the table.

"Your gal pal's pretty," Lester said. "Though my tastes tend toward the guy she's with."

It was my first good look at Nicholas Geier in the flesh. I disagreed with Katya—I didn't think Nick was that handsome. His scarred chin was too weak and the bushy hair was out of control. But he had an animal magnetism and he moved with a grace that reminded me of Felix the cheetah, aware of his movements and the impression he made.

Katya had dressed up for the occasion, swapping out her street clothes for a low-cut blouse that clung to her breasts, a short skirt, and the kind of high-heeled shoes my female friends called fuck-me pumps. She wore mascara, dark eye shadow that accentuated her blue eyes, and a bright shade of coral pink lipstick.

Nick hadn't gone to as much trouble, but I had to admit that his body rocked, in sharply creased jeans and a light blue polo shirt that stretched tight across his chest.

Lester and I talked idly as I observed the body language between Katya and Nick. They smiled a lot, and she often leaned forward intimately. At one point he took her hand and squeezed.

I was dying to know what they were talking about, but I wasn't close enough to hear anything.

"Not to be rude, because I know you're working, but we are on a date, aren't we?" Lester asked after I'd been ignoring him and the piece of prime rib in front of me.

"You're right," I said. "Sorry. So tell me what's new in Lester-world."

"I decided it's time to act like a grown-up," he said. "You inspired me, you know."

"How so?"

"You figured out that you didn't like accounting and found something better," he said. "I need to do that."

"So what's your new plan?"

"I met this guy at Eclipse," he began, and immediately I felt jealousy rising in me. I sliced into my beef so hard that the knife skidded against the plate.

Lester didn't seem to notice. "He's a sales rep for this new line of premium liquors," he said. "The same thing is happening with hard liquor as with beer. You know, the whole microbrew thing. These independent small-batch distillers are coming up with new versions of bourbon, gin, whiskey, and vodka. There are literally hundreds of them around the country, with more coming online every year. And our generation is going for them in a big way."

I loved his enthusiasm. "Sounds cool."

"This company has distribution agreements with a bunch of small outfits. He's getting promoted to district manager and he needs a guy to take over his job, going around to bars and talking about the products, running tastings, doing social media."

"You're interested?"

He nodded. "I met with him on Monday for an interview, and we did some product tasting, too. There's a lot to learn, but he's willing to send me to seminars run by some of the manufacturers, and the company will pay for classes at the hospitality management program at FIU. I might end up getting a master's degree."

"That's awesome, Lester. I'm impressed."

"It's going to be hard at first. I have two weeks of training before I start going out to meet with customers, and he warned me the hours are going to be long if I'm taking classes and working."

"If there's anything I can do, let me know," I said. "I can help you study. I wouldn't mind learning more about that kind of stuff myself."

"And you'd be cool if I couldn't go out with you too much, at least at first?"

"You still have to sleep, right?"

He cocked his head. "Uh, yeah."

"So do I. If all we have for a while is pillow talk and the comfort of sleeping together, then that's OK."

He smiled broadly. "I really dig you, G-Man," he said.

"Right back at you." I lifted my water glass and we toasted.

We ordered a slice of key lime pie to share, and I looked over at Katya and Nick. They were finishing their entrées too, but Nick mimed writing in the air for the check.

He gave his credit card to the server, and Katya stood up. It didn't look like they were parting on friendly terms. She grabbed her tiny purse and stalked toward the front door on her high heels.

"I'll be right back," I said to Lester, and I headed after her.

Katya wasn't leaving though—she was going to the ladies' room. I hovered outside until she came out. "Everything OK?" I asked.

"He knows," she said. "And he's not happy about it." She suddenly pulled me back into the shadows. I turned and saw Nicholas Geier stalking out of the restaurant, letting the big glass front door slam behind him.

"Did you find anything out?" I asked, as we watched him go.

"I had to read between the lines because he wasn't going to say anything incriminating. But from what I can figure out, Verenich was the middleman between Kurov and a lot of his operations, like the porn house. With Verenich out of the way, Kurov needed somebody to fill in, and Nicky got the call."

"I agree with that." I told her what I'd learned from the manager at The XXX Factor, and what Eric Morozov had said about Geier during the interview with Ana Cespedes.

"He didn't mention anything about that kid who was killed on the beach, did he?" I asked. "Dorje Brewer?"

"No. But if Nicky killed Verenich then I wouldn't be surprised if he killed Brewer, too."

I was trying to work out all the connections when my phone rang. I thought for a moment it was Lester, worried that I'd been gone from the table for too long.

When I saw it was an unfamiliar number, I was tempted to ignore it. But with so much going on, I knew that was a mistake.

"Angus? It's me, Dimetrie. The shit's hit the fan here and I don't know what to do."

"Slow down, Dimetrie. What's going on?"

"I got a text from Ozzy a couple of hours ago. Frank couldn't get a reservation at this hotel in Key West he wants to go to until Sunday, so they're camped out at the apartment building where Dorje was staying."

"That's great, Dimetrie. Thanks for letting me know."

"I told Shane, and he freaked out. He said he's going to go rescue Ozzy. Angus, he has a gun! I don't mind if he shoots Frank but I don't want Ozzy to get hurt and that boy is the kind of nut who'd do something dramatic."

Craptastic. "Don't worry, Dimetrie. I'm going to head over there right now."

# 37.
# MANAGED

"What's going on?" Katya asked as I stuffed my phone in my pocket.

"That was one of the boys from the porn house. He got a text from the other boy that he's still in town with the older man who was running things. They're camped out at an apartment building by the beach—the place where Dorje Brewer was murdered. I've got to get over there right away."

"I'll go with you. Just give me a couple of minutes to change. You have your gun?"

I patted the holster on my hip. "You?"

"In the car. See you in a couple of minutes."

I hurried back to the table. "Sorry, I've got to run." I explained the situation as I pulled cash out of my wallet to pay the bill.

"Be careful, G-Man," Lester said. He walked outside with me, and we kissed quickly. At my car, I pulled my Kevlar vest out of the trunk, shucked my shirt, and belted the vest in place. I felt a familiar twinge of pain as it pressed against the nerve that had been damaged when I was shot.

I was buttoning my shirt again when Katya joined me. She'd changed out of her high heels into a pair of sneakers, and the shoulder holster with her gun edged against her low-cut blouse. As I pulled out of the restaurant's parking lot, she looked up the street address for the Morningstar.

"This is where the boy was killed," she said. "And you think Nicky is the one who shot him?"

"Yes, it's where he was killed," I said. "But you know Nicholas

Geier better than I do. Is he that kind of stone cold killer? Slice a beautiful boy's face up then shoot him in the head?"

She blew out a big breath. "I wish I knew. When he was with me, Nicky could be tough, but gentle, too. He picked up stray cats from the beach, took them to be cleaned up and neutered, then pestered people to find homes for them."

"A regular Mother Teresa," I said.

"I know. I sound like an idiot because I fell for him."

"Love makes us all fools," I said. "Look at this boy Ozzy, chasing after the man who abuses him and makes him act in porn. Why?"

"Because this man makes him feel," Katya said. "I've talked to a couple of girls who act in porn and they're so numb to what they do. The sex has no meaning. Sometimes the only way they can feel anything is when they get hurt."

There was a lot of traffic heading to the beach, and I worried that Shane would get there first and get into trouble with Frank Cardone. Shane was obsessed with Ozzy, and that was not good. He had been abused, but he seemed to have come through it and became a good guy. Even though he'd told me he grew up around guns, I worried that he'd do something stupid, and one dumb move could destroy everything he'd built over the last few years.

When I pulled up beside Shane's car in front of the Morningstar, the night hummed with the sound of distant trucks, an owl's hoot, and Latin music floating in from beachfront bars. In the shadow of the trees, the Dumpster was almost invisible. "Follow me," I said.

I hopped up and legged it over the fence, with Katya right behind me. Once I was on the ground I listened again, and this time I heard raised voices. I crept forward, trying to minimize the noise I made through the dead leaves. When I rounded the corner, I saw the pair of plastic lawn chairs where Shane and I had met Dorje before.

Only a sliver of moon illuminated the area, but it was enough to see Frank and Ozzy against the wall, Shane across from them. "Come on Ozzy, come with me," Shane said.

"I hate you!" Ozzy said. "You're a monster." He reached out for Frank's hand. "Frank is going to take care of me."

There it was, the emotion that Katya had mentioned. Frank made Ozzy feel something—so Ozzy was sticking with him.

I looked back at Katya and nodded down along the fence. She moved quietly forward and I turned my attention back to the three men in front of me.

"Come back to Lazarus Place with me," Shane said. "The other kids miss you. We can get you back in school, help you work through whatever you're feeling." He paused, and I could hear his voice catching in his throat. "Let me take care of you."

"Yeah, like you did before."

My heart was racing and I regretted not calling for backup before Katya and I came to the apartment building. It was up to the two of us to make things right.

I stole a glance down along the fence and saw that Katya was in position. When I looked back, Frank Cardone had put his arm around Ozzy's shoulders and pulled him close. "Leave the boy alone," Frank said. "He's with me of his own free will. Now beat it before you get into trouble."

I drew my gun and stepped forward. "FBI!" I called. "Everybody stand down."

With my eye on Frank Cardone, I didn't see Shane raise his arm and fire his gun until it was too late. I was stunned to see Ozzy fall to the ground instead of Frank. I knew it. Shane had done something stupid. He'd shot the very boy he was trying to protect.

I rushed ahead and tackled Shane. We both fell to the ground and the impact knocked his gun from his hand. Out of the corner of my eye, I saw Frank Cardone turn to run from the scene. I managed to get up on one knee and aim at him. "Freeze Cardone, or I'll shoot!"

Katya rushed at Frank and grabbed his arm. I was impressed at the way she was able to keep Frank's arm immobilized behind his back, while at the same time whipping Frank's belt off. Then she flipped Frank around and used the belt to tie his hands behind his back.

I followed Katya's lead, pulling out my own belt and using it to tie Shane's hands together. "I didn't mean it," Shane kept repeating, tears streaming down his face. "I never meant to hurt him."

"Your aim was off," I said. "Ozzy and Frank were too close together to get a clean shot. That's why you should leave the shooting to the professionals, Shane."

Katya called 911 and requested an ambulance. I left Shane tied up on the ground and hurried over to where Ozzy sat slumped against the building. His left hand was soaked with blood as he grasped his right bicep. "It'll be OK, Ozzy," I said. "My name is Angus and I'm a friend of Shane's. I want to help you."

He moaned in pain as I quickly unbuttoned my shirt. "I'm going to tie a tourniquet around your arm to stop the bleeding." I ripped a strip above the hem of my shirt. "We'll get you all fixed up and then take you back to Lazarus Place."

"No!" Ozzy screamed. "I won't go back there. Frank rescued me!"

"It's OK," I said, backing away a bit. "Nobody's going to make you go anywhere except to the hospital to get treated."

Ozzy looked panic-stricken, his eyes wide. "Where's Frank?"

"Don't worry. He won't hurt you anymore."

"Frank isn't the one who hurt me. It was Shane."

Shane? Well, yeah, Shane had shot him. But did Ozzy mean something more?

I looked over to where Shane was lying on the ground. Tears were streaming down his face. "I didn't mean to hurt you Ozzy," he said, between gulps of breath. "I wanted to take care of you."

A funny phrase, take care of. Nicholas Geier might have "taken care of" Alexei Verenich and Dorje Brewer. But the phrase could also be so good—the way I felt taken care of when I was with Lester. Even that could go too far though—and I had a feeling I knew which way things had gone between Shane and Ozzy.

"Shane. What did you do?"

Shane didn't answer.

"He made me have sex with him," Ozzy said. "He'd tie me up and beat me. He said it was the only way he could show me that he cared about me."

"Shane. Is this true?"

Shane curled up in a ball as the ambulance siren keened in the distance. I left Katya in the courtyard and went out to the front to wait for it. I unlocked the front door and tore down the yellow crime scene tape on the outside.

I'd gotten it all wrong. I'd thought I had special insight into this case because I was gay, but I was looking at everything that had happened through the lens of my own experience, growing up with a loving family, never being assaulted or forced to have sex against my will.

Though I hated Shane for what he'd done to Ozzy, I knew that he was as much of a victim as the boy he'd tried to save. He was reenacting those awful scenes from his childhood, when his cousin had raped him repeatedly. Was that the only way he could feel now—to cause someone else pain?

A big red ambulance came down the street, lights flashing. When the first EMT jumped out, I showed him my badge and told him that Ozzy had been shot. He and his partner got a stretcher from the back and carried it into the lobby, then out to the courtyard.

Katya had rolled Frank and Shane together, both still cuffed by belts. She sat on the ground beside Ozzy, speaking to him in low tones. I put my torn shirt back on as the EMTs opened up the stretcher and checked Ozzy's vitals.

Ana Cespedes arrived before the EMTs took Ozzy away, and she spoke to him briefly.

Then she came over to me. "Mr. Perez has an interesting story," she said. "You have any evidence to back it up?"

"I have a video where Frank Cardone has sex with Ozzy, who is underage. That should be enough for statutory rape, right?"

"Absolutely. I'll need a copy of the video as soon as you can provide it. What about his allegations against Shane McCoy?"

"That's tougher." I thought back over what I had heard. Shane had only said that he tried to take care of Ozzy. When Ozzy told us about the way Shane had raped him, and I'd asked Shane if it was true, he hadn't answered, just curled up and sobbed. "I think it's going to be Shane's word against Ozzy's," I said, though I hated to admit it. "For now, you'll have to use the shooting. And then once you've mirandized Shane, maybe he'll admit to something."

She nodded, and walked over to speak to a couple of officers in uniform, who cuffed Shane and Frank and led them away. An EMT told me they were going to take Ozzy to Broward General for treatment of his gunshot wound.

Cespedes interviewed me and Katya as the CSI guys set up big lights and collected evidence. I began with my investigation into the flakka distribution, and how that had led to the porn house in Wilton Manors. "That's how I got to Lazarus Place," I said. "Shane McCoy was the only guy dealing with homeless gay teens who was willing to talk to me. He was desperate to get in touch with Ozzy Perez. Now I understand why."

I shook my head. "I had it wrong," I said. "I thought Shane was rescuing these boys from the street, but according to Ozzy, he was being abused. And that makes me wonder if other boys are in the same situation." I explained what Shane had told me about his own abuse as a kid.

"That's no excuse," Cespedes said.

"I know. And I'm not defending him. Just trying to understand." I shook my head. "I should have suspected something."

"No way you could have known," Katya said.

"Maybe I'm not cut out for this job," I said. "I had the abuser in my sights and I didn't recognize it."

"Humanity is what makes a good law enforcement agent," Cespedes said. "Now. About the murder that took place here a couple of days ago. You ready to give up the information on the guy Eric Morozov mentioned? Nicky?"

I looked at Katya. "It's time," I said to her.

# 38.

# BAD DECISIONS

"The man you're looking for in the murder of Dorje Brewer is Nicholas Geier," Katya said. She spelled the name and gave Cespedes Geier's cell number. "I don't know where he's staying, but he's driving a rental car." She pulled out a small notebook and recited the make, model, and plate number.

"What's the status of Antonio Cruz?" I asked Cespedes. "Is he still in custody?"

"He bonded out yesterday, and immediately demanded to know what happened to his cheetah," she said. "The cat's recovering at a veterinarian's office that specializes in exotics. Since Mr. Cruz did not have a permit to keep a wild animal in his home, when the cheetah is recovered, he's going to a shelter in central Florida that accepts wild cats."

"I'm glad I didn't kill it," I said.

"I'm just as glad you shot it," Cespedes said. "What do you need Cruz for?"

"It looks like he's the man behind the LLC that runs the porn house. I'll need to meet with Frank Cardone after you've booked him. I'd like to get him to confirm Cruz's place in the operation before I get an arrest warrant for Cruz."

It was nearly midnight and I was wiped out, but I didn't want to go home. I texted Lester to see if he was still awake, and he was. He invited me over, but I called him and said, "I need a long, hot shower to wipe all this crud away from me. But by the time I finish that I'll be in no condition to drive."

"Then I'll meet you at your house," Lester said. "And if you need a hand in the shower I can help with that, too."

• • •

I woke beside Lester Sunday morning, and I wondered if this was going to be my future—waking up beside this big sexy guy who made me feel protected. I thought about what had happened the night before, the awful way that everything had turned out. Shane and Frank would end up incarcerated—Shane for shooting Ozzy, and perhaps for the sexual assault that Ozzy alleged as well. The statutory rape charge against Frank was only the tip of the iceberg once the prosecutor got hold of all the videos and computer files we had confiscated at the house in Wilton Manors. Frank would probably have the chance to make a plea bargain if he could give up Antonio Cruz or anyone else higher on the food chain than he was.

What would happen to Ozzy once he was discharged from the hospital? With Shane out of the picture, could he go back to Lazarus Place, or would there be too many bad memories associated with it? There weren't many other options for a kid on the edge of adulthood with no education and no skills other than the ability to perform sexual acts on film.

I picked up my phone from the bedside table as Lester slept on his back, tiny snores rippling from his mouth. A text had come in at two o'clock from Ana Cespedes asking me to come in and meet with her later that morning.

Lester woke up and I leaned over and kissed him on the lips. "Morning, sunshine," I said.

He yawned. "Is it morning already?"

"That's what the sun says." He got up to use the bathroom and while he was gone, I called Broward General. After jumping through a few bureaucratic hoops I was able to find out that Ozzy Perez had undergone surgery to remove a bullet from his chest. He was sedated and in guarded condition.

When Lester returned, I got up and we both grinned as we bumped hips. "You have time for a workout this morning?" he asked.

"We didn't get enough of one in last night?"

He laughed. "I was thinking of the gym. But hey, if you're up for more fun…"

"I wish I could. But I've got to go meet with a police detective."

"You're an awesome guy, Angus. You're smart and you have a big heart. You know how to handle yourself in a crisis and you're not bad looking either." He grinned.

"We're a mutual admiration society then." I wrapped my arms around him and pulled him close to me. I loved the way his body smelled, the way his skin felt against mine. I could live in those arms.

"What's your schedule this week?" I asked.

He was working a couple of late shifts at Equinox. "But tomorrow morning I'm meeting with the liquor distributor again. If they offer me the job, I'll quit Equinox as soon as they can replace me."

"I'll keep my fingers crossed for you, then."

Lester left soon after, and I showered, dressed, and drove to the Fort Lauderdale Police Station to meet with Ana Cespedes. There were dark circles under her eyes, and her cream-colored blouse was wrinkled, with a coffee stain on the right cuff. She introduced me to an assistant district attorney named Vivian Walsh, a statuesque woman with a Jamaican accent.

I spent nearly an hour telling Walsh everything that had led me to the Morningstar Apartments the night before, stopping periodically as she asked me to clarify certain points.

"There are a lot of crimes here and a lot of perpetrators," she said when I was finished. "Some of them will go up on federal charges, some on state charges."

"I believe that Antonio Cruz, who's out on bail for participating in an illicit poker game, is behind the operation of the porn house. If Frank Cardone can give us Cruz, will you make a deal with him?" I asked her.

"That's certainly on the table, depending on what he has to offer." She looked at her watch. "I have time now if you want to accompany me to the jail."

Walsh made arrangements to have Frank Cardone brought to an interview room like the one where Cespedes and I had met with Eric Morozov. Walsh and I met in the lobby of the jail a half hour later.

I had already told Walsh about the investigation into the flakka distribution, which I had handed off to Colin Hendricks. "Can we ask him about that, too?"

"Let's see how things go. I don't want to muddy the waters by bringing in too many cases at once, and since I'm not the prosecuting attorney on that case, I don't have the authority to make deals on it."

Cardone looked like shit. The orange jumpsuit wasn't a good color for him, and he was pale and sweaty. A clump of dirt remained in his hair from when he'd been wrestled to the ground.

Walsh introduced herself and me for the tape. "Depending on what we find after a full analysis of the videos you produced, you're looking at numerous counts of unlawful sexual activity with certain minors, as well as lewd and lascivious molestation," she said. "Each count could include a fine of up to $10,000, up to 15 years in prison, or both."

"You've gotta help me," Frank said. "I can give you lots of information if you can work on those charges. I don't want to spend the rest of my life in prison."

"We'll see, based on what you have to deal with," Walsh said. "Why don't you start by telling us how this operation got started?"

"I met Antonio at a bar in Lauderdale," he said. "Second Star, on Andrews Avenue. We discovered that we had similar tastes, if you know what I mean."

"For the tape, please specify," Walsh said.

"Cruz likes young boys," he said. "Preferably right on the edge of puberty. He plays the daddy, gives them gifts." His mouth curled into a sneer. "Fucks their little asses until they start sprouting pubic hair. Then he dumps them."

Walsh was impassive. I imagined she heard a lot of awful things in her job. "How about your own tastes?"

"I'm no pervert," Frank said. "Yeah, I like my boys young, but older than Antonio's for sure. Fifteen, sixteen, seventeen. You know, in the old days people used to be able to start having sex as soon as they hit puberty. Our society is so fucked up about sex."

"Let's go back to the original question," I said. "You met Cruz at Second Star, discovered you had similar tastes. What happened next?"

"At the time I was working for a web company making instructional videos. Cruz was impressed with my skills and told me he had connections with a guy who distributed porn. He asked if I was interested in making some movies. That there was a lot of money in it for me if I could do it right."

He cleared his throat. "He found the house in Wilton Manors and paid for all the equipment. I started cruising around downtown Fort Lauderdale and the beach, looking for boys to participate."

He led us through how he'd recruited boys, then let them go when they aged out. From what he said, the house had been in operation for at least five years.

He wasn't a stupid guy—he made it clear that Cruz was behind everything, even going so far as to say that he had tried numerous times to get out of the business but Cruz had threatened him to keep him making movies.

Eventually, Walsh said that she would review the evidence and get back to him with further questions. "Looks like we made a bad decision in releasing Antonio Cruz," Walsh said as she and I walked out of the jail. "I'll put out an order to have him picked up again."

She reached out to shake my hand. "Good work, Agent Green."

I shook it, and thanked her for her help. But if I'd done such a good job, why did I feel there was still so much to do?

# 39.
# SINUOUS GRACE

I called Katya and made arrangements to meet with her at the office in Miramar to make sure our details matched. "I spoke with Frank Cardone this afternoon at the county jail," I said, when we were in my office together. "He implicated Cruz in the operation of the porn house. The DA is having him picked up again."

"Lots of people made bad decisions in this case, and they're all going to pay."

"Nobody rides for free," I said.

Katya looked confused.

"It's something my stepdad says. Back in the day, he hitch-hiked across country, and one of the drivers had a big sign on his car. 'Cash, ass, or grass—nobody rides for free.' He used to tell my brother and me that we weren't going to get a free ride from him."

"This case has cash and ass, and flakka in place of grass," Katya said. "And those boys sure didn't get a free ride anywhere."

None of us did, I thought, after Katya left. We all paid a price for the lives we led. Guys who had been victimized, like Shane, Ozzy, and Dimetrie, were trapped in many ways by what had happened to them—whether it was abandonment, abuse, or just making bad decisions.

That night, I remembered my conversation with Katya and the way I'd mentioned my stepfather and my brother. I realized I hadn't spoken to Danny in a while and I called him.

"Awesome news," he said, after we'd said hello. "I applied for this scholarship for my summer program and I got it!"

"Wow. From Penn State?"

"No, from this Italian-American group that wants to foster closer ties with Italy. They fund a bunch of scholarships to programs like the one I'm going to. With their money and what I've got saved, I've got all I need."

"That's great, Danny." I was happy for him—but at the same time I'd enjoyed playing the role of big brother, sending him my extra cash to make sure his dream could come true.

"I was thinking, Angus," he said. "I'm going to have enough cash to cover an extra week in Rome at the end of the course. That is, if I'm careful and I have somebody to share expenses with. You think you might be able to get some vacation time in August and come join me?"

"The Green boys take Rome," I said. "I should have some time coming to me. That could be wild, bro. You and I haven't had a vacation together since...when?"

"I came to visit you at Penn State when I was a senior in high school," he said. "Remember? You borrowed a car from somebody and we went camping at Stone Valley?"

"Oh, yeah. But I gotta tell you, bro, I'm going to need indoor plumbing on this trip. No more peeing in the woods for this guy."

"It's gonna be great, bro!" he said, and I had to agree.

• • •

Monday morning I met with Roly to explain the events of the weekend. "It looks like all these cases are tied together, and if we're lucky, the lower level guys will rat out the upper echelon. The porn house, the flakka distribution and the money laundering will all get wrapped up."

"That's a lot of work for one weekend," Roly said.

It took a couple of hours to go through the evidence I'd collected and determine which prosecutor got which materials. When I left Roly's office I texted Lester to ask about his interview, and a moment later he called me. "I got the job," he crowed. "I start next

Monday, and I already got another guy to cover my shifts. For the moment, I am officially unemployed. But I've got a lot of studying to do this week."

"I can help with that," I said. "Product tasting? Flashcards?"

"All of the above. We just have to make sure we don't get too distracted."

I thought of Lester's rocking body and how much fun we had together. "That could be a problem. But we'll figure it out."

I hung up and went back to work.

· · ·

Government paperwork being what it is, it took most of the month to wrap up the investigation that had begun with Brian Garcia's flakka-induced rage.

Colin Hendricks handled the flakka investigation. Garcia would face charges for the assault, but fortunately the woman he attacked had made a complete recovery.

Nicholas Geier was arrested for the murders of Alexei Verenich and Dorje Brewer, and he implicated Vadim Kurov in both cases. Katya was going to be pulling together evidence of Kurov's many illicit businesses for a long time to come.

By providing evidence to the DA, Eric Morozov managed to evade prosecution for letting the cheetah loose on Ana Cespedes and me, and there wasn't enough evidence to implicate him in the porn filming. One of the guys at the gym told me Eric had left town for a fresh start somewhere else.

I went over to Lazarus Place once a week to hang out with the boys there, and I was pleased that Ozzy had gone back to school and appeared to be thriving. Dimetrie had opted to test for the GED instead of finishing high school, and got a scholarship to study with a Cuban ballerina who ran an elite program in Pompano Beach. One of the dance moms there had offered him and Lucie a room in her house, and Lucie had been able to get away from her nasty grandmother and enroll in an arts magnet school where she could study voice.

Shane had been unable to post bail, so he was in a detention facility waiting for his trial. Franny, his co-director with the big gauges in her ears, had taken over the operation of Lazarus Place and was looking to hire someone to replace Shane.

Lester and I spent a lot of time together, tasting different artisanal spirits, then quizzing each other on the details. I thought I knew about liquor from my time behind a bar in State College, but there was a whole new angle I didn't know about, and it was fun to explore that with Lester.

I accompanied him to a three-day seminar in Orlando sponsored by one of the bourbon brands, and on our way back to Fort Lauderdale we detoured past the wildlife refuge outside Ocala where Antonio Cruz's cheetah had been sent.

I didn't know what I was doing there, but I guess I needed to see for myself that the cat had survived getting shot. We made it there in time to catch one of the tours of the facility. The volunteer who led us around told us that Felix was the only cheetah there, but there were lots of lions, tigers, ocelots, and other wild cats to keep him company.

The preserve took up nearly eighty acres in the middle of nowhere, and the cats were allowed to roam freely within designated areas. I was disappointed that we didn't see Felix on our tour, though the guide assured us he was out there somewhere.

The rest of the group continued on, but I stopped by a wire fence in the area where Felix was supposed to be. "Felix!" I called. "You out there?"

No answer, of course. "I wanted to say I'm sorry I shot you. I know you didn't mean to hurt me or Detective Cespedes. You were doing what came naturally to you. No hard feelings, OK?"

I turned away, ready to rejoin Lester and the rest of the group, when I heard a chirping noise, and I looked back. I recognized Felix from his tan coat and dark spots—and well, the guide had said Felix was the only cheetah there.

He moved sinuously toward the fence, his expressive brown eyes focused on me, and I wondered if this was what a gazelle felt like out on the savannah. I was glad that the chain link fence was between us.

"Hey, Felix," I said. "You happy here?"

He chirped again, then stretched his head out as if he wanted to be petted.

"Sorry pal, but I can only go so far," I said. "All my body parts stay on this side of the fence. But you look good. I hope they take good care of you."

He sprawled down on the thin grass on his side, looking up at me.

I stood there for a moment, communing with him, until the tour guide called, "Sir, we're ready to wrap things up. I need you to come with the group."

"You take care of yourself, Felix," I said.

He got up and stalked away, moving gracefully, not looking back.

Good advice for me.

# ACKNOWLEDGMENTS

This book would not have been possible without the insights I gained as a participant in the FBI's Citizen's Academy, as well as through my membership in the Citizen's Academy Alumni Association and attendance at InfraGard presentations—where the idea for this story first began. I'm grateful for all the great speakers, the lab visits, and the chance to shoot and watch SWAT demonstrations.

Christine Jackson, Kris Montee, and Sharon Potts provide valuable feedback on every piece of writing I share with them, and their comments are always in my head as I write and revise. Thanks to Jim Born for technical help, though I take full responsibility for all errors and improbabilities.

Additional thanks to Randall Klein and Lia Ottaviano for their editorial input as well as to everyone at Diversion Books who has helped get Angus out to the world.

And of course, Marc, who makes it all possible.

CPSIA information can be obtained
at www.ICGtesting.com
Printed in the USA
BVOW08s1204170917
494971BV00001B/1/P